PREY DRIVE

USA TODAY BESTSELLING AUTHOR
JEN STEVENS

CONTENTS

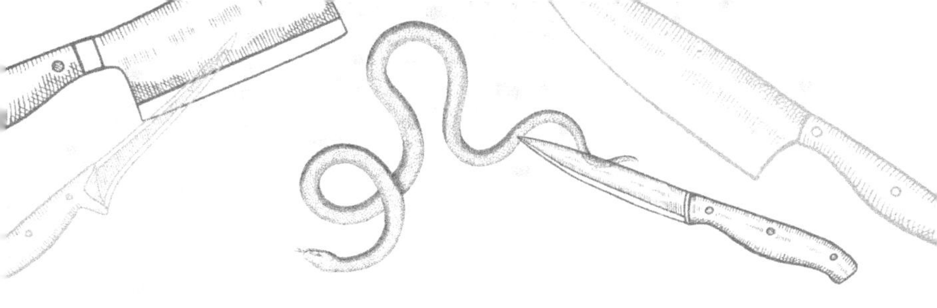

C O N T E N T
W A R N I N G S

This book is intended for a mature audience only. Anyone who considers themselves as a sensitive reader should review the list of content warnings below prior to starting this book.

Stalking & Hunting, Dubious Consent, Mention of Mental Health Hospitalization, Mention of Suicide Attempt, Depiction of an Abusive Relationship (Physical, Emotional, Verbal), Drug & Alcohol Addictions, Drug Abuse, Needles, Overdose, On-page Death & Murder, Blood & Gore Depictions (Flaying, Drowning, Knife Violence, Torture, Mutilation), Physical Assault, Gun Violence, Cut Mentality, Hazing, Profanity, Sexually Explicit Scenes, Grief & Loss Depictions, Sexism, Mention of Childhood Neglect, Mention of Poverty, Fire

Please read at your own risk.
xoxo, Jen

MULTIVERSE
(M U L · T I · V E R S E)

a theoretical reality that includes a possibly infinite number of parallel universes.

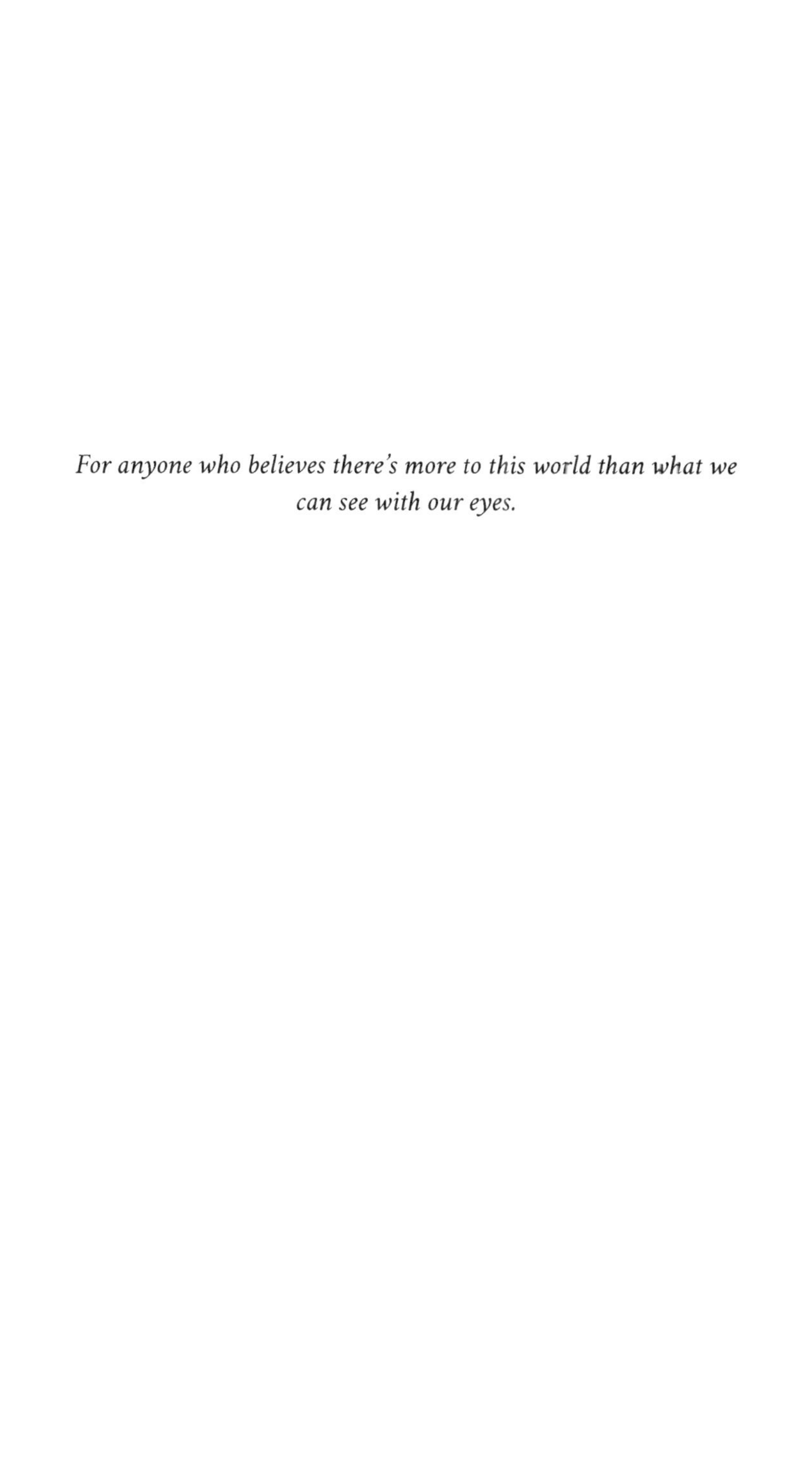

For anyone who believes there's more to this world than what we can see with our eyes.

PAST

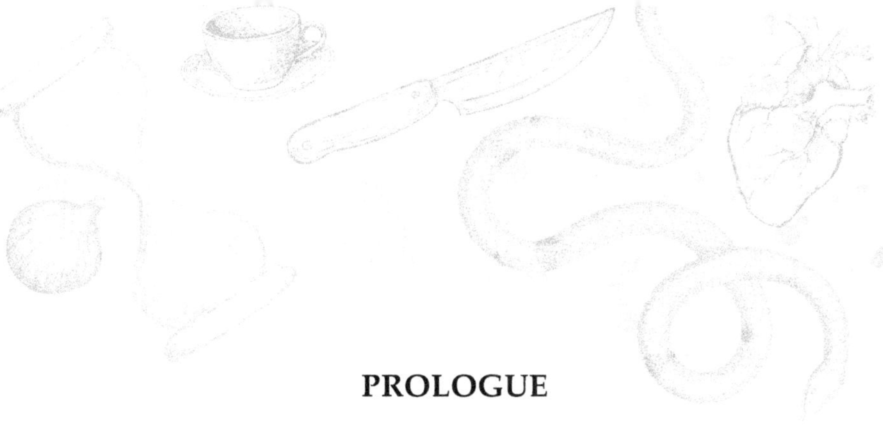

PROLOGUE

The Lamb
  One year ago

DARKNESS BLANKETS the house as I pull my car into the driveway. Once again, Gabe didn't bother leaving a single light on for me, despite the countless times I've asked. When I reach the door, I'm surprised to discover that it's unlocked.

Flipping the light switch in the kitchen, I hear my mother groan from her spot at the kitchen table as the unforgiving bulb comes to life above her head. She blinks owlishly, slowly uncurling herself from the awkward position she was slumped into over the table. She fell asleep here. Or rather, passed out. Who knows how long she's been lying there in the dark?

I want to kick her out, but Gabe guilts me about it every time I even mention the idea of sending her packing. I'm starting to think their relationship is getting a little too cozy, but I can't bring myself to feel any sort of jealousy. I truly couldn't care less, and that scares me worse than the idea of losing my boyfriend to my mother.

"What time is it?" she croaks, rubbing her forehead. There's a clock on the stove right beside me, but she can't be bothered to look at it.

"It's past midnight. You should go to your room if you're tired," I tell her, my voice more gentle than she deserves. Especially when her nose curls up and her mouth tilts down in the scowl she seems to reserve only for me.

"Don't tell me what to do," she spits defiantly, grabbing for the pack of cigarettes sitting right beside her. A disappointed groan erupts from her throat when she turns the box upside down and discovers it's empty. Then her eyes find me again, glaring as if I'm the one who smoked them all. I've told her more times than I can count that she can't smoke in the house, but it always falls on deaf ears. At this point, my entire security deposit is going to go to her addictions.

Refusing to engage in another argument with her, I huff out a frustrated breath and walk past her toward the living room just as Gabe walks through the front door.

"You're home late," I greet, not bothering to slow my steps down the hallway.

He glances toward the kitchen, where my mom is mumbling nonsensical words to herself, and then back to me.

"I got caught up. Are you going to bed?"

"Caught up" usually means he stopped for a drink with his friends. I'm sure my theory will be proven correct when he climbs into bed, reeking of whiskey. Hopefully, I'll be asleep before it can bother me too much.

When I nod, turning for the bathroom to take a quick shower, Gabe walks toward the kitchen.

"I'll be right behind you," he calls out, but I've already closed the door.

Twisting the handle all the way over, I lean away from the scalding-hot water and strip out of my work clothes. Steam fills the cold bathroom immediately, and I quickly jump in before the chilly air bites against my skin.

And I stand there. Completely and utterly exhausted. Debilitated. And safe, at least for the time being.

Twenty minutes pass, and I take my time washing all the scum of the day off my body. I had to work a double today, bartending at the gentlemen's club to make enough to pay our electricity bill. After begging my boss for the extra shift, I managed to scrounge up just enough to cover my half of it. Gabe was supposed to come home tonight with his half, but judging by his state just now, I'd wager a guess that it went to tonight's bar tab instead.

We'll have to ask for an extension. Again.

Just as I'm turning the water off, a hand snakes through the curtain and wraps around my middle, pulling me out of the tub. I scream as loud as I can, flailing around just enough for my assaulter to lose his grip. When I see that it's Gabe, I relax the slightest bit.

But something about the look in his eyes makes my relief short lived. As soon as he's standing straight again, he comes after me, wrapping his arms around my shoulders in a bear hug that makes it nearly impossible to escape from. Panicking, I kick my feet around, nailing him in the shins multiple times before he throws me onto the ground and my head smacks against the ceramic tile with a loud crack.

And everything goes black.

I'm not sure how long I'm out of it before regaining consciousness. My head lolls to the side, my eyes searching around desperately for some indication of where I am and what just happened. But everything is still a little too out of focus.

"This is the only way, Jovie," Gabe coos from somewhere above me. "I promise you'll be safe."

The bathroom. I'm in the bathroom with Gabe.

And he hurt me.

I try to lift my arms and push him off me, but they're being held down by something too heavy for me to lift.

"Hurry up and do it," my mother urges in a rushed tone.

I feel Gabe's hand wrap around my thigh, and I try to kick him away, but my movements are too delayed to reach their mark. My brain and my body are no longer working in sync. He grabs my ankles and shoves them against the cold tile, then I feel his weight settle across my legs.

"I'm trying," he grinds out, sounding irritated.

Something bites into my inner thigh, and then a cold liquid floods my veins.

Everything slows all at one. My body relaxes faster than my mind—which is running wild with the comprehension of what they've just done.

They're drugging me.

Why are they drugging me? Why the fuck are they *attacking* me?

Why, why, why?

"Grab the other one," Gabe's gruff voice says from somewhere far away.

Blood whooshes into my ears, drowning everything else out with a high-pitched ringing.

There's a shuffle around me, and then more poking along my inner thigh. My mom mumbles something above my head. Gabe relaxes atop my knees. They exchange a few words, and then I feel someone's lips against my forehead.

"Stay with me, baby. It'll all be okay soon."

Hours and seconds pass by in synchronicity. Time flows all around me. Fast and slow. In and out.

I'm not sure where I am or what happens in the time it takes for Gabe and my mom to leave the bathroom and the medics to come rushing in with a stretcher.

Words are spoken from somewhere above my head, but none of it sounds like English. It might not even be real. Maybe I made them up in my head.

Maybe no one came to save me from this nightmare.

My head lolls around against the hard tiles, and I try to open my mouth to tell my saviors what happened, but no words come out. Just a garbled mess of vowels move past my swollen tongue, and then I'm lifted onto a stretcher and carried outside with the flashing red lights.

They planned it all.
They attacked me.
They tried to kill me.
They're going to get away with it.

THE WOLF
One year ago

"I KNOW, I know, I'm late," Sienna calls out to us as she weaves her way to us through our parents' penthouse, gracefully dodging the mess of furniture our mother keeps scattered all around.

"You nearly missed the entire meal," our father reproves as she breaks through the balcony doors, not bothering to glance at her before he's shoving another piece of steak into his mouth. He knows he won't be able to hold up his act when she gives him her signature look.

Our mother stands up and pulls her into a hug before pointing to the chair beside mine and her cold plate of food.

"We're glad you could make it at all," she smooths, shooting a scolding look at our father for his rough greeting.

My sister turns to me and rolls her eyes, and we exchange a silent conversation about how irritating our father is. She truly has no idea. I've done my best to avoid him lately, since all he wants to talk about is The Order. The pressure has been put onto him to get me initiated, and he has no answers to offer his fellow brothers because I have no intention of joining them.

It's caused a lot of tension between us, though he shouldn't be surprised. I'm not interested in doing anything the same way he does.

"This looks delicious," Sienna compliments, and my mom beams at her proudly.

She sends the personal chef away to cook our family meals herself, and even if she served us cardboard, Sienna would accept it with a smile and make sure she feels good about it.

They talk casually across the table about Sienna's school schedule and what she'll do after graduation in a couple of months while me and my father stay silent, locked into our own standoff.

I wouldn't even come to these dinners if it weren't for my mother. There've been periods when weeks will pass without me seeing my parents, despite the fact that we live in the same city, mere blocks away. Sienna has gone even longer, milking the convenient excuse of grad school. But where my father is controlling and insufferable, my mother is sweet and comforting. She misses us—misses the chaos that came with raising us and realized too late what a mistake it was to send us away to school each year.

She set up a standing date for us all to meet twice a month to have dinner and catch up, and neither me nor Sienna wants to disappoint her, so we show up every time. Even if we're two hours late, like Sienna was tonight.

"What are you doing for your last night of spring break?" she asks Sienna once all our dinnerware is cleared away, resting her chin on the backs of her hands to give her full attention.

Sienna shrugs, shoving a chocolate truffle in her mouth to avoid answering for a moment.

"Come on, you've got to do something special. It's quite possibly your last spring break ever."

"Unless you decide to go back for more schooling. Again," I jab in a playful tone, though my message is clear. I've never understood why she bothers with school.

She rolls her eyes at me, swatting my forearm with a little more force than necessary. "Actually, *asshole—*" she starts to say, pausing when my mom chastises her for her language. Without bothering to apologize, she straightens her back and goes on. "I was waiting to announce it until I figured out my housing, but I've been accepted into the Yale School of Medicine for my doctorate. I'm going to be a plastic surgeon."

My mother squeals, propelling herself from her seat to round the table and pulling Sienna into a tight hug. I mumble my own congratulations that get lost in the mix of their excited conversation, while my father sits across from us silently, a rare, proud smile spread across his lips.

"I'm going out to celebrate with Mallory and the girls tonight," Sienna explains once things die down, and for some reason, those words pique my father's interest enough for him to lift his gaze back up from his phone.

"In Styx?" he asks, his hopeful expression falling when she shakes her head.

"Jamie is in from L.A. for the weekend, and she wants to go to some new bar."

"Maybe you should sit this weekend out…" he urges, his eyes pleading.

Sienna laughs, bringing her martini to her lips. "Come on, old man, you've taught me well. I can handle a night out," she teases. "Besides, they're celebrating *me*. It would be weird for me not to show."

Sitting back in his chair, his face still holds the same troubled look as before. "Just promise you won't stay out late."

"Okay, Daddy. I promise." She flashes her megawatt smile at him, the same way she always does when she wins an argument. Which, in my dad's case, is every time. He's never been able to deny his little princess a single fucking thing.

As we're leaving, Sienna invites me out with her and her friends, but I've got too much work to do by Monday to justify the hangover, so I decline, promising her that we'll celebrate her accomplishments another day. And with that, we kiss our mother goodbye and head in different directions.

Five hours later, I receive what would be my last call from my sister. And the last time her name flashes across my screen, I swipe the red button and ignore it.

It's ironic how many of us take advantage of the time we have with those we love. How we assume there's always more. Always a *next time*. If I knew the way the night would end, I would have made so many different choices.

Starting with insisting that she never step foot in that club.

PRESENT

1

The Lamb

"The offer still stands for you to stay in the apartment," my sister, Halen, reminds me, peeking her nose through the thick curtains covering the sliding glass doors to gaze out at the private, misty lake.

One look at her wife standing beside her tells me they've already discussed having me extend my stay in their finished basement and didn't land on an agreement.

"I'll be fine," I assure through an uncomfortable laugh.

It's not that me and Kennedy don't get along. In fact, it's the opposite. Ever since my… accident, my sister has been helicoptering my every step. Kennedy knows I need this. I need my freedom back, whether Halen thinks she can trust me with it or not.

Halen steps away from the view and stands beside Kennedy, subtly nudging her in the side in a silent urge to step in. I still catch it, though, and my stomach turns in response, the way it always does when I see that look of concern cross her face. She shouldn't be worrying about me like this. No one should. But spending three months in a rehabilitation facility for attempted suicide makes people think they need to take ownership of your well-being.

Even if it was all built on a misunderstanding.

"It *is* really creepy out here," Kennedy agrees, her nose scrunching as she looks around at the backyard.

It's not creepy. It's just quiet. Isolated. And very different from their townhouse in the small city we've always lived in.

I love it. The view is beautiful, and the privacy is exactly what I've been craving after spending six months post-rehab, holed up with Halen and Kennedy, and the past seven years with my ex-boyfriend or various roommates as I struggled to get on my feet and finish community college. And the rent is an amazing deal.

"It's secluded," I amend, walking over to the door that Halen just left to push the drapes open and let some sunlight into the large dining room.

Specks of dust puff out of the luxurious fabric and float all around us, settling into the small layer that seems to coat everything else in the home.

The surrounding trees create a canopy over the house that blocks most of the natural light, but it also keeps it cool in this blazing summer heat. Besides, there's a private beach at the end of the small strip of grass that's been cleared from the yard to create a hangout area. If I want sun, all I have to do is walk twenty feet out my new back door.

"I'm just afraid you'll be lonely," Halen whines, pivoting her approach. She swipes her finger along the buffet beside her and gapes at the amount of dust that she picked up before quickly dragging her hand across her jeans to wipe it off.

"The owners said they haven't been able to get out here in

some time. It'll just take a Swiffer and a vacuum to be good as new," I defend, irritated that she's being so nit-picky at this point. The decision has already been made. "And it's not like I'm moving out of the country. You'll only be twenty-five minutes away. Close enough to reach me in case of an emergency."

Twenty-five minutes can feel like a lifetime when it comes to emergencies, and Halen knows that just as well as I do. Still, she should be grateful, that after all the suffocating she's done in the past few months, I'm not moving out of the state. Or even the country, like I said.

The house is owned by some ridiculously rich couple from New York. He runs an investment company and works far too many hours, according to his wife. They said they haven't been able to get out here in a couple of years and figured it was time to see the place get put to good use.

That's it. No weird ghost stories, no dead bodies buried in the backyard. No dangerous foundation issues. Just a busy couple.

It's perfect for me. A fully furnished home, three times the size of any apartment in the city, and half the rent. I have a private beach on a small, crystal-clear inland lake, and don't have to deal with the constant hustle that overwhelms me in the city. With all utilities included, all I have to do is pay the deposit, pack a bag, and swipe a damp rag over all the neglected, custom-built furniture. It would have been stupid to pass up.

"I'm glad you're finally getting back on your feet," Kennedy says a little more brightly. She's trying to ease the tension radiating off my sister, though she should know by now that's an impossible feat.

As best-friends-turned-lovers, Halen and Kennedy are the perfect balance of yin and yang. They know each other on a level far beyond anything in this physical realm and they play to each other's strengths perfectly. They're lucky as hell to have found each other. But that kind of connection doesn't come without qualms. They usually have two very different perspectives on things—namely me.

"There could be a serial killer hiding out in those woods, and you'd have no idea. Look at how big this window is! Anyone could be watching you from out there."

Halen scurries over from the dining room to the family room, holding her arms out to show the floor-to-ceiling wall of windows that overlooks the lake and surrounding trees. I admit, it's a little intimidating to think about being fully exposed like that, but the lake is private and it'll be off-season for tourists in no time. No one will even be in any of the neighboring homes in a few months.

But Halen is justified in her fears about leaving me alone. I'd be the same way with her if I'd been given the same story she was.

Still, I tell her, "I'll get some curtains."

"You're not going to back down, are you?" Her tone is dejected, her shoulders slumped when she turns her attention back toward me.

Shaking my head, I offer a small smile. "I need to do this, Hales. It's time."

She can claim to fear serial killers and dust and loneliness all she wants, but what she's truly afraid of is losing me to the darkness that she thinks hangs above my head. The demons she's convinced whisper temptations into my ears.

They don't.

No matter how many times I scream at her that I don't want to die, she doesn't listen. No one does. Because of that one night that was completely out of my control. The one night that destroyed the life I loved so much and led to three months in *real* hell, I've been labeled the girl who doesn't want to live. I haven't told anyone the truth to protect my attackers—the people who have stolen all my credibility—but this is the first step to gaining my confidence back and reclaiming my life.

One day, she'll hear my words and find the truth hiding between them.

2

The Lamb

MOVING my things into the house takes almost no time, especially with Halen and Kennedy's help. A couple of suitcases full of clothes, two crates of linens, a few miscellaneous boxes, and some groceries I picked up to fill the fridge is all I have. I think it took longer to drive here than it did to unpack Halen's van.

Growing up with a mother who was more concerned with scoring her next hit than holding on to school projects or taking milestone photos, Halen and I didn't start our adult lives with much. Of course, she's been able to accumulate her own special keepsakes throughout the years between her and Kennedy. Anything of value that may have crossed through my hands was either lost or stolen in my various moves. That's what I'm hoping to change with this new start.

Halen has tried to convince me not to move here at least a dozen more times since I first showed it to her last week, but

I've stood my ground. She just doesn't get it—this need to settle. She's never been *un*settled enough to feel it.

The stillness doesn't sink in until they leave, and I'm left alone for the first time in years—and then, it lingers. I thought I would get used to it after some time, but it continues to haunt in the next couple weeks. The house is so silent, it pulsates and rings in my ears as I walk through each room, deciding what will go where, the same way I've been doing each night since I moved in.

It's a fun, distracting game to move things all around until I find the perfect spot. Every moment I'm not working, I'm turning this place into my own little sanctuary.

There're two extra bedrooms and an entire living room that I've decided I have no use for. They sit on the opposite side of the house from my master bedroom, family room, and kitchen. I keep each door pulled shut, closing off the setting sun's natural light from the small hallway. It's an odd habit I learned from living with my mom and the number of random roommates she always kept. Bedroom doors were never open, because no one wanted us seeing what was happening behind them.

I'm pulling the last door closed, when the distinct clatter of something metal hitting cement echoes throughout the kitchen, where the garage is attached. I stop in my tracks, holding my breath to listen for any other noise to follow, but nothing does. My heart is punching holes through my chest as I take the three steps into the kitchen and grab a knife from my new butcher block, then tip toe over to the door.

I haven't turned on any lights yet, though the sun is quickly descending behind the trees and blanketing my new home in hazy, dark shadows. Maybe someone didn't realize I was home, and they're trying to break in. Or, the owners did admit they haven't made it out here in quite some time… maybe there's a squatter that's been living in the garage.

Any scenario I come up with in my head terrifies me. But standing here frozen with my back to the wall isn't going to save me from the impending murder I've convinced myself is coming, so I've either got to move or hide.

I allow myself to take three deep breaths before swinging open the door and stabbing the knife into the black, empty air.

Okay, so my self-defense skills are lacking. *Sue me*. I've never lived on my own before, and I've always been in the city, where anyone could hear me if I screamed loud enough. Here, I bet I could be slaughtered right on the back patio and no one would be the wiser.

Fortunately, there's no one in the garage. An old oil can is lying on its side in the middle of the floor, clearly having fallen off the storage shelves. I quietly walk over and pick it up, taking the opportunity to look around.

The owners made it clear that this was just an unused vacation home for them. In fact, there's hardly been any trace of them throughout the entire house. No family pictures, no meaningful knickknacks, no forgotten clothing. The shelves are scarcely peppered with random things that no one really has any use for anymore, which doesn't shock me. It was all probably left behind by the people who lived here before.

What does surprise me is the light peeking through the bottom crack of the door on the other side of the garage. I walk across the dusty cement floor to turn it off, assuming it's just a storage room or shed and that they forgot to flip the switch the last time they were here. That obviously isn't helping the energy bill, though what should I care? I'm not paying it.

As I get closer, I could swear I hear the deep rumbling of a man's voice. I pause in front of the door, listening carefully to see if that's where it came from. But there's no noise on the other side. I lean forward to check the cracks beneath the door for any moving shadows against the dim light, but again, I find nothing. Assuming I misheard something over my dragging footsteps, I twist the handle to open the door and turn the light off.

Only to find that the door is locked.

I wiggle the handle a few times, hoping that maybe it's just jammed. Still, it doesn't give. With a sigh, I start back toward the house, making a mental note to ask the owners where the key to that room is.

3

The Wolf

A LOUD, distinctive crack echoes off the walls when my hands jerk to the left, and I watch as life instantly fades from my victim's eyes.

This is my favorite part. When I get to witness the flicker behind their eyes disappear into nothingness. My own eyes roll to the back of my head, and I release my hold from his jaw. His head hangs awkwardly to the side, his neck now completely broken and useless.

I pause for a moment to hear the soft sigh pass his lips as he sags over enough for his final breath to leave his lungs. Blood drips onto the tattered, gray Armani suit he so proudly wore into the seedy gentleman's club I found him in, then splatters onto the plastic-covered floor.

It took me a while to learn the perfect force and angle to use for the cracking effect. When their soul exits their body and it's so close, I can feel it—it's an addictive feeling unlike any other. Far better than any drug I've ever consumed. And I've consumed plenty.

I wasn't always like this—ruled by this murderous need for revenge. In fact, if we ran into each other on the street, you'd have no clue how many lives have been lost by my hand. All you'd see was another too-rich, New York business-district asshole who barely mutters an apology as he passes by. Sure, it's not polite, but manners aren't necessary where I come from. Not when money and social status rule everything. Besides, I work hard to keep people away from me. The world I come from is cruel and incestuous, with little regard for anything beyond the bottom line.

And for what it's worth, as long as you weren't involved in the brutal killing of my sister, you'd never have to worry about my face being the last you saw.

There're six, to be exact. Six times, including this one, I've been secluded in this room with my victims. With the men who were there on the night my twin sister died and took part in the grotesque display. Men who we both grew up with in the same schools and country clubs and vacation towns. Six times, I've taken justice into my own hands because the fucked-up system allowed it to slip through the cracks. Next are the ones who had a hand in covering it up.

I have a plan and tunnel vision to get me through it. I'm the judge, the jury, and the executioner for Sienna's case. All it costs me is my soul, which I'll gladly hand over when the time comes. It means nothing without her, anyways.

I sat with my grief. It almost consumed me. Until anger came in and numbed me, then began to fight back, breeding a strong and insatiable need for vengeance. I may be dead inside, but I have a purpose—at least for now.

But this man—this *group* of men—they deserve far worse than the fate I've afforded them. And I have no doubt they'll receive it. I'm just initiating them into Hell before the devil gets his hands on them.

Or Sienna does. My sister is likely as ruthless in death as she was in life.

"He was useless," almost as if my thoughts conjured her, the eerie feminine voice scoffs from the corner of the room.

I used to jump when she did that, but it's become part of our routine. I kill them while she watches from a distance. Only when they're good and dead does she interrupt me anymore. She used to hang over my shoulder and try to micromanage the process, but I quickly put an end to that. This might be about finding answers for her death, but it's a sacred process for me. I don't need her muddling it up with her constant nagging.

That's one thing about her I don't miss.

My sister may be dead to the world, but she still haunts me.

I can already see you rolling your eyes.

Fine... Go ahead and laugh. I know you are.

I laughed and cried and raged—among taking countless mind-altering drugs in an attempt to chase her away.

It doesn't make sense. In fact, it goes against everything taught to us in the ridiculously expensive Catholic boarding school we were sent to. But she's here. Sienna was brutally murdered, and then somehow found me in the afterlife to carry out the punishment for everyone involved.

Did you get that out of your system?

Okay, good. Let's get back to the story.

"He confirmed a few things that were unclear," I reply, annoyed she's interrupting my moment so soon.

Sienna moves to stand before our newest victim, eyeing him skeptically.

Logan Simon.

His father is a shareholder at my family's investment company and a long-time member of The Loyal Order of the Serpent. I've never liked him, personally. He's always been a whiny little prick who takes whatever he wants with zero consequences and his father is even worse. This time, they took too much.

"He ordered my drink that night," she muses, absently running her fingers down his pale, stubbled cheek. "He must have been the one to choose me."

I can hear the hurt in her voice as she stares into his face. I already knew he was the one who picked her that night for their weird ritual. He admitted as much while I cut the hideous Order's snake tattoo off his arm and dangled the bloody chunk of skin before his eyes. It's the same tattoo my father and grandfather wear proudly on their backs—concealed from view, but there to declare their allegiance to the misogynistic group. The same symbol they so desperately want to see branded into my skin one day, so I can take over for them.

Follow in the family footsteps.

Turns out, my feet are too big to fit into their footsteps, my stride too long. I'd rather die than shrink myself down to fit into the life they want for me. They just aren't ready to admit that yet.

Logan originally tried to claim she'd been a random victim. A prospect needed to be initiated into The Order that night, and he was the one leading their sickening ceremony —one that included brutally beating, raping, and murdering a "random" woman of the leader's choosing. According to him, Sienna was just in the wrong place at the wrong time. He had no idea it was her until the bag was pulled off her head.

But that's bullshit.

He's been around me and Sienna since we were in diapers, and he started going after her shortly after. Thankfully, my sister had better taste in who she dated than some spoiled, arrogant asshole who waves daddy's money around to excuse his horrific behavior—though not much better. She always rejected him in the most public ways, and he wanted her to pay for it. *That's* why he picked her.

If I didn't know that going in, I would have figured it out fairly quickly based on his body language as he spewed the well-rehearsed lie. In the subtle way his eyes darted to the left. Or the slight tilt of his head when I prodded further.

That was when I knew I wasn't going to get much out of him with my usual tactics and, unfortunately for him, it was when I upped the ante.

I smirk at the distant sound of his screams as I extracted the information I wanted out of him, habitually pulling the smooth, cold metal necklace out of my pocket. It's the last piece of her I have to hold. A heart-shaped locket our grandmother gifted for her twelfth birthday that she wore every day since. When the case fell through and the police returned her belongings, this was carefully folded into the dress she had been wearing that night, still coated in her dried, brown blood.

I never cleaned it. I wanted the harsh reminder of what happened to her that night so I never wavered in my quest for revenge. But the blood has worn off from all the times I've taken it out of my pocket, flipping it around in my hand. It's become a part of me now, just as it was a part of her.

Sienna's moment of vulnerability quickly ends. She straightens her spine and pushes her shoulders back stubbornly, and I already know what she's thinking. She's done giving this piece of shit any more of her time—something she now has a lot of. Her ghostly eyes take in the space and her nose scrunches up in disgust at the blood splatters all over the tarp I hung from the ceiling. At the crimson pool at his feet.

My eyes follow her lead, only I look on proudly at a night well spent. This is a form of art. One I've perfected in the past few months. It's something I'm actually good at, and if you ask my father, that's a rarity in itself. If I could frame this cheap plastic and hang it in my penthouse without repercussions, I'd do it.

But alas, I have a large cleanup ahead of me. Technically, I'm not even supposed to be in Styx right now. I would hire someone to do the cleanup for me, but I'm not ready to risk being exposed just yet. Bringing another person in on the process only makes me more likely to get caught, regardless of how discreet they are.

My gaze falls to my watch to check the time, clearing away all the missed calls and texts from my assistant. Sienna and her best friend, Mallory, shared an apartment on the east side of Styx, and Mallory kept it for herself after Sienna passed. My assistant thinks she's the reason I keep coming back to this shitty place.

My parents bought a cottage down the road to spend weekends when Sienna decided to go to the University of Styx for her master's degree. She was planning to be a plastic surgeon or some shit. I have no idea, honestly. It just seemed like an excuse for them to continue the college parties beyond the usual dedicated four years.

I never went to college, so I have no clue.

Our mother fell in love with Styx when she visited the campus with Sienna. She bought the lake house as a spot for our parents to visit without intruding and even went as far as naming it The Crystal Cottage. My father added this workshop off the back of the attached garage to butcher and process whatever animal he was hunting that season. He was usually into bigger, less common game than anything you'd find in Styx, so I couldn't ever understand why he bothered going through the trouble. Once I started using it for my own version of hunting prey, I started to appreciate it more.

Though, I have found it to be a little *too* convenient for my uses. I doubt processing deer required so much sound-proofing of the walls. It seemed like the perfect place to bring the bodies of the men who killed my sister after I hunted them. The hour drive from New York has been the only downfall.

"She's probably going insane," Sienna says, her brows raised into her forehead with irritation.

She's never liked the middle-aged woman who teeters the line of assistant and mother, always taking my mom's jealous side on the matter. But that's the good thing about her being dead. I don't have to listen to her opinions about how I'm living my life.

Well, I guess in a way, I still do. But I don't have to comply.

"She'll get over it. I have a lot to do tonight." I gesture my arm to draw her attention back to the dead body sitting beside us to prove my point.

We're in the middle of negotiating a contract with a huge firm in New York, so I should at least be responding to Eliza in case something pops up with that, but it can wait until I wash the blood off my hands.

"You got messy with this one. You're starting to show more rage than control," she chastises, crossing her arms over her chest. "Maybe you should take a break."

I can't help my eyeroll. I really don't have the energy for this.

"If you're going to nag me, you can just leave. I'm sure you have better things to do nowadays anyway."

Her smartass response is cut off by the doorknob rattling behind us. My heart immediately drops into my stomach as I swing around to double check the lock.

It's securely flipped into place, but the knob still slightly twists back and forth while whoever is on the other side tries to get in.

I'm stuck to my spot, stunned silent with the blood of my victim drying onto my hands. What am I going to do if they find a way in here? I instantly decide that I'm killing them, and the thought sends me spiraling.

"Who the hell could it be?" Sienna wonders. Her stunned expression mirrors mine as we share a look.

But I can't speak. I have no idea if whoever is out there has already heard me before, and I can't risk letting them know I'm here in case they haven't realized it yet.

Sienna's right, though. Who the fuck is on the other side of that door?

With the only entrance to the room coming from inside the garage, there's absolutely no reason for anyone to be trying to open that door. Not to mention, the house has been sitting empty for years.

The rattling stops and dragging footsteps echo through the garage. I turn back to Sienna, my eyebrows practically in my hairline as I ask, "Can't you use your weird little ghost powers and check?"

Scowling, her mouth pops open in offense. She hates when I bring up her deadly state, but what the fuck good is it to have a ghost hanging around if they can't go through walls and make sure you aren't about to be caught murdering someone?

We stare at each other in a stubborn standoff, each of us refusing to be the first to break eye contact until she scoffs, rolling her eyes to the ceiling.

"You're such a jackass," she spits before her translucent

form disappears right before my eyes. A moment later, she returns with her eyes widened in alarm. "There's a woman here. It looks like she's squatting or something. She's got her things moved in."

Fuuuuck.

4

The Wolf

"ARE you aware there is someone squatting at the Styx property?"

I hear my father's disappointed sigh reverberate through my car's speakers, and I know he made sure to breathe right into the phone so I didn't miss it.

"And what would make you think that?" There's some rustling in the background, then a woman's voice mumbles something into his other ear.

He should be home with Mom right now, keeping her company. It's the whole reason he's taken a 'step back' from his business—a process that has resurfaced a lot of resentment toward me for not being the perfect, prodigal son to hand his work off to, the same way his father did with him. But that wasn't her voice I just heard.

"I was driving past the house and every light seemed to be on." The lie falls easily from my lips, just as they always have.

I panicked after the door handle rattled while I was there.

Once enough time passed that I was absolutely positive no one was waiting outside for me, I looked around the property for any sign of the intruder.

Imagine my complete and utter horror when I walked to the back of the house and found a half-naked woman sprawled out on the couch, staring into a computer screen like she owned the place. I still can't decide if I'm disgusted or enamored by her.

She made no attempt at hiding herself from view. The wall of windows off the back remained uncovered to avoid any obstruction of the private lake and still she was lying there, completely exposed.

"No one is squatting. I rented out the place," my father explains distractedly, as if he can't be bothered with giving me his full attention.

"Why would you do that?"

"Why does it matter to you, Sebastian?" he snaps, and it only adds to my growing list of suspicions about him. This whole situation feels like too much of a coincidence.

"It would have been nice to know," I say tersely, irritated that I've already given too much away.

My grasp on the situation in Styx is slipping. The delicately balanced charade I've created is starting to go dangerously off kilter. If I'm honest with myself, it has been for a while.

Each person I kill is leading me deeper into the wormhole, exposing far more people in the situation surrounding my sister's death than I ever expected. People I know and once respected. People like my father.

There were never supposed to be this many victims. I wasn't supposed to enjoy it this much.

And now this. This low-class, aloof girl who has stumbled right into my path and planted herself directly in my way. She's meaningless in the grand scheme of things, but she's the one thing that finally sets me off. The first domino to fall.

"I wasn't aware you were still going to Styx."

His tone is mocking. He thinks he's caught me doing something I shouldn't be. To his credit, I am. But he doesn't need to know how spot on he is.

"Just for the night." I don't try to muster up a weak excuse. He won't listen anyway.

Another sigh, and then a door closes in the background. The familiar squeak of his office chair assaults my ear, and I can practically see him crossing his ankles on his desk and leaning backwards, that sinister smile splitting his face. He's set his trap and I fell right in.

"Your mother can't bear to visit that city anymore," he begins, the weight of his words hanging between us. Since Sienna's death, Mom hasn't been able to bear much of anything. "I decided to rent it out until she's ready to sell. Get some money out of it."

"I'll buy it," I say without thinking.

I'm instantly regretting the outburst. The last thing I need to do is further attach my name to the place I've been torturing and butchering people in, especially when my father is involved with it. But I need control. I need something to go my way.

My father scoffs, but thinks it over for a moment. "Your mother would never agree to sell. I've already tried."

"She won't mind so long as it stays in the family," I press, for no reason other than I refuse to allow him to deny me.

"I doubt you could offer anything close to what I paid," he tries again. I can tell he's starting to give in.

I have far more money in my accounts than even he knows about. Ever since I abandoned the family investment business to start my own cyber security company, it's been a pissing contest between us to prove who's worth more. I decided early on that I didn't want to spend my life making other people money—I wanted to make my own, and I wanted to revolutionize the world while I did it. He still resents me to this day. When I brought him my first design for my software, he threw his head back and laughed.

Billions of dollars later, I'm the one laughing.

I know he'll start with some ridiculously high number for the cottage, but I don't really give a shit anymore. It has more value to me than any amount of money could offer. Besides, my ego won't allow me to back out now.

"Send me what you want for it in an email, and I'll have my realtor look it over and draw up a contract."

"There's still the issue of the tenant," he points out. The quick flick of a lighter goes off, and then a second later, his Zippo snaps closed. I hear him take a sharp inhale. "I have a contract with her," he strains through his exhale.

I've seen him do the motion so many times, I can imagine every detail of him lighting his cigarette as the familiar sounds travel through the line. It's disgusting. A repulsive habit I had hoped would kill him by now.

Yet, here we are.

"I'll have my lawyer worry about it."

There's another pause, as if he's waiting for me to back out on the deal already. Or maybe he's trying to figure out my angle, though I'm fairly certain he already knows. Either way, I wait.

"Fine. You'll be hearing from me shortly," he finally says, and then the line cuts short.

I tilt my head against the headrest of my seat just as there's a break in the landscape and I can see the distant New York skyline.

Control.

All I need is a little bit of control, and then I can figure out where to go next.

5

The Lamb

I'M LATE AGAIN.

I've only been working at Old Soul Cafe for a couple of weeks, and I've already gotten three warnings about tardiness. It's really not my fault this time, though. Mrs. Botless, the woman I dog walk for, kept me tied up in a riveting conversation about her upcoming bingo tournament. She wouldn't stop rambling until I was already walking twenty feet away from her, promising her that we'd continue the story tomorrow, but I *had* to go. I hopped into my beat-up, ancient Volkswagen that Kennedy's mechanic friend agreed to accept cash payments on, and raced over to the cafe before she could mutter a single word.

It's seven minutes past the start of my shift by the time I'm swinging the front door open and jogging behind the counter to begin taking orders from the growing line of people. Rosie, my boss, looks over at me from the espresso machine with a disappointed scowl that tells me she'll be pulling me into her office the second I get this line down.

She's a thirty-something single woman with bright pink hair and the most eccentric wardrobe I've ever seen who has poured everything she has into Old Soul. When she isn't laying into me about being late or getting yet another order wrong, she's actually a really cool person to talk to. We share a lot of things in common and work well together when it matters. Time just passes quicker when we're both on a shift.

That's not why she hasn't fired me, though. Her sister was my roommate at Sunnybrook. Genny's been to the facility three times already, but can't seem to overcome her vices just yet. On my last day, she told me to talk to Rosie about helping out at the cafe, knowing she would need the extra hands with her being tied up in rehab. I had no plans to follow through, but not many people are willing to hire someone fresh out of a facility with a huge, otherwise unexplainable gap in their resume, so I really had no choice.

Old Soul is ten minutes past Styx and over a half hour from my new home, but the tips alone make it well worth the drive. If I can get here on time.

Especially after dog walking for Mrs. Botless, Halen and Kennedy's neighbor. I might have to pick Ollie up earlier to account for his chatty owner. Once I finish my shift at Old Soul, I'll be rushing back across town to fill in a bartending shift at the sports bar that Halen works at.

I feel like I've called in every favor I have since moving into my own place, just to make ends meet. Don't get me wrong, my rent is insanely cheap. I'm not complaining even in the slightest. But it's still a struggle to cover all by myself without a steady, full-time job. I've applied everywhere with zero callbacks, and each day in the job field looks more and more grim. I'm terrified the favors will dry out before I can find something stable and I'll be stuck back in

Halen's basement just when I've finally caught a taste of freedom.

So, I spend my evenings glued to my computer, applying for every open position I can find until I pass out and have to do it all over again.

Except this evening.

After being threatened with my last strike from Rosie and a horrible shift at the bar, where I was groped and yelled at by a table of drunk bachelors, I'm finally home alone and enjoying the silence.

So far, Halen has been wrong about serial killers living in my woods or the boogeyman hiding under my bed. I never got around to buying curtains for the enormous living room windows, but I haven't minded it yet. The property is private enough without them, and I rarely even see my neighbors, if they're home at all.

It's taken me a while to get used to the silence of living alone. I never realized what chaos my life had been, always sharing my spaces with someone else. The peace was unsettling at first, but I've easily become addicted to it. I love the freedom of coming home and stripping my sweaty clothes off the instant I walk through the door, just because there isn't a single person who will stop me. Or leaving my dishes in the sink until I feel up to washing them.

It's quite liberating, being a slob. Everyone should try it at least once.

The house itself makes a lot of creaks and groans that I've grown used to. The opposite end where the other bedrooms are remains closed off as my backup plan in the event I run out of favors to pay my bills, and that's where most of the noises come from. I don't want roommates, especially now that I'm used to being alone, but I also refuse to fail.

I'm returning my dishes to the sink when I first see the figure in my backyard. I walk by the sliding glass doors so fast, I nearly miss it. But something urges me to turn my head at the very last second, and that's when I notice him. I freeze, my heart dropping down to my toes as my lungs seize up.

Dressed in all black with a hood pulled over his head just far enough to conceal his face, a man stands in the middle of the back lawn. He's peering into the house, directly at me.

My stomach flips as I squint to get a better look. It's not *him*—my bully ex-boyfriend. I've memorized his stature enough to tell the difference. This figure is taller and leaner. My ex is short and stocky, with a head full of long, platinum blond hair that even the biggest hood couldn't conceal.

What are the chances a second man could be hunting me?

His stance is wide and comfortable, as if he's been watching me stuff my face in front of the TV for some time now. His head turns and tilts the slightest bit, bobbing like he's talking to someone. But I don't see anyone else around. I turn away for a split second, gauging how well he could see me from where I was just sitting on the couch. Without anything covering the windows, he would have had a completely unobstructed view. I'm surprised I didn't notice him before.

When I turn back, he's gone. It's as if he's disappeared into thin air.

What the fuck?

There's no way anyone could move that quickly.

…Right?

I'm shuffling closer to the window despite the terror I feel in my gut, trying to catch another glimpse of him, irritated when I fall short. The bastard was too quick.

My survival instincts finally kick in, propelling me toward the couch to grab my phone, and I'm dialing the police in the next breath. But just before I hit the green button, I stop myself, doubting every second of the past ten minutes.

Why the hell would anyone want to watch me shove down a carton of ice cream in the middle of the night? I don't have anything of value in this home, aside from the ridiculously heavy furniture the owners left behind. I also have no reason to think anyone would want to stalk me. And the guy moved so fast… I'm not even sure how he did it.

Maybe I've imagined the whole thing.

Would a police officer even believe me if I told them? Or would they write me off like another crazy person from the loony bin?

Dropping my phone, I look out the window for any sign of him again. Of course, there isn't anything visible from this far away, and while I'm not fully convinced he was there in the first place, I have no intention of going outside and getting taken by some psycho on the off-chance he's waiting for me in the woods. I may be dumb, but I've seen enough horror movies in my day to know that's not the right move.

Instead of making the call, I lock my phone and sneak back into the kitchen to grab my knife. If the man is real and still watching, hopefully he'll see the knife and realize I'm not afraid to use it.

Or, it'll ruin the only element of surprise I have.

Before I get too far into my head, I run to my room, shut the door, and hide under my covers like any other rational person would do.

6

The Wolf

It's a risky move to be making the drive into Styx for the second weekend in a row without a good excuse, but I need to get my affairs back in order. Luckily, I can hack the GPS in my car and erase the trip from its history. I left my personal phone at my penthouse and picked up a burner with cash, spoofed it, then forwarded all my work calls to it. I've gone through this routine so many times, it hardly takes a second thought.

I'm just usually traveling with a person tied up in my trunk when I do it.

I drive straight to the cottage, not bothering with parking down the street and walking there on foot, the way I usually would to keep my identity concealed from any nosey neighbors. It seems pointless when I'm buying the place next week. If anyone questions me, I've got the alibi of checking out my newest investment. I do, however, make sure to park across the street instead of pulling into the long driveway, just in case the tenant is home. I don't want to scare her just yet.

The neighbors can ask questions, but they don't need to know that my visit has nothing to do with the house and everything to do with the person inside of it.

I want to see her. Study her. Determine if she's a real threat and how much she potentially knows.

I'm the hostile wolf with an insatiable prey drive, and she's the little lamb that's accidentally wandered into my path.

I've caught her scent and now I can't stop until I take her down.

First, I check the workshop. The door is still securely locked, and nothing appears to be out of place. All traces of the dickhead I tortured in here last weekend are completely gone, and aside from the slight metallic smell that lingers in the air from the sheer amount of blood he lost, there's no sign that anyone has even been in this room recently.

Good.

I was unstable when I packed up the body and scrubbed the place down. With no access to my usual tools or the freedom to come and go as I needed, I couldn't destroy the body as methodically as I should have. Instead, I had to wrap it in plastic and dump it into one of the barren fields just outside the city.

It's the same place The Order uses when they're through with their victims—not far from where my own sister was found. I hated giving them the chance to find him and draw their conclusions. I enjoy the mystery of plucking them off one by one, leaving them wondering where their sons and brothers are being taken and why they aren't popping back up. That was all ripped away, thanks to *her.*

Every time I had a second to think this week, my mind

strayed to any potential mistakes I may have made. I'm glad to see that my insecurities were misplaced.

It gives me just enough of a confidence boost to close the door and head for the house.

"What are you doing?" Sienna's sharp, haunting voice stops me just as I pull the door to the hunting room shut.

My shoulders instantly tense. "Go away."

I can't deal with her pestering me right now. If it weren't for her incessant need to micromanage everything I do, I might have been able to catch my father's new tenant *before* I brought my victim here.

She almost cost me everything.

"You can't go in there. She's home." Sienna points toward the door I'm facing. The one that leads right into the kitchen, where she could be standing right now.

"Oh, *now* you can warn me?" I bite back sarcastically.

Forcing her lips into a grim line, Sienna stares at me for a moment before insisting, "She can't see you here."

I sigh, scowling at my dead sister because she's probably fucking right. What am I going to do? Waltz right in there and tie her up? I have no real reason to kill her. *Yet.*

"I'll go around back," I mumble, mostly to myself. Sienna attempts to object, but I walk through her and out the door leading to the backyard.

The girl is lying on the couch again. The artificial light from the TV flashes across her skin and illuminates her face every few seconds before dying back down again. I'm only watching for a few moments before she stands from the couch, grabs a bowl from the coffee table, and then drags her feet toward the kitchen. I stand still in the middle of the lawn, adrenaline pumping through my veins like pistons in an engine at the way the moonlight exposes me here, out in the open for her to see at any moment. Still, I can't bring myself to move into the shadows.

Then, to my complete horror, she abruptly stops in the middle of the dining room and swivels her head directly toward me, as if someone had called her name. As if something inside of me silently called to something inside of her.

And her eyes land right on my dark figure.

I can see the wave of fear crash down on her all at once. The way her expression crumples in wonder and disbelief that I'm actually here, watching her. I want to move, but my feet feel rooted to the earth. I'm too enthralled with her to be the first to break eye contact.

Why is she just staring like that? Shouldn't she be calling the police? Running away? Grabbing a gun, for God's sake?

Do something to defend yourself, little lamb.

But she doesn't do any of that. She just stares.

Finally, when her head turns back toward something in the house, I'm released from her invisible grip and logic creeps its way inside my head. I quickly walk over to one of the trees off to the side, leaning against it so I can observe her without being detected again. At least if she tries to look out the window, I'll be able to slip into the shadows before she sees me.

"You shouldn't be here," Sienna hisses from my side.

"I need to make sure she doesn't know anything."

"She clearly doesn't. She would have gone to the police by now if she saw anything. You're risking too much. What if someone sees you lurking out here? You've already been caught once before," she fires off, holding her arm out toward the window I was just staring into.

My gaze cuts over to her. "Why didn't you tell me she was living here last weekend?"

The words come across as an accusation more than a question.

Crossing her arms over her chest in the same stubborn

way she would do when we bickered before, her bottom lip juts out in a pout. "I didn't know," she says defensively.

I consider her ghostly form for a moment. We've never talked about what it's like for her—what sort of things she can or cannot do. I haven't even asked about where she goes when she isn't with me. But I assumed, at the bare minimum, she'd be able to tell me if someone else was around. That she could sense them or something.

That was a foolish assumption. She doesn't seem to know anything more than I do.

I don't mention any of that to her, though. Instead, I look back toward the door and release a sigh.

"I need to cover my ass."

"You're making a mistake. At least wait until you have ownership of the place before you go scaring the girl."

"Why don't you leave the worrying up to me? Go do whatever the hell it is that dead people do with their time, and leave me alone," I snap, not bothering to turn back toward her.

I don't have to look to know she's glaring at me and, within seconds, I can feel the weight of her presence disappear from beside me.

She can be such a fucking pest sometimes.

At some point during our argument, the light from the TV went out in the house and the girl is nowhere to be seen. Unfortunately, Sienna *is* right. She could already have the police racing to catch me peeping into her windows for all I know. It would be unwise to let myself into the house before I even have ownership over it, especially when I'm not sure what she has against me.

After a few weighted moments of debate, I jog through the woods along the driveway and get back into my car instead of walking through the garage and slinking in through the side door, the way I want to.

Another day, little lamb. I'll be back to finish this another day.

7

The Lamb

I WASN'T late for a shift at Old Soul once this week, which put Rosie in a much better mood. I've adjusted my schedule enough to account for drive time—and extra talking time, in Mrs. Botless's case—and while things are still chaotic, I've settled into a routine that feels more manageable.

I've taken the night off from waitressing, opting for a solo Gilmore Girls marathon instead. By the grace of God, I managed to make enough this month to cover my rent, and it's only the twenty-first. Every dime I make after this can either go in my pocket for things like groceries or gas, or I can add it to the jar for next month's rent. Either way, the weight has been temporarily lifted, and I can breathe for a minute.

So I'm taking that breather alone and in peace with a pack of Truly and Netflix. It's going great.

Until it isn't.

I'm three deep when I hear a noise in the garage again.

Pausing the TV to end Lorelei and Rory's constant banter, I crane my head to listen. Five full minutes pass before I decide that it was nothing. I turn the TV back on, but lower the volume just in case.

Three episodes and two more Trulys later, I realize I haven't even been watching the show because I've been so paranoid about the imaginary noise in the garage.

Or was it imaginary?

Finally, I decide I'm wasted enough to go to bed and pray that I was right before, back when I was still sober, and could convince myself it really was all in my imagination.

But if that's the case, why do I have this eerie feeling I'm being watched again?

I've been living in ignorant bliss this whole week, refusing to allow myself to believe there really was a man standing in my backyard, or that he was staring right in at me. It was easy to do when I've hardly been spending any time in the house outside of sleeping and rushing through a shower or shoving food in my mouth as I walk out the door. Now that I'm alone again, the creepy feeling has returned tenfold, and it refuses to be ignored. Suddenly, Halen's teasing about me being all alone in these woods with a serial killer seems much more plausible.

I'm racing toward the back of my house and leaping onto my bed as my intrusive thoughts get the best of me. I'm convinced there's someone in my house waiting to kill me.

But sleep is weighing too heavy for the fears to consume me once I'm comfortable in bed, especially with the alcohol running through my veins. As soon as the room stops spinning, I feel sleep take me under, and I'm passed out in what feels like minutes.

Something wakes me a couple of hours later. There's a long, discombobulated moment where I'm confused about the time and whether I really fell asleep or not, my consciousness still hazy from the alcohol. But when I realize it was a creak in the floorboard that woke me, I shoot up in bed and look around the room.

It's still dark. My clock reads 3:33, and I'm instantly reminded of all the times Kennedy rambled on about the witching hour. Maybe the noise wasn't a killer at all… but a ghost.

Could there be a ghost in the house? That might explain the light…

Would that be better or worse than someone breaking in?

No. I shake my head in an attempt to rid myself of the thought.

Ghosts aren't real. No one's breaking in.

The man isn't back.

You're drunk. Go to sleep, I think. Or maybe I said it out loud, I don't know.

I lie back and turn away from the bright, moonlit window. Within seconds, sleep takes a hold of me once more, and I don't wake again until the morning.

8

The Wolf

My father wastes no time sending over a ridiculously high number for the Styx cottage. I'm barely settled in my office for the day when I receive the email.

It took longer than usual for me to get my own car parked in my carport on Monday morning after driving back into the city from Styx last week before my driver, Sterling, pulled up to pick me up in his. We drove straight through New York morning traffic to my building, already two hours late for my meetings. I have no issues driving an endless number of hours on the expressway with no breaks, but New York City traffic is enough to make me want to blow my head off. Road rage is a real thing, and it's something I've yet to get used to since moving here. I hired Sterling within my first year of moving Lancaster Tech into an office and out of my old apartment, and I haven't looked back. He's far better equipped to handle the ridiculously congested city than I am.

I was immediately met outside the elevator by my

assistant, Eliza, who wasn't shy about letting me know she was irritated with my late arrival. She prattled on about my adjusted schedule since I got home later than expected, and I barely sat down on my chair after getting my ass chewed out before my phone vibrated with his email.

I'm not even dignifying his request with a response. Instead, I forward the email to my realtor and ask her to pull up comps in the area, then head into my next meeting for the day, avoiding Eliza's glare from her open office door.

She's a middle-aged, single mother of four adults who doesn't take shit from anyone. Her personality is more akin to a rottweiler than a personal assistant, and I'm waiting for the day she realizes I'm hardly worth her time. She's also the only person who is allowed to talk to me the way she does—more disciplinary than my own mother. But she cares about my company and what we're doing for the world and, thankfully, that's been enough to get her to stay.

I always manage to thaw her ice-cold attitude.

The rest of my week follows the same chaotic pattern. I'm caught up in meetings and work that goes well into the night, barely taking time to sleep in my own bed before I'm back in the office the following day.

My realtor has a deal settled with my father by Friday afternoon and promises to have the paperwork ready by Monday.

"Your dad really didn't want to negotiate much. You're overpaying by a lot, and the area isn't the best. Are you sure this is what you want?" she asks over the phone.

She thinks I'm making a mistake. And maybe I am. But I'm too deep into it to give a fuck about that right now.

I can't have his tenant snooping around. Not when I'm this close to the finish line.

"I'll pay whatever he says. It has sentimental value," I explain to Chantel as Sterling pulls up to my home.

I'm already planning on jumping into my car and driving upstate as soon as he pulls away. I barely managed to thaw Eliza's cold shoulder for arriving so late to the office on Monday before she found out I was leaving again. She's made it well-known to me that she's pissed. We're supposed to be preparing for our presentation next week to take over another tech firm and expand our reach. I should be spending the weekend making sure I'm ready, and she knows it.

When I packed my laptop into its case and told her I'd be unavailable for a little while, the glare she sent my way could have burned holes into my chest.

"Are you sure you want to forgo the inspection and appraisal?" Chantel asks, interrupting the memory.

"Positive. Let Eliza know when the papers are ready, and we'll get a carrier to pick them up."

We end the call just as Sterling stops the car. Eliza's worries are misplaced. I know my company well enough to make that presentation blindfolded. Even if I hadn't spent the past two weeks looking over data, I'd be well prepared. Besides, I have more pressing matters at the moment. The house may not be mine yet, but I'm still going to make sure everything is in order.

I should take her car in the driveway as a sign to leave. It's late by the time I'm coasting down her street, and I have no idea if she's told anyone about our encounter last weekend. So, I should go.

But I don't.

Instead of turning my car around and remaining undetected the way I know that I should, I'm fastening the mask over my mouth that I use when I'm stalking or collecting my victims, then sneaking through the garage again, testing the door to the kitchen. My heart kicks up when I find that it's unlocked and I take that as a sign to keep going, carefully stepping into the dark room.

Small traces of her stand defiantly against the lavish pieces my mother and sister curated for the space. I remember them talking obsessively over it the first time we were all dragged out here, when Sienna moved into her apartment with Mallory and started her first semester. The place was completely bare, the rooms outdated. My father hadn't added the workshop then, either.

Within two months, the cabin was gutted and remodeled. It was such a frivolous waste of money, given the place would hardly be used any more than the other properties our family owned. But it gave them something to bond over. An experience I'm sure my mother looks back on and appreciates now that Sienna's gone.

Now, with this new tenant's belongings sprinkled about, everything looks much more ridiculous and out of place. This is Styx, not our beach house in the Hamptons. They were clearly trying to make it something it wasn't.

Alcohol cans line the counter and a pile of dirty dishes sits in the sink. Her shoes have been haphazardly kicked off along the wall and three coats lay flung across one of the kitchen chairs. I walk past her small messes with equal parts wonder and disgust. Grabbing one of the jackets, I inhale her scent—a strong mix of coconut, vanilla, and coffee.

I can't stand how addictive I find it. Such a stark contrast from the strong floral scent of Chanel No. 5 that Mallory and all the other women I've hooked up with douse themselves in.

Carefully placing the jacket back onto the chair, I tell

myself it's part of the hunt. Just a step in the process. Though, I've never gone this far with my previous victims. Not until right before I captured and killed them.

Before I can get any more confused by my feelings, I push on through the house. Most of it remains untouched by her.

She's taken the master bedroom. Her sleeping form is sprawled across the mattress, her soft snores the only sound that fills the cool night air. Even my footsteps are silent as I make my way across the plush carpet and into the nearly empty walk-in closet.

It's scarce. No designer dresses or one-of-a-kind pieces. No ridiculously priced shoes or outrageous hats. She's nothing like the women I'm used to. There's a pile of dirty clothes sitting in the corner, as if she can't even be bothered with aiming for the laundry basket right beside it. A cheap pair of black heels rests beside a beaten-up pair of snow boots, and the few hangers only hold jeans and cotton t-shirts.

Whoever she is, she doesn't have much. I can't imagine she can afford whatever ridiculous price my father is surely charging her for rent on her own.

Which makes me wonder if she has any roommates. Maybe a boyfriend…

I turn back toward her so my eyes can openly roam over her body—scantily dressed in a simple white tank top and underwear. The tank has ridden up her abdomen, exposing tanned skin and a pierced belly button. Dusky nipples peek through the translucent fabric, leaving little to my imagination. Her legs are slightly spread open, offering a teasing taste of what's between without fully exposing her.

I'm hoping that, if anything, it's the former. I suddenly can't stand the idea of another man having access to her like this now that I've decided she's my prey.

As if I'm magnetized toward her, my feet move on their

own accord to take me to the bed, but a floorboard creaks and I'm stopped in my tracks, slinking back into the safety of the shadows. She releases a quiet moan, the sound of it going straight to my groin as I linger in the doorway, shrouded by darkness. She sits up and squints like the movement hurts her head. Based on the number of cans I saw in the kitchen and the alcohol she's likely consumed, it probably did.

Why are you drinking alone, little lamb?

Her dark eyes scan the room once, skirting right past me, before she falls back onto her pillow, tugs the blanket over her body, and falls back asleep.

I wait until she's snoring again before I walk toward the bed, staring down at her with so much resentment for what she's making me do to her. For how I have to destroy her. Under different circumstances, I would love to devour this woman. I have a feeling she's scrappy enough in bed to give me exactly what I need. What the others never could.

My fingers lightly grasp the blanket and tug it back down, exposing her top half to me again. Her chest rises and falls with each steady breath, the tank top tightening against her breasts every time it does. I hover my hand over her neck, tempted to close the distance and end this right now. It would take the smallest amount of pressure in just the right spot to cut off her airways. It would be over before she even realized what was happening.

I almost do it. My skin lightly brushes hers as I line my fingers up with the exact place they need to be.

But she stirs beneath my touch, shifting my hand from her neck onto her chest, and I freeze in place above her. Her heartbeat thumps against my palm, her skin warm beneath my icy touch. Those long, dark lashes flutter open, revealing round, near-black irises.

She gazes up at me—not in horror, but something else entirely. It's like she's looking at me, but doesn't quite *see* me. Her eyelids stay at half-mast as she grabs my wrist and slides my hand down, over her breast. And then, she shocks me even more by pushing her tit against my palm.

Her head falls back to the side, eyes closing as she arches her back, applying more pressure. Another breathy moan escapes her lips as she snakes her hand down her abdomen and beneath the blanket.

I'm stunned silent. My eyes track her movements under the blanket while she pushes herself into my hand and I'm genuinely confused.

Do you know I'm here?

My fingers trail over her hardened nipple, testing her reaction. She hisses out a breath and shoves herself back against me.

I notice her hips moving back and forth as she rides her own fingers, and I'm ripping the blanket off her with my free hand before I can stop myself. This entire display has shifted me into a different type of predator.

My erection presses so hard against the unforgiving material of my jeans, I have no choice but to undo the button and let it out.

I need relief.

Relief and control.

I can't even begin to think of the consequences of her fully waking up and finding me like this. Standing over her with one hand kneading her breast while the other strokes my cock. I shouldn't be witnessing this. I sure as hell shouldn't be touching her.

But holy fuck, is she hot right now.

One hand works beneath her panties, hips bucking forward as her orgasm builds while the other twiddles the breast I'm not touching. The pure, unadulterated way she's pleasuring herself speaks directly to a primal side of me that

I never knew existed. It's like her body senses I'm here, and it's simply reacting to me.

I've never seen a woman so brazen. Sure, she's half-asleep and likely unaware she has an audience, but something tells me she'd act the same way regardless.

I can tell she's getting close by the way her breaths quicken, her movements more desperate. My balls tighten, the familiar heat of an orgasm wrapping around my spine as if the knowledge I'm about to watch her fall apart is enough to make me do the same. I'm debating whether it would be less noticeable if I pulled away from her now, or after she finished, when she goes still beneath me. She shudders out a breath, thrusting her hips one last time before a loud moan fills the room, and then she relaxes again, her breathing evening out.

My own orgasm follows shortly after, with no warning. I was so caught up in hers, I barely noticed until my cum sputtered out onto her sheet. I quickly rip my hand away from her to catch the rest of it before I make an even bigger mess, stifling a moan as my eyes roam over her center and I notice the wet spot on her panties.

I decide then that I have to taste her before I kill her.

Not now. It would be too risky, and I won't violate her any more than I already have.

No, when her juices finally coat my tongue, it'll be because she begged me to do it. Then, I'll take her life.

For now, I pad over to the master bathroom and clean myself off. My reflection feels like a feral stranger looking back at me. I hardly recognize myself anymore, don't know the side of me who pleasures strange women while they lie there unknowingly.

I felt the same way the first time I murdered someone. Perhaps this is the same thing. A new addiction to feed.

I don't even know her name, but I will soon.

Adjusting myself, I give one last look in the mirror before I head back into her room. I was going to attempt to clean my cum off of her sheets, but decide against it at the last minute.

There's something incredibly satisfying about knowing she's sleeping with my seed. I almost want her to wake up and find it. To run her hand through the sticky puddle and wonder what the hell happened. My cock tightens again at the mere thought.

No, I'm not cleaning it up.

9

The Lamb

I WAKE up with a pounding in my head, my mouth completely dry.

I hate this part. The getting drunk part is fun. The *being* drunk part is great. But the hangover? That always leaves me promising myself I'll never do it again.

My alarm doesn't go off, so instead of nursing the hangover the way I want to, I'm forced to scramble around and get ready for my Saturday shift at Old Soul as my head and stomach protest. I'm chugging water and throwing the first pair of jeans I can find, cursing myself for drinking so many Trulys instead of just going to bed like a normal fucking person.

I run a brush through my hair and speed out the door, determined not to disappoint Rosie when I've been having such a successful streak. After breaking several laws and possibly running over a bunny, I'm walking through the front doors at the exact time my shift starts.

"You're late," Rosie barks, but there's no one in the cafe to hear or wait on.

"No, I'm right on time." I round the counter and grab my apron, quickly throwing it over my head. With my hands on my hips, I look over at the clock above to prove my point. It's exactly 8 a.m. Right when I'm scheduled to start.

Rosie huffs out a laugh, shaking her head. "Fine, you win."

I don't even attempt to hide my triumphant smile. "What did I miss?"

"Nothing at all," she says in a heavy sigh. "Just the usual morning rush."

Toying with the syrups lined against the back wall, I admit, "I got drunk alone and had the weirdest dream last night about a guy in my house."

I can't help the word vomit. The dream has been bothering me all morning, and I need someone to talk to about it to prove I'm not going crazy.

Well, not *that* crazy.

She cuts her gaze to me from the opposite end of the counter. "Should you be drinking?"

I shoot her an incredulous look. "Of course, I can drink. I went to Sunnybrook for attempted suicide, not an alcohol addiction. And besides, I didn't even really try to commit suicide in the first place. I shouldn't have even gone there…" I explain for what feels like the millionth time.

It doesn't matter how many times I scream from the top of my lungs that *I don't want to die*, people will think what they want either way. Especially with the black mark of Sunnybrook on my record.

Rosie holds up her hands in mock surrender. "Fine, fine. It was all an accident, I get it. So what about this dream?"

I blow out a breath, calming myself from the spike in adrenaline. I shouldn't get this upset, but I've grown so tired of living under a microscope and having my every move questioned since that miserable day. Still, Rosie doesn't deserve to have that anger taken out on her. Especially when she's still dealing with the aftereffects of her own sister's unsuccessful attempt.

Genny is, without a doubt, living with one foot on the other side.

Finally, I'm calm enough to explain, "I don't even know. There was a random hot stalker guy in my room, watching me. It felt so real, though."

I leave out the part about a creepy guy standing in my backyard and the terrifying thought that the two incidents might be related. I'm still processing that detail, and I'd rather consider some other alternative than my stalker possibly coming into my house and watching me finger myself. Isn't it more realistic to believe that I may have had some distorted wet dream?

Yeah, I don't think so either.

"Are you sure it *wasn't* real?"

"I'm here, aren't I?" I joke, holding my arms out. "If there was an intruder in my house, I'd probably be dead."

Or half my stuff would be missing. Well, half of the house's stuff. I don't own anything of value. And as far as I could tell, everything was untouched this morning. I've already considered that as a possibility.

"True." Her lips tip up in a smile. "So, like, a lucid dream, then. One you can interact with and control. I've never had one, but I have a friend who trained himself to lucid dream every night."

"Yeah! I've never done that before. It was kind of hot." My teeth graze my bottom lip as I recall how the dream-man touched me, allowing myself to fall headfirst into this theory. The way his eyes darkened while they tracked my hand between my legs.

I squirm against the counter, tightening my thighs

together at the memory. That was definitely a dream. I haven't been with a man since well before I was taken to Sunnybrook. Even then, it wasn't nearly as arousing.

Rosie doesn't seem to notice the direction of my thoughts. Instead, she's focusing on the customer who just walked through the door, and I busy myself with washing the smoothie pitchers sitting in the sink.

Lucid dreaming, huh? I'll have to look more into that.

10

The Lamb

I've been so busy flying across town from gig to gig, I haven't had a moment to think about the mysterious light in the garage since the night I found it. When I checked again the following morning, the light was off, and I could only deduce that the bulb either burnt out, or I imagined the whole thing. Which isn't too far-fetched considering how exhausted I've been.

Except, when I think about the mystery man standing in my backyard the following night, the pieces fall together too nicely for my liking.

He hasn't returned this week. Granted, I've been getting out of work much later, desperate to collect any extra wages I can to cover my bills. I don't allow myself any time to look around when I pull into my driveway late at night, and dash over to the front door like Freddy is on my tail. I've also invested in some new, thicker window coverings from Goodwill to go over the sliding glass doors and back window. They're a little worn and out of date, but they do the job. I make a point to close them before I leave each day, and don't bother opening them again until I'm home long enough to enjoy any of the scarce sunlight they let in.

Perhaps he *has* come back, and I just haven't allowed myself to see him.

Is that the healthiest approach to having a potential stalker? No. But I'm sure it's not the worst thing I could do.

I don't have much time to obsess over it today, either. It's my first full day off in weeks, and Halen is coming over to hang out. If I mention anything about a weird noise, a mysterious light, or a creepy guy in my backyard, she'll be packing my bags herself.

"Have you talked to Mom recently?" she asks from the dining room table as I'm walking our lunches over from the kitchen. She's making her best attempt at seeming casual, but I don't miss the way her fingers lock together beneath the table, or how her heel is incessantly tapping against the floor.

"Nope." I haven't spoken to my mother in almost a year, and she's made no attempt to reach out to me, either.

Why would she, after what she did? Or I should say, what she was unsuccessful at doing.

I carefully set her plate down in front of her before I take my seat across the table. We're having grilled cheese and tomato soup—the same meal I always made for us when we were younger. Mostly because a loaf of bread, cheese, and a can of soup were some of the few things I could scrape together enough food stamps to buy that would last longer than one meal before Mom sold them off for cash.

I assume it's what led Halen to bring up our mother. She's always had a warped view of the past. Where the meal reminds me of a time when I was forced to mature well beyond my years to ensure both mine and Halen's survival while our mother lay passed out on the couch, she probably sees it and thinks of how she would eat it beside her sleeping form.

Memories can be tricky like that.

"We never know how much time we'll have with her. Especially with how far downhill her health has gone in the past few months," she begins to guilt, as she always does when the topic comes up.

I hold up my palm to signal for her to stop talking and roll my eyes. Truthfully, I don't give a fuck how long my mother has to live, and I'd rather pour this boiling, acidic soup in my eyes before I ever see her again. Especially after what she's done to me. If I had to wager a guess, I'd say she'll outlive both of us, just so she can torture us with her manipulation.

"She's family, Jovie," Halen adds. I can tell she has more to say on the matter, but thinks better of it when I shoot her a warning glare.

"Keep your relationship with her all you want. Just don't drag me down with you." My tone has a stern finality to it that lets her know the conversation is over.

Her thoughts play clear across her face, but she never puts a voice to them. Instead, she asks, "Have you heard from him?"

It seems like a change in subject—and as far as Halen should know, it is—but it's not. And it's not the first time she relates my mother to my ex-boyfriend in a conversation, alluding to the fact that she knows more about what happened that night than she should.

Casting a long, suspicious glare at her, I bring my soup spoon to my lips and slurp. "Nope," I finally say, popping the 'p' at the end.

Gabe didn't take our breakup well. He didn't want things to end and didn't see anything wrong with what he did. But that's the thing about living in a free country—I don't have to give a shit about his feelings. I was done.

Done with the arguments. Done with hiding the cuts and bruises. Done pretending I deserved it all.

With a satisfied nod, Halen drops her eyes back to her plate and busies herself with eating. She may not agree with me distancing myself from our mother, but she sure as hell is glad I'm done with Gabe. They never got along.

We finish the final half of our meal in silence as the cloud of anger lingers over our heads. I hate that our mother can do this to us. That she has so much influence over Halen, she can drive a wedge between us without even lifting a finger. It's the way it's always been. She keeps us divided because that makes it easier to manipulate the situation.

Halen is the first to break the silence. She points toward the kitchen, her eyes squinted in confusion.

"What is that?"

I turn in my chair to look at whatever she's seeing, scanning the area for anything out of place. When I come up short, I turn back to face her. "What?"

Halen stands, and I watch with rapt attention as she walks to the corner beside the fridge and picks up a piece of fruit. At least, I think it's fruit. I've never seen it before.

"Since when did you start eating figs?" she asks playfully, her lips breaking into a smile as she holds the purple thing up in her palm.

It's a running joke between us and Kennedy that I'm a picky eater. So picky, in fact, that Kennedy refuses to cook for me. I blame it on the fact that I grew up only being exposed to basic meals with minimal ingredients. Less ingredients equals less cost, and every cent matters when you're trying to fill an empty stomach with spare change. That bland palette has followed me into adulthood, unfortunately.

So no, I would never have picked a fig out in the store and wasted money on it just for it to sit on my counter.

How the fuck do you even *eat* a fig, anyway?

For some reason, I can't bring myself to tell Halen any of that. There's a revelation rolling through my bones as she holds up the odd fruit and examines it like it's going to sprout legs and run off. My blood stills in my veins for a millisecond as I realize there's only one other person who could have left something like that here. Out in the open, yet tucked away enough for me to find at the perfect moment.

Him.

It's no coincidence that he chose a fig. The infamous forbidden fruit.

It's a message. That much is clear. I just can't piece together what it might mean through the blood pumping into my brain and whooshing in my ears.

The fear jolting through my body fights beneath my skin to lash out and take Halen under with me. I refuse, though. Dropping my face into an emotionless mask, I grab the fruit from Halen's hands and toss it into the air, catching it in my palm like a baseball. I just want to get it away from her. I hate the idea of her touching anything he did, spreading his darkness onto her.

"I saw it in the store and thought it looked weird enough to try. I figure if I don't eat it, I'll let it sit on my counter for decoration." A perfectly formed lie within seconds. I can thank Gabe for that skill.

I may not have an abusive ex-boyfriend anymore, but I do have a stalker. One that has now made it nearly impossible to believe is only a part of my imagination like I so desperately want to.

I can't decide which is worse.

11

The Wolf

I CAN'T STOP THINKING about the girl in the cottage.

My beautiful, deadly little Stardust, as I've decided to call her. A representation of the complicated supernova of feelings I've experienced since first laying eyes on her. Like the dusty remains of a star's chaotic explosion, she's somehow managed to coat every piece of my existence with her bejeweling presence, and she doesn't even know who I am.

My brain goes back and forth between wanting to drive to the cottage and stab my knife into her chest and wanting to fuck her. Sometimes, I imagine doing both at the same time, which is even more jarring.

I need time. Time to process. Time to gain control. Time to make a plan and get back on track.

Sleep doesn't come easily for me, and when it finally does, it's fitful and short-lived. I'm up and dressed before the sun even bothers to peek its head over the horizon. In all my tossing and turning, I've decided that the best way for me to gain control over the situation with Stardust is to succumb to the instincts I'm feeling toward her. To lean into these odd, uncomfortable reflexes until I bleed them dry. See how they can strengthen me.

Because there's one thing I'm certain about: strength comes from the most uncomfortable circumstances.

I'm a hunter, after all. And she's just another prey.

So if the feral beast inside of me wants to play with its meal before devouring it, then so be it. I'll play.

That's the thought process that leads me to spend the entire day working on my presentation for next week in a sports bar across from the coffee shop I followed Stardust to this morning. Mostly because Eliza sends me periodic reminders of the things I need to add, and I'm genuinely afraid of what she'll do if she finds out I was watching a woman I don't even know instead.

Even serial murderers have fears. Mine just happens to be a five-foot Italian woman from the Bronx.

I can see Stardust behind the coffee counter perfectly from my spot against the bar window, smiling at customers as they walk in, then chatting with the pink-haired girl she works beside once they leave. At 4:05, they walk out of the café, laughing about something Stardust said, and I'm so caught up in the way she tilts her head back and throws her entire body into the laugh that I completely ignore my waitress standing beside me with the bill. It's only when Stardust shuts her car door that the waitress clears her throat and earns my attention back.

"Is there anything else I can get you?" she asks in an irritated tone that tells me she's repeating the question. I've been taking this booth up for her all day and haven't bothered to order anything besides a salad I finished hours ago.

With my friendliest smile—one that's likely not friendly

at all—I shake my head and set my credit card on the table. "That will be it, thank you."

The girl takes the card and walks away, swinging her hips as she passes a table full of men who openly gawk at her ass. When she returns with my receipt, I write out a two-hundred-dollar tip and gather my things, rushing to follow my little Stardust down the road.

12

The Lamb

THE DREAM MAN IS BACK.

Or perhaps it's more appropriate to call him a nightmare, since I'm pretty sure it's impossible to deny he's the same man I found standing outside my window.

I settled into the couch the moment I got home from my shift at Old Soul and worked on applying for more jobs while Halen and Kennedy kept me company on speakerphone. One thing I miss the most about living together is being able to talk to them whenever I wanted. Before, even if one of them was rushing out the door to get to their next shift or run errands, I could still sneak in small conversations and hear every menial update about their life. Now that I'm on my own, I spend most of my time at home in silence, and those easy conversations we once had have become something that needs to be scheduled into our busy days.

I miss them. Just as much as I love my private solitude, I miss constant human contact. More than I ever expected.

Maybe that's why I keep obsessing about this man. Maybe that's also why I haven't called the police.

Tonight, when they offered to call and talk my ear off, I couldn't pick up the phone fast enough. There are no weird noises outside or creaks inside the house this time. I'm not sure if it's because I'm still too hungover to drink again, or if I was imagining it all in the first place. Either way, I'm off the phone and ready for bed by eight o'clock. I'm so insanely exhausted that the moment my head hits the pillow, sleep takes me under.

And I don't wake up until there's a noise in my closet. My eyes find the alarm clock on the bedside table and confirm I've only been asleep for a few hours. I might even still be asleep now, because the man is back.

He's standing across the room, his dark and familiar silhouette relaxed against the doorframe of my walk-in closet. I blink owlishly, clearing the sleep from my eyes, and he remains still, staring directly at me.

I looked up ways to control lucid dreams the way Rosie suggested after I got home from the cafe, but everything I read completely dissipates from my mind now that he's here. In fact, every conscious thought seems to fly away in his presence.

It feels so incredibly real. How can I be asleep?

Maybe I'm not.

Maybe he's a ghost.

Or maybe there's really a man standing in my bedroom, watching me sleep.

Fuck, I don't know. This is insane.

"Hello, Stardust," a deep, commanding voice greets, startling me out of my thoughts.

His tone is confident and direct. Where I'm floundering, he knows exactly what's happening here.

"Wh-who are you?" I ask dumbly.

Who are you? As if that matters.

He's the guy who's going to kill you, that's who he is.

He doesn't answer the question. Instead, he pushes off the doorway and starts toward me. "I see you've started without me."

Tilting his head toward my hand, which I'm now realizing is stuffed between my legs, his brows inch upward.

I quickly pull it out, mortified that he found me like that, and twist my palm in front of my face, staring at it in complete shock, like it betrayed me. Since when do I masturbate in my sleep?

He snickers, stopping at the side of my bed just before his thighs hit the mattress. Every move he makes feels calculated, as if he's planned this whole thing out.

"I'm going to tell you what's about to happen, little Stardust, and you're going to obey," he begins, tugging the blanket farther down my legs. I'm too frozen with fear to protest or stop him.

His face is stunning. Well, at least what I can see of it. Perfectly symmetrical and free of any imperfections. He's got to be the most beautiful man I've ever laid eyes on.

Dark hair that I can tell was slicked back at some point now hangs over matching thick, arched eyebrows. I can't see the color of his eyes, but I can tell their light against his long black eyelashes. The lower half of his face is covered by a black mask that hangs down to his broad chest, but I have no doubt it's just as appealing.

He certainly isn't from Styx; I can guarantee it. That kind of face screams privilege and money.

"You're going to lay back on this bed and spread those pretty legs for me."

He stares down at me expectantly, waiting for me to comply. But I can't seem to wrap my head around his words.

"Um… what?"

A low growl rumbles in his throat as he digs his fists into the mattress beside me, lining his masked lips up with my ear without actually touching it. "I don't repeat myself. That's rule number one. And take off those hideous fucking boxers before I rip them off you. I don't ever want to see you in another man's clothing again, do you understand?"

I'm not sure if I'm supposed to be horrified or turned on, but the sudden harsh words appear to invoke both emotions simultaneously.

What the fuck is wrong with me?

With a stiff nod—mostly because I'm terrified of what he'll do if I hesitate any longer—I begin slipping Gabe's old boxers down my legs, fully exposing myself to the crisp night air. I'm instantly regretting my choice not to wear panties to sleep.

Fear as deep as my marrow and metallic as my blood creeps into every fiber of my being.

He moves around the bed to stand at my feet, giving himself a full, uninterrupted view of my body.

"Good girl. Now, rub your fingers over that pretty pink pussy for me," he says, gaze trained between my legs. I pause for a second, and his eyes snap back to my face.

"Now." His growl is deep and impatient.

This has to be a dream. It *has* to. There's no way a man with this much wealth and entitlement would waste his time with a girl like me. In a place like this.

That's what I tell myself as I lean my head back into the pillow and gently move my hands over my thighs. I hiss out a breath when my fingers meet the swollen, sensitive flesh beneath my legs, immediately coating them in my arousal.

Men don't speak to me like this.

Any man I've hooked up with before has found me to be

too intimidating in bed. The instant they realize I'm a woman who actually knows what she wants, they clam up and submit. I fucking hate it.

I've yet to find one who can match me in the bedroom. Which is another reason why it's so easy for me to convince myself this isn't real. Because men like the one standing before me simply don't exist in my world.

So I decide I'm going to lean into this. Play along, even if it's just a survival technique. I'm going to continue to fool myself into believing he's a figment of my imagination, simply because any other alternative is absolutely terrifying.

Deny, deny, deny. That's what I'm best at.

"That's it, baby," his rough voice encourages from below.

I don't bother looking at him. Instead, I focus my gaze on a crack in the ceiling as I caress my clit in the exact way that I know will send me over the edge in minutes.

I'm waiting for him to move closer. To feel his weight dip on the bed as he crosses the invisible line between us. To have his hands on my skin. But none of that happens.

Only when I feel myself skirting around the edge, do I gain enough courage to drag my eyes away from the ceiling and back down to him.

He's unbuttoned his pants and taken himself out. My eyes track his hand as it moves up and down his long, thick shaft. Even shrouded in darkness, I can tell he's larger than any man I've ever met. That should scare me.

"Are you imagining my cock inside you, Stardust? Is that why you're digging your fingers deep into that tight pussy?"

I moan, bucking my hips forward as if the movement will bring me closer to him. Because he's right. I *was* imagining how it would feel for him to fill me up, and I can't make sense of *why*.

"Soon. So soon," he promises, and his hand begins moving

faster. "For now, I just want to watch you make that sweet pussy come all over your hand. Can you do that, Stardust?"

I have no idea where he's come up with this nickname, but the way it flows off his tongue is becoming my newest addiction.

"Yes," I whimper, my hips grinding farther into my hand as my orgasm builds.

"Good. Now come with me, baby."

And I do. Not because he tells me to, although that gravelly voice is hot enough to send anyone over the edge. I finish because this situation is fucked up and dangerous and has me questioning my sanity. Because if I don't, I'll succumb to the fear and then there won't be anything left for him to kill anyway.

Seconds later, I hear his quiet moans as he finishes into his hand, and I sit forward in my bed to watch as he comes undone. My teeth work against my lip, and he groans even louder. The mask over his mouth moves with his lips when he says, "I can't wait until those lips are wrapped around me and my cum is shooting down your throat."

He reaches backward to grab a discarded shirt off my dresser and cleans off his hand, then throws it back down and moves toward me. I flinch when the same soft palm wraps around my jaw, squeezing a little too hard.

"Sweet dreams, little Stardust," he whispers into the space between us, then he turns and walks out my bedroom door.

I fight the urge to follow him, confused with the way this entire exchange has left me desperately wanting more, yet shaking with nerves at the same time. I sit as still as possible in my bed, listening. There're no other sounds inside the house. No footsteps, no door closing, nothing. It's like he walked out of the bedroom and disappeared into thin air. I reluctantly lean back against my pillow, doubting the past hour of my life and begging for sleep that never comes.

When it's time to get ready for the day, I muster up the courage to leave my room and walk out to find a lone, dark purple fig sitting in the center of my dining room table, and I know for a fact that everything was real.

13

The Wolf

I ARRIVE HOME in New York late Sunday evening, and I'm immediately swept up in preparations for the presentation with Power Tech on Wednesday. My father drags his feet with accepting the offer on the Styx house that Chantel presented to him last week, countering with his own ridiculous number I'm forced to agree to.

Work consumes me, the way it always does when I'm processing things in my personal life. Eliza and my team have me in back-to-back meetings from morning until night to iron out any issues we run into with our data and testing.

Part of the reason my company has been so successful is because I used it as an escape from Sienna's death. Sure, we were doing well before. But the concentrated effort I threw into it gave me a boost that wouldn't have been possible if I weren't detaching from my personal life. I'm sure a therapist could have a field day with that.

Nevertheless, we land the deal. My team celebrates by

going out for drinks on Wednesday night. I celebrate by going home and choosing my next victim.

Judge Matthew Greene was in charge of overseeing Sienna's case. Despite the indisputable evidence our lawyers presented, he refused to rule in our favor, allowing her killers to walk free.

That's the shorthand version. His attitude toward the case was one of my first indicators that something was off. The more I dug, the more corruption I discovered.

He was paid off. I want to know who's pocket he's in.

Lucky for me, Judge Greene happens to be staying alone in New York for some bullshit religious conference this week.

Since Stardust took over the cabin in Styx, I've been struggling with how to move forward with my process. I've looked into renting warehouses downtown to take my victims under a pseudonym, always ruling it out as too much of a hassle. I've considered just killing everyone involved without trying to get answers out of them. I've even imagined a thousand ways to kill *her*.

But I'm not some senseless murderer, and I owe Sienna more than that. It's clear the corruption runs far deeper than some random street gang in the ass crack of America. I just need to recalibrate.

Having Judge Greene come to me in the city feels like a sign from the universe to keep going. And who am I to deny the universe?

I know I have to move quickly on the judge or I'll lose my shot. It takes almost no time to figure out his schedule and hotel information. My plan is laid out and I'm resting in my bed within an hour.

Tomorrow is the day. Once I kill the judge, I'll regain some semblance of control of this shitty situation and be able to get back into my routine.

14

The Lamb

ANOTHER WORK WEEK passes with no sign of the mystery man. Not outside on the grounds or in my room. It's just enough time for me to convince myself that I imagined him again. I almost do too, if not for the two figs that taunt me from their spot on my table. Nothing is missing from my home, nothing has been touched, and I don't get the sense that I'm being watched again.

I swear my mind is playing tricks on me, or maybe I'm just going insane. I suppose there's no way for me to truly know. No one is really conscious of the fact that their sanity is slipping until it's already gone. I saw it plenty of times in Sunnybrook. The crazy people never *knew* they were crazy.

But there's no other explanation. Why else would I allow some stranger into my home and to watch me like that? Why else would I look for him in the shadows and hope he's come back?

I'm either insane or extremely fucked in the head.

He has a pattern when he visits. So far, it's mostly on weekends and almost never in the middle of the week. That must mean he has a job. I have a hard time believing there's any place in Styx that affords him the type of wealth that radiates off of him, though I have no idea where to even begin with searching. New York City is only about an hour away. Is it a stretch to assume he's making that drive?

I've looked into having security cameras installed, at least on the outside of the property, but the price is astronomical. I'd have to take on a separate job just to pay the subscription fee. There're quite a few do-it-yourself alternatives online that I've begun to set aside savings for. It's impossible to get ahead when you're hardly keeping your head above water to begin with.

Rosie is the only person I've told about him, though only bits and pieces. She's convinced he's a part of my imagination, and I'm not sure if that offends or relieves me. If she knew the rest of what I've experienced, she would probably be telling me to move out and call the police.

For example, I haven't told her about the figs.

I think they make it too real, a physical token to go along with his haunting presence. It's too hard to deny his existence and what the thought of it does to me when I can hold the evidence of it in my hands.

So I lie, carefully disclosing enough information that if something *were* to happen to me, there would at least be one person who could lead people in the right direction. Especially if it happens before I can install my cameras. And Rosie makes me feel better by assuring me it's all in my head. Perhaps, it's easier for her to believe that than to admit the possibility that I *do* have a stalker.

I'm mostly scared. Terrified, in fact.

But not in the way I should be, and that's what alarms me

the most. The feelings he invokes in me are like nothing I've ever experienced.

Fear.

Lust.

Longing.

They run deeper than ever before, cutting into my flesh and marrow like sharp blades. And like a true masochist, I fall to my knees, ready to beg for more each time he returns.

Instead of reporting the stranger who appears to have formed some sort of obsession with me, I'm protecting him, just how he wants me to. He somehow knows I'm too weak to turn him in. That I'm too intrigued to end whatever is going on between us.

It's a sick thought. How can I accuse him of being messed up when I'm just as fucked in the head—if not more, because I'm enabling his behavior? Yet, here we are.

My vibrating phone dances on the coffee table before me as yet another call lights up the screen. I refuse to drop my eyes from the TV to check. I don't have to look to know who it is. This is the fifth time he's called in the span of twenty minutes after his obsessive texting all afternoon. If there's one thing Gabe hates, it's being ignored. It's a good thing I'm not his girlfriend anymore, and therefore don't owe him shit.

Still, I've been properly trained to answer like a good little pet. There's that internal struggle brewing in my chest—the anticipation of what comes when I don't pick up his calls. I have to remind myself each time the phone flashes with an incoming call that he doesn't have that hold over me anymore. I'm safe from his fury.

The screen darkens as his call ends, and I cringe when it vibrates again three times to alert me to a new voicemail I'll be deleting as soon as I can hold my phone without feeling like it's on fire.

He's getting desperate. Calling me like this, leaving

threatening messages that anyone could see or hear. It's not his usual, calculated approach. The one where he convinces everyone I was the insufferable problem in our relationship. I'm not even sure where he got my new number from. Everyone who has it has been sworn to secrecy.

Realizing my back has gone ramrod straight, I relax back into the couch and take a few deep breaths to clear my head, reminding myself once again that he can't get to me here.

He doesn't bother calling again, though that doesn't make me feel as good as it should. I'm sure if I bothered to listen to the final voicemail he left, there would be some empty threats for my lack of response, but I refuse to hear it. Hitting delete in my voicemail box, I have the fleeting thought that if it was this easy for him to find my number, how difficult could it be for him to discover my address and show up here? Would he even go that far?

Maybe I should have listened to his message just to decipher how unhinged he's become. Clearly, calling me this many times in such a short span of time alludes to some level of insanity, right?

Apparently, he'd have to get in line for stalking me, since there's someone else who has stepped in to take that role. Perhaps they'd have to reach some sort of agreement on who gets to gaze into my windows on which day. I'm not sure what the protocol is for being a creepy asshole.

Ah, shit. When did life get so messy? And when did I get such a horrible sense of humor over it?

In an attempt to avoid looking at my phone at all costs, I stand to bring my dinner dish to the sink, deciding which creep I'd rather find standing outside my window. At least I know the mystery man doesn't want to hurt me. Not yet. And I've unintentionally been giving him ample opportunities. Gabe has taken every chance he's been given to hurt me in some way—physically, emotionally, verbally... you name it. There's a saying that you should go with the devil you know, but I don't even think the *actual* devil would choose my piece of shit ex in this scenario.

Of course, the best option for me to choose would be *no creepy stalker*, but it seems like the universe, or God, or whoever the hell is up there, doesn't want to give me that.

Once my bowl is securely nestled in the dishwasher and the sink is clear, I turn to the fridge and notice that the photo I had of me, Halen, and Kennedy at a concert is missing. I came across it last week when I was unpacking a box I missed in my bedroom, and I stuck it there to remind myself to grab a frame.

But now, it's nowhere to be found.

Climbing down on my hands and knees, I try to peek underneath the fridge, but the space is too small and dark to see anything. I could swear it was here just this morning.

As I'm pulling myself back up, I hear the floor creak in one of the spare bedrooms.

I've kept the doors shut since I first moved in, only ever bothering to use that end of the house when I need to rummage through the linen closet to find something or to clean out the bathroom. Otherwise, it stays dark and cold. I haven't even had any guests stay over yet.

Granted, the house usually makes random creaks and groans that are light enough for me to chalk up to the bones of it settling. It's an old building, and the temperature is changing with the seasons. But I'm not sure if it was my crassly joking thoughts earlier, the missing photo, or because there aren't any other noises around me to drown it out, but this one sounded more significant. Like something moving instead of settling into place.

"Hello?" I call out in a broken voice.

No one responds, obviously. I've either given myself away and let the potential intruder know that I'm onto them, or

I've become insanely paranoid. Either way, I'm paralyzed in fear.

With my heart beating faster than what should be humanly possible, I dash back into my bedroom, grabbing my phone from the coffee table on the way. This is the shitty part of living alone. What if someone murders me tonight? How long would it take for anyone to notice I was gone?

Throwing myself against the pillows, I pull my legs up to my chest and listen intently for any other noises to follow.

With all the fear and anger I can muster, I send a strongly worded prayer up above for whoever the hell is in charge to give me a break. And even though there aren't any more weird noises in the house, I don't sleep at all.

15

The Wolf

FOR A MAN who has made a career of hearing cases about brutal murders and persecuting true criminals, Judge Matthew Greene is a disgustingly easy target. He moves through the city like he owns it, filled with an arrogance no man with a bald spot the size of the Empire State Building should possess. Interesting he's so confident, considering he left the bullshit Jesus convention with a woman who I happen to know for a fact *isn't* his wife.

Usually, the scummy assholes are the ones looking over their shoulder every few minutes, ready for an attack that no one gives a shit about executing. The only people who aren't paranoid about being taken down are those like me—the ones who *do* the taking.

The devils in the night. The demons lurking in the shadows.

Which confirms my suspicions that Judge Greene and I are one of the same: predators at the top of the food chain.

The woman is a roadblock in my plan. I have no intention of killing an innocent and soaking my hands in any more blood than necessary, so I have to wait for their little rendezvous to end before I can break into his room. Luckily for me, the judge puts next to zero effort in making sure his mistress is satisfied, and she leaves his room within the hour.

I know I need answers from him. Each kill before him has proven that the situation surrounding Sienna's death went above The Order prospect's heads, and the judge is the first rung up that ladder. But I can't use my usual tactics to pry the answers out. Not in a hotel where anyone can hear his screams and come rushing in to save him.

Instead of my usual bloody affair, I've got the judge tied up with his sock shoved so far down his throat, he's fighting for each breath as I fill the jacuzzi tub with ice cold water. I've hogtied him with a set of handcuffs that I bought with cash in a sex toy shop a few streets from here while he and his mistress played. My original plan was to simply drown him and stage it as a suicide, but this plays out much better. I guess it worked out that he's a piece of shit husband.

He doesn't recognize me, which should come as a relief. I hardly made an impression on him in those two weeks of Sienna's trial, and likely won't be tied to his death in any way by the detectives who will inevitably take his case. Especially since I hacked the hotel's security cameras to play on a loop and entered through an employee entrance in the back. I'm a ghost in this place, moving freely without consequence.

Still, it would have been nice to see the fear in his eyes when he realized I had come back to haunt him.

Oh well. I'll just have to make him remember.

He squirms on the floor when I turn the faucet off, panicked moaning noises reverberating from his chest as I lift his flabby body and throw him over the edge of the tub with a loud splash. In his restraints, he can't turn around quick enough to keep his nose out of the water. I patiently stand over him as he thrashes around the small tub in an attempt to flip himself upright. After a few moments of struggle, his movements go sluggish as he takes on too much water, and I have to step in before he fully drowns.

With a gloved hand, I grab him by the arm to flip him over in one swift move. Widened, terrified eyes roll up to meet my face, and he tries to speak through the soaked sock, which sends him into a coughing fit.

Reaching forward to rip the sock out, I warn in an even tone, "If you try to scream, I'll cram it right back down your throat."

When he nods his agreement, I tug it out and throw it off to the side as he coughs to work out all the fluid that's hopefully building in his lungs.

"This will go much easier for you if you cooperate," I promise, leaving out the small fact that he won't live past the hour either way.

When he doesn't acknowledge me, I shove my hand in the water beneath him and tug on the handcuffs so the metal bites into his skin. It's possible he can't hear me through all his hacking, but I don't give a fuck.

"Okay," he angrily shouts, then quickly cowers back down from his outburst when he sees the look on my face.

"You presided over Sienna Lancaster's case," I begin, but the shake of his head stops me from going on.

My brows raise in question, offering one chance for him to explain before I just shove him under and call it a loss.

"I take on tons of cases. It's impossible to remember them all," he says in a rough voice.

"I'd recommend wracking that tiny brain of yours for the details of this one…" I grit out through clenched teeth.

What a fucking bastard.

The day he threw out her case changed the entire course

of my life. I've hunted and killed because of that decision, and here he is, pretending it was just another day on the job for him.

"I'll try to refresh your memory. Sienna Lancaster was brutally murdered by six men. We had everything to prove it was them—security footage, fingerprints, their fucking cum was still inside of her when she was found. *You* ruled they were not guilty and allowed all of them to walk free."

I can tell the exact moment he remembers. I can also see the instant recognition hits and he realizes who I am. His eyes widen again, ping-ponging across my features as it all comes back to him.

"Good, you remember."

"I-I didn't—" he blubbers, but I quickly cut him off.

"Save your excuses. Someone bought your verdict that day. I want to know who it was."

"Don't do this, son. Don't get involved," he tries to rush out the warning through trembling lips, as if he truly cares. "You have no chance against those guys. They'll have your head hanging from your ceiling within hours."

I move away to pace a few steps across the floor, running my fingers over my jaw as I consider how much I can mark his body and still make his death look like an accident.

"Oh, you haven't heard? I've already taken care of them. All six, actually. If I had to guess, I'd say their bodies are probably mutilated by some wild animal in the Atlantic by now. The ones who weren't destroyed are probably rotting away in a field not too far from here."

Leaning my hands against the edge of the tub, I lower myself until we're nose-to-nose.

"You see, I was already *involved* when those assholes murdered my sister. I know everything there is to know about them. But I'm a much less forgiving man. In fact, you'll be meeting the same fate in a few short minutes. Your cooperation will determine how brutal your death is."

"I don't know anything…" he tries to say, but I release a frustrated growl that stops him from going on.

"I don't think you understand, *Judge*. You're going to die tonight because you chose to protect those entitled wastes of skin over my innocent fucking sister. You think those pieces of shit were dangerous? I fucking gutted them while they were still alive. They were crying, begging for death when I was through with them. The level of torture in which I use to bring you to Death's doorstep will be determined by how much information you give me about the people I *know* paid you off…"

He begins to sob as I'm speaking, and I have to stop to regain my composure. It's always the men who think they own the world who fall to their knees first. If the roles were reversed here, he'd be lucky to get a single fucking reaction from me, let alone a sloppy mess of tears and snot.

Pinching the bridge of my nose, I roll my eyes and try again.

"Just tell me who the fuck paid you," I say on a sigh.

"I don't know…" When I start toward him with the knife that I pull from my pocket, he begins to stutter again, finally offering something of value.

"Someone dropped a wad of cash in my office with a picture of my wife and kids taken from inside our home and a note that said I had to let them off. I wasn't going to do it. I was prepared to bring it all to the police to sort out and pull from the case. I'm a man of God… But the next day, I got word that the girl's lawyer was about to drop the case anyway. Something about all the evidence being lost or compromised. I couldn't risk my family getting hurt."

"A man of God?" I mock his panicked, rushed tone. "Is that why you brought another woman back to your room tonight? Because you're a *man of God* who loves his family so much?"

With brows raised, he releases another sob and throws his head into his chest in a pathetic show of weakness. I tuck the tip of my knife beneath his double chin and force him to face me again, careful not to penetrate his skin. This has to look like an accident.

"How do you think your precious wife and kids would feel knowing you're hooking up with some other Jesus-loving whore the second you're away from them? How would they react to knowing you allowed six known rapists and murderers to roam free after directly threatening their lives? Is that your twisted version of a man of God, Judge?"

"N-no. I've made mistakes, but I can learn from them. I can repent. Please, let me go and I'll find out everything I can about your sister. I'll help you bring justice."

I release a sardonic laugh, so loud it bounces off the walls and echoes back into my ears. "Don't you remember? I've already brought her justice. And you've already given me everything you can."

Pulling out the rolled-up fabric I've been keeping in my back pocket, I shift my weight to rest against the floor as I carefully uncover the syringe and vial I picked up earlier this week. I could have gotten much higher quality drugs from anyone in my father's social circle, but that would give too much away about my identity. A man like this could never afford that kind of quality drug, so I stooped to his level and found a dealer on the street. It was quite humbling.

My hands fumble with the small glass, filling the syringe with more than enough to sedate a man of his size. My victim's dilated eyes track my every move so carefully, I think he forgets to blink.

Once I'm finished tapping the air out of my syringe, I set the vial down beside me and reach into the freezing bath to grab his restrained arm. The move tilts his whole body over to the opposite side, and spit gathers all around his mouth as he quickly mumbles a worthless prayer for his God to save him.

That earns another laugh from me, which only grows louder as I inspect his inner arms and find a pre-existing line of track marks. This truly couldn't have gone any better for me. His disgusting, unsavory lifestyle will make getting away with his murder that much easier.

I shake my head, *tsk*ing at him in mock disappointment. "Hasn't anyone told you that drugs are bad for you, Judge?"

"Pl-please," he weakly begs.

"You've already sealed your fate."

Tapping his skin until I feel the elasticity of his veins, I pick my spot and don't waste any more time slipping the needle into it, sending the drugs straight into his bloodstream.

He struggles against my hands for a brief moment before the depressants take their effect and calm his system, slowly shutting it down. I sit back and watch as his eyes drift closed, limbs going slack against the tub and restraints. His large body slips farther into the water, mouth agape.

I put my hands against his chest until his mouth and nose sink fully beneath the water, then I hold him down, waiting for the precious moment that his heart stops beating and his soul passes over.

It finally comes just as his body stills and the water settles around him.

The rest of my night is spent soaking up any of the mess that escaped the tub, releasing him from his handcuffs—a task that's much more difficult under water and beneath his dead weight—and erasing every trace of myself from his room. I find a housekeeping closet on the next floor up to dump the towels in, and then I leave before the sun rises.

Sienna doesn't bother appearing at any point during my clean up to go over what was revealed, so I don't allow myself to consider what he said until I'm walking back to my apartment. It sounds like The Order was trying to pay him off, just as I suspected. But then why did our lawyer try to pull the case early? That part doesn't add up. I remember the day the case was dropped.

Our lawyer, Arthur Lewis, hunted down information against The Order and that night no one should have ever had access to. He was a shark with the scent of blood in his nostrils, ready to obliterate anyone in his path. I thought it was odd when he accepted that the case was dropped so easily, but my father stopped me from confronting him that day. I suppose that was a mistake on my part.

It looks like I've found my next victim.

16

The Wolf

THE INK on my last contract is hardly dry before I'm driving back to Styx, officially marking my collaboration with Power Tech and nearly tripling my company's worth. I'm in the mood to celebrate, and what better way to do that than to spill the blood of my enemies and have some fun with my darling little prey?

Styx is quickly morphing into more of a reprieve from my normal life than the nuisance it's always been. I'm not too proud to admit the shift started with one annoying roadblock.

Stardust has become an oasis in my otherwise barren life. A refreshing drink of water to quench the thirst I've been living with for longer than I'd like to admit.

Now, I'm hooked.

Her drive, her tenacity… her sheer will to live when every sign points to just giving up.

Every time I allow myself to soak in the memory of her pleasuring herself, I'm instantly hard.

I'm sitting in my car outside the coffee shop she works at, gazing at her through the large windows as she prepares the hundredth coffee order of the day for whatever asshole stomps his way through those doors. My attention flickers between her and my laptop, where I'm gathering information on my next victim. Though, it's remained more on her in the past hour than anything else.

I'm simultaneously pissed and jealous, my nerves grated down to nothing as I watch each interaction she has unfold.

Jealous, because they get to interact with her during normal waking hours without freaking her the fuck out—which, thanks to my impulsively, I can't do yet. I'm pretty sure she thinks I'm not real.

And pissed, because every time I watch one of them treat her with an ounce of disrespect, and that little crease between her eyebrows forms as she swallows down her smartass retorts, forcing a tight smile instead, I want to walk in there and strangle the person who put it there.

I found her leaving the cottage when I arrived early this morning and decided on the spot that whatever plans she had for the day were far more important than anything I was going to do. So, I followed her.

She appears to be finishing up with the coffee shop, hanging up her apron and rounding the counter with a small goodbye wave toward the pink-haired girl. I'm parked right against the curb in front of the tiny building, sitting in plain view. I don't bother to cower or hide as she passes, either. There's a thrill in knowing she's so close to becoming aware that I'm watching her. How will she react? All she has to do is lift her gaze from her feet, and she'll see me here.

Of course, she doesn't.

Instead, she strolls right around the front of my vehicle

and back to her own pile of rust directly across the street from me. Once she fights the lock and falls onto the driver's seat, the dilapidated car sputters to start filling the street with the sound of its low rumble as she prepares to drive. I'm so close to buying her a new vehicle for the simple fact that this one belongs in a junkyard.

Pulling away from the curb, she leaves a cloud of black smoke behind for me to follow.

"She's boring," Sienna comments from my passenger seat, and I resist the urge to swerve as I jump from the sudden interruption.

"She is not," I argue, recovering before she can notice.

"Yes, she is. I don't understand your sudden interest in the charity case. You should be focusing on the next victim. Who is it, by the way? The lawyer?"

A hungry look crosses her eyes, and I'm reminded that this thing with her has already gone too far. She's getting too fixated on revenge for a ghost who should be off frolicking in the clouds or having orgies or some shit.

I blow out a breath. She's not wrong. Killing the judge gave me a ton of information I didn't have before. I should be following that trail of breadcrumbs before someone realizes I'm onto it and cleans it up. But like I've had to remind her a million times before, Sienna is dead. She doesn't realize how consuming this whole chase has been for me. Every move needs to be calculated. Every kill is precise.

I need an escape. One that has no connection to this clusterfuck. That's why I've clung so tightly to Stardust.

She flicks on her blinker and takes the next left turn and I follow close behind.

"I've got a plan for that. Why else would I be here?" I ask Sienna, my voice tight. I hate explaining myself.

"You haven't done anything to prepare for the next kill," she points out. Her lips turn up in a smug, knowing smirk.

She's right again. I've been so busy with signing the deal with Power Tech and following Stardust, I haven't had time to look into our lawyer. Even today, I hardly gathered much outside of his address and some bullshit Facebook photos. My plan was to drive back to New York and work on it at my apartment tonight, but seeing Stardust this morning threw me off. She's so much more interesting.

"I have a good idea of his schedule. I'll set aside some time tomorrow to confirm it," I promise. Sienna rolls her eyes as I take the next turn with Stardust.

"She's probably just going to another one of her million jobs. Are you really going to sit here and watch her all day?"

"I have to tread lightly with her. I don't have the luxury of moving around unnoticed like you." I cut my eyes toward her pointedly, then back to the road.

"Don't pretend this isn't anything but another odd obsession you've formed," she admonishes.

Stardust pulls up to a dumpy sports bar and parks her car in the back of the nearly full lot. I drive a loop around as she gets out and runs toward the front door, presumably late, if I know her at all.

She was late to the coffee shop too.

I hate people who can't delegate their time efficiently enough to respect others. It's another skill I'll have to teach her when I finally get my hands on her.

"What are you doing, Bash?" Sienna asks, reminding me of her presence again as I grab my laptop bag and push the button to turn off my ignition.

Swinging the door open, I don't bother looking back as I say, "I'm going to have a drink while I gather some more intel on the lawyer." I turn to face her with my hand on the corner of the door. "Is that okay with you, Boss?"

Her lip lifts in disgust, and I slam the door before she has a chance to make another smartass comeback. It's pointless, really. She can always just appear beside me again, but I like the effect it has on her inflated ego to be cut off. She's always needed more discipline when it came to running her mouth.

Entering the bar, I'm immediately hit with the pungent smell of stale beer, burning oil, and piss. The fucking things I do for this girl, I swear...

She needs a new job.

Tossing that idea around, I take a spot in the far, dimly lit corner and work on my computer while Stardust tirelessly works the bar.

Yeah, my girl needs a career change. Preferably one with less of a stench.

17

The Lamb

I ROUND the corner from the doorway of my bedroom and am instantly hit with the sweet, syrupy smell of vanilla. The room is illuminated by the soft, flickering lights coming from the dozens of candles lining the bathroom counter and the sides of the tub that's nestled into the back corner of the room. Water is pouring out of the spout into a sea of bubbles that's nearly full, and a glass of white wine is perched on the ledge.

And sitting right beside it is another perfectly ripened fig.

I have no idea what to make of this.

Stepping into the bathroom, I reach down to turn off the spout, and then spin in place, taking the scene in.

It would be incredibly romantic if there were actually someone here to explain themselves. If I didn't live alone in this house. If I didn't forget to even give Halen and Kennedy the spare key.

Instead, I'm left reeling.

Because no one should have access to my home to do this. Someone was here. In my space, without my permission.

Of course, my mind lands on one person. Someone who shouldn't even be a blip on my radar. Someone I finally convinced myself wasn't even real. That thought alone nearly sends me spiraling. But he's the only person who would use the fruit as a message.

But... how?

How did he time it perfectly for me to show up just in time to turn the water off?

I suppose he's done it before. Though, why did it feel so much less violating when I was home?

"What are you waiting for? Get in," that familiar, rough voice startles me from behind.

I whip around to face him, jumping when I find that he's standing less than a foot away from me in the doorway. From this close, I can see he's got to be at least a foot taller than me, his shoulders twice as wide.

"What are you doing in my house?" I immediately confront, scowling. My hands are trembling so badly at my sides, I have to ball them into fists so he doesn't notice.

He tilts his head, carefully considering me for a moment. He's wearing his black mask to cover his nose and lips, but I can still read his expressions.

"Running you a bath," he explains slowly, as if I'm dense.

"I mean, why are you *here*? What do you want from me?" I hate the way my voice shakes—the weakness it shows.

I'm not sure why this feels any different from him sneaking into my room while I slept, but it does. I feel like he's crossed an invisible line here. A much larger, more intimate line than before.

"You've had a hard week. I figured you could use a break."

I want to ask what he means by that. How does he know how my week has been? How did he know when I'd be home tonight after taking on a last-minute shift? But fear has my mouth clamped shut, trapping all my burning questions inside until they're scorching my tongue.

He walks around my frozen body to lean his weight onto the counter across from the tub, then stares at me expectantly.

"Well, now that that's settled, you can get in."

"I'm not stripping in front of you and getting in that tub," I insist, crossing my arms over my chest.

His face drops, all emotion wiped from his expression within a millisecond. A cold, hollow mask takes its place, and my breath hitches at the dangerous gleam that's filled his eyes.

How the hell did he do that?

"You're going to get in that tub and you're going to relax, or else I'm going to rip your clothes off and throw you in there myself."

"Who the hell even are you? *What* are you?"

Those eyes cut over to me. "Me? I'm your worst nightmare, little Stardust."

"Why do you keep calling me that?"

"Would you rather I use your real name, *Jovie?*"

I don't know how he does it, but my name sounds like a threat. A promise for something more—something *worse*—if I don't obey. I still, swallowing through the lump of fear lodged in my throat.

Why should it bother me so much to hear my name on his tongue? That he even knows it in the first place? He clearly has no boundaries, breaking into my house at all times of the day, watching me as I sleep, expecting me to strip bare in front of him.

"Point taken. You know about me," I finally push out through the fear.

"I know *everything* about you," he corrects in a cocky tone.

The statement sends chills rumbling down my spine, because I have no doubt that it's true.

"Then it's only fair that I know something about you…"

His brow quirks up. "Do I look like the type of man to bargain with?"

Not at all, the voice in my head screams, but I don't let the words leave my lips. Instead, I jut my chin out and nod toward the steaming bathtub.

"One answer for every piece of clothing," I offer, fully expecting him to decline.

He surprises me by rolling his eyes and pinching the bridge of his nose. "Why can't you just let me do this one nice thing for you?"

"Is that a yes?"

"Fine," he says with a stiff shrug, shaking his head.

I don't waste any time asking, "What's your name?"

"Bash. Start with your shirt."

Glaring at him, I grab the hem of my shirt and pull it over my head, exposing the lacey, white bra I'm thankful I had the urge to put on this morning.

Did I really just say I'm thankful?

Fuuuuck.

"Bash? Bash what?"

Slanted, feline eyes—which the candlelight reveals are an impossibly light shade of green—bore into my face. His jaw flexes beneath his mask, as if to further prove his point.

He's not telling me his full name.

"Fine. Where do you live? I know it's not Styx."

He doesn't hesitate this time. "New York."

I push my jeans down my legs and step out of them.

"That's a far drive to be making this often…" I fish, hoping he'll give me more.

"I have business here that requires my attention," he says

in a response that doesn't really answer anything. He knows exactly what he's doing.

He raises his eyebrows at me expectantly, like I'm supposed to be taking off more clothes, but I shake my head.

"I didn't get to ask another question," I whine, placing my hands on my hips.

His eyes openly roam over my chest and abdomen, a hungry look flashing across his features before he buries it away.

What is it about him that turns me on so easily? I should be putting distance between us. I should be having him arrested for breaking into my home and running me a *bath*, then demanding I get naked in front of him. Instead, I'm going right along with the psychosis, stripping my clothes off and sharing random facts.

"Maybe I should ask you questions instead. Why don't we start with what happened the night you were brought to Sunnybrook? With your mom?"

I freeze. How could he know about that? Sure, it's public knowledge that I went to the rehab facility. I suppose he could have somehow even dug into my medical records and saw the injuries I was brought into the hospital with that night. But there's no way for him to have known who was there with me before the ambulance came. I never told a soul.

Is it because he really is a stalker? Because he's a figment of my imagination, burrowed deep into my subconscious, where all my secrets hide?

Either way, I'm not reliving that night. Not even for a man who looks like he would kill me if he grew too bored of my company.

His gaze darkens. "I thought so. Get in the tub. I won't say it again."

18

The Wolf

STARDUST SLIPS out of her underwear and climbs over the edge of the bathtub without another word. I'm watching her every move with rapt attention, studying the minute details about her that I've missed from afar.

I can tell I unnerved her when I brought up that night. She thought her secrets were protected—buried deep beneath the web of lies she's spun. She should know nothing is safe with me.

Once she's fully submerged, I walk around the edge and crouch behind her.

"Relax, little lamb. Let me take care of you," I whisper against her neck, earning a small moan that seems to hit me in all the right places.

I feel guilty for scaring her when all I meant to do was help her unwind. This is all new to me, and I'm just fumbling through it.

Every reaction she has to my presence feeds my addiction. The sharp intake of breath when my hands wrap around her shoulders. The way her head tilts back as my fingers dig into tightly wound muscles. The tightening of her thighs as my hands venture across her skin.

I haven't allowed myself to touch her since that first night. I tell myself it's about not having her permission, but it's deeper than that. A sick internal game I'm playing—a test of my resilience. But the anticipation of feeling her beneath my fingertips was enough to drive me mad. I spent multiple nights wide awake as I imagined how she would taste when I finally got my mouth on her.

This bath is just as much about me as it is about her.

My hand moves along her collarbone and stops at the top of her left breast, feeling her heartbeat. She sucks in a breath, subtly pushing her chest forward to move my palm downward the same way she had done in her sleep. I comply, gently closing my fingers around her nipple.

"Do you like when I touch you?"

"Yes," she hisses the admission, and it's like the sound is sent straight to my growing erection pressing against the tub.

My other hand comes down and kneads her right breast. I'm leaning over her with my arms wrapped around either side of her head, which is thrown back against my shoulder, hair brushing my neck where my mask has been slightly shifted. Eventually, her hand disappears somewhere beneath the surface of bubbles between her legs and I want to fucking kick myself for adding so much of the useless soap.

"That's it. Rub your fingers all over yourself, little lamb. Imagine those are my hands bringing you pleasure."

I can feel every unsteady breath and irregular heartbeat thrumming against my skin in a symphony curated just for me as she works her fingers against her clit and pushes her chest into my hands.

This wasn't my intention when I started the bath for her

this evening. I'd been following her around for three days, watching her bounce from one place to the next—one random job to another. It was exhausting. I wanted to do something nice for her. I can't even begin to explain why. I don't *do* nice. Even Sienna, who I respected more than anyone else, never received this kind of treatment from me.

I told myself it was because I was preparing to kill her. She deserves a moment of luxury before I steal everything away. But now that I'm here, it's like my instincts have taken over and I couldn't find the will to kill her even if I tried.

She appears to experience the same conflicting feelings toward me—distrustfully questioning me one moment, then pleasuring herself in front of me the next.

Every moment I've spent denying myself the taste and feel of her over the past few weeks has built up to this insatiable need to have it all. And she's so goddamn willing to hand it over.

I pull away from her to move to the other side of the tub and face her, relishing the frustrated growl that leaves her lips at my disappearance.

"I want to touch you so bad," I admit through a pained breath, my gaze pinned on the cluster of soap between her legs.

"Then touch me, Bash," she urges.

Hearing my name on her lips is intoxicating. I almost didn't tell her, too afraid to give her anything she could dig into and find more information about. But whatever fallout might come from having her discover who I really am is worth it. This is worth it.

Soon.

"You should be afraid of me. I could hurt you... In fact, I probably will. I'm not the hero in this story," I warn, shrugging off my black hoodie to prevent it from getting any wetter.

For a moment, she simply stares up at me with that frustratingly indistinguishable look I've seen her wear countless times. Her eyes track my movements as I grab her shampoo from the floor and squirt it into my palm. I can't stand that I don't know what's going through her head.

She should run. I wouldn't even blame her for it. Of course, I'd chase her. But at least then I would know she possessed some semblance of self-preservation.

I'm almost positive that's what she's about to do, as she hesitates to answer me. Instead, she surprises me by saying, "I'm not afraid of dying. I've already done that. I'm afraid of not living."

I move back behind her and fall to my knees, using the excuse to escape her punishing gaze as I analyze what those words mean.

"Wet your hair," I command.

She obeys, dunking her head backward into the water so she can look up at my face hovering above her. There's a long moment where we just stare at each other, our expressions soaked in understanding.

I'm afraid of not living.

So am I.

Ever since Sienna died, it's like my soul has gone missing. The very thing that makes me *me* is nowhere to be found. I came into this world as one half of a whole and when she left, half of me left with her.

I've been telling myself that these murders have been retribution for her death, but maybe that's not entirely true. Maybe they're also retribution for *my* death as well. Because the instant my twin sister took her last breath, I may as well have taken mine, too.

Now I'm stuck here, a fraction of myself—living, but not entirely alive. It's like Stardust somehow understands what I feel without ever making me admit it.

Once she's satisfied with whatever she was looking for in my face, she lifts her head out of the water and faces forward again. I clear my throat, massaging the shampoo into her scalp before I unintentionally reveal anything else to her. She relaxes into my touch, moving her head around to give me better access. It's somehow the most erotic thing I've ever experienced with a woman. The way she blindly trusts me to care for her, even after I've broken into her home and violated her privacy.

I can't decide if she's absolutely insane or just as dangerous as me. The most unsettling part is that I don't give a fuck either way.

When I'm finished shampooing, she dunks under again to rinse, then we repeat the process with the conditioner. Neither one of us speaks a word the entire time. Where the silence should be uncomfortable—deafening, even—it feels the exact opposite. It's like I can hear her thoughts dancing off the tiles around us, and I'm sending my own signals to her in the same way.

Only when her hair is fully washed, do I dare to speak.

"Done," I tell her softly, but she doesn't bother moving away from me.

My fingers trail down the sides of her neck, and she leans her head against my wrist. Without thinking, I move her hair to the side and lean forward, pulling my mask down far enough to place my lips behind her ear in a gentle kiss.

She exhales a breath, turning her head away to allow me better access as I run my mouth down the column of her throat, teeth grazing against her skin. When I make it to her shoulder, I clamp down, earning a squeal.

I move away from her again, readjusting my mask to grab a rag as her eyes track me carefully. I'm fighting every instinct I have to rip her out of the water and throw her onto the bed so that I can finally have my way with her. But patience is a virtue, and forcing myself to use restraint will only make it that much sweeter when I finally consume her.

With as much delicacy as I can muster, I begin to scrub the rag against her skin, starting with the wrist closest to me, where her hand is tightly clutching the edge of the tub in anticipation of my next move. I make quick work of washing her, and she doesn't ever seem to fully relax against my touch. I'm not sure if my presence beside her unsettles her or if she's simply not used to being taken care of, but both scenarios are enough to push me to continue.

Once I reach the apex of her legs—the spot I *really* want to be caressing—I'm extra careful not to brush my skin against hers. Still, the thin fabric is the only thing between us, and my resilience is hanging on by a thread until I finish my task, dropping the rag into the water.

My eyes lock back onto hers, and I'm moving toward her before my brain can catch up.

19

The Lamb

LARGE HANDS WRAP around my back and beneath my knees, hoisting me out of the water before I realize what's happening. The cold air against my wet skin shocks me, pulling a gasp from my lips. I should fight against him more. I should fight *for myself* more—to care like I used to. Somewhere along the way, I just gave up.

Bash is unpredictable. If I take my eyes off him for one second, I'm left flailing around and trying to catch up. He said I should be afraid of him. I don't doubt that's true, and if I'm completely honest with myself, I think he's quite terrifying. But there's also this electric thrill that trails along my spine with my terror, and it's just strong enough to make me want to stick around and see what he'll do next.

I've never met anyone as contradictory as him. Someone who I'm completely unable to read. He's like an impossible puzzle I want to solve—a riddle I want to crack. It pisses me off that I haven't.

He carries me over to the bed, completely unconcerned with the puddles of water he leaves behind or the way his clothes are being soaked and melded against our skin.

"I want you," he says in a deep, lusty tone as he releases me from his hold and drops me onto my bed.

Just like before, the words come out like he's admitting something taboo. Like, for some reason, he can't stand the fact that he holds any desire for me.

You and me both, Stalker.

I gaze up at him, too afraid to let him out of my sight. "So take me," I dare, and I immediately want to take the words back when his shocked gaze crashes against mine.

This man broke into my home, demanded I strip in front of him, and then insisted he give me a bath like some child. Not to mention the probability of him stalking me outside of the cottage. How else could he have timed all of this so perfectly?

But deep down—like, really deep—I still want him. I'm drawn to him in a way I can't even begin to describe and refuse to put words to. Perhaps it's the desire burning in his stare every time we meet. Maybe it's the fact that I'm not entirely convinced he's real. Or maybe it's because I'm completely fucked in the head from all my abandonment issues, and the idea of *anyone* wanting me is enough to make me spread my legs and hand myself over to them.

Even if they're likely a psycho, stalker, killer.

Okay, that's probably it.

Regardless of the reason behind it, that's exactly what I do as he moves toward me on the bed, positioning himself between my legs. Long fingers stroke my thighs while his eyes openly roam over my body. His gaze feels like an extra hand caressing my skin. Goosebumps pebble my skin, and I shiver when he reaches my slit and runs his finger down the middle.

"So wet for me," he muses, bringing his hand back up to rub my clit. "You'll be my undoing."

"I'm already undone," I admit in a voice soaked in sex, one I don't even recognize.

I'm trying to figure out how he thinks he'll be the one walking away from this destroyed, when the admission falls from my lips. If I'm going to Hell, I might as well have a good time on my descent.

He cocks his head to the side.

"I don't think you get it, Stardust. The second I coat my tongue with your cum, you're going to be mine. No other man will ever touch you again and live to talk about it. When I eat this pussy"—he glides his finger down my slit again, and I shudder out a breath—"I'm taking ownership of it."

His hands fall onto the bed as he leans over my body to cage me in, dropping his face until only a few inches separate our mouths. His is still covered by his mask, but I can still feel the heat from his erratic breaths over my lips.

"Do you understand now?"

Once again, I can't tell whether I should be afraid or aroused. Why does the idea of being *owned* by him sound so fucking appealing?

I won't show him my fear, though. Something tells me that's exactly what he wants to see. Instead, I swallow roughly and nod my head, then thrust my hips into his so he knows what I want him to do next.

His understanding hums from his chest. "Mm. Good girl."

There is no other warning. In one blink, he's off the bed and kneeling on the floor, his shoulders nestled between my thighs as his tongue makes one long, thick stroke over my entire center.

I jump at the sensation, sending my pussy farther against his hot mouth, and the bastard laughs.

"So sweet. So fucking delectable," he says into my folds as I'm arching my back into the mattress with a moan.

He's devouring me, just as he said he would. Kissing, licking, biting me in the most erotic way. This is a man who knows how to manipulate my body into doing exactly what he craves. A man who is used to getting what he wants. His face is obviously uncovered now, and I'm frustrated with myself for being so incapacitated by his mouth on my pussy, I can't even lean forward to see it.

"Fuck," I drawl, bucking my hips forward to find some sort of relief from his constant attention.

His large hand drapes over my stomach, anchoring me onto the bed as he drives his tongue and fingers into my pussy. I'm sitting on the edge, ready to fall apart against him, when the low rumble of his knowing voice vibrates against my center.

"Come for me, baby. Scream my name so everyone in this shitty, Podunk town knows who you belong to."

It's all the encouragement I need to take a nosedive off that cliff and fall into a euphoric state. My legs clamp together against his head and my hips fight the hand holding me down. Deep moans like I've never made before fall out of my mouth, and just when I think there's no way it can get any better—that I can't *fall* any further—he jams another finger inside me and hooks it against the perfect spot.

I see stars. Balls of fire explode behind my eyes, igniting a whole new wave of ecstasy to course through me.

"Holy shit, Bash," I moan.

I can't think straight. Hell, I can't even open my eyes until the shock waves stop reverberating through every limb. And when I finally do, Bash is standing over me with his mask pulled down for the first time.

A cocky, unguarded smile graces beautiful, plump lips.

He's licking his fingers in a crass show of ownership. My legs are still spread wide open, my breathing inconsistent.

He's right. No other man will compare to what he just did. That shit terrifies me worse than anything else he's done. I'd chase this high to the ends of the earth.

I'm afraid I'll wake up tomorrow and realize this was all a dream. What then?

Bash comes around the side of the bed and leans forward, hovering over me while taking great care to make sure we aren't touching at all. "Tell me… who do you belong to, little Stardust?"

I don't even hesitate to answer. "You."

"That's right, baby." Green eyes flick down my body as he brings his palm down to cup my center.

"This pussy is mine." His hands move up my body in a long, teasing caress that has me dripping all over again. When he reaches my throat, his fingers wrap around either side.

"*You're* mine."

I want to touch him. I want to wrap my lips around his cock and repay the favor. To make my own feeble attempt at staking my claim on him the same way. But before I can do anything, Bash steps away from me and disappears into the bathroom. Seconds later, I hear the spout for the bathtub turn on, and he walks back into the room to grab me up from the bed again.

Wordlessly, he brings me back to the bathroom and lowers me into the warmed bath.

"Relax."

It's all he says before turning his back and leaving me alone.

20

I WENT TOO FAR last night with Stardust.

And yet, I walked away feeling like we didn't go far enough. It seems like every time I make a move to bring whatever I feel for her to an end, I just crave more.

Just watching turned into *just touching* turned into *just tasting,* and now that I've done all that, I want to consume her. I want all of her in every way I can get it. I showed her my fucking face, for God's sake.

The look in her eyes when I was finished with her was clearly one of longing. She wanted to go further, and I couldn't allow that to happen. At least, not yet. I wanted to taste her, and I did. So I put her back into the bathtub and walked away before we did anything we might end up regretting.

I keep telling myself that I did it for her. That it's out of respect for her emotions, her privacy, her boundaries. It might be time to admit it's more for me than anything.

Because I know that the second I give in to this monster and let him in, it'll overrun me. I told her she should be afraid of me, but if I'm being completely honest with myself, the way I feel about her terrifies me.

I've already crossed so many lines. None of this was ever supposed to get this far. I shouldn't still be in Styx. I shouldn't be buying property here. I definitely shouldn't still be killing people here.

The worst part is that I'm so fucked up that I'm *enjoying* it. Every last, damning part of it.

Stardust's life is chaotic and restless. It's an infuriatingly mundane pattern of work, sleep, eat, repeat.

Over and over and over again.

I hate following her around to each odd job she has, watching her serve people who don't deserve it. It's like looking through a window at a completely different world—one I've admittedly avoided eye contact with for as long as I can remember. The housekeepers and cooks were just background noise in our household. Busy bees that buzzed around us and made sure everything was exactly how we liked it.

I realize now that the only difference between me and them is the number in my bank account. The blood running through my veins is somehow considered more valuable to the world than that of the people who have always worked below us and made it possible for us to live these ridiculously lavish lives. Where their life always seemed so drab and lacking any real sustenance, I find myself on the opposite end of the societal spectrum. My gluttonous, rich peers get to enjoy life *too much*. It's disgusting and unjust. A thinly veiled illusion to make you think they're living better than the people they employ, when in reality, it's the rich who lack any true value or emotions. And now, I have to sit helplessly and watch my obsession churn around like another cog in the machine.

Or do I?

I'm still working through the thought as I click on Eliza's photo in my phone, and it begins ringing. She answers on the third ring.

"It's after hours, asshole. I'm off the clock," she greets in her grainy voice, heavy from all the smoking she's done throughout the years.

"I have someone I want to offer a job to," I say into the line, knowing she's already opening her computer to help me. We don't ever bother with pleasantries, and I prefer it to stay that way.

"Okay…" she drawls, keypad clicking in the background. "Who? What job?"

"I don't know yet," I admit, realizing I haven't thought this through. What if Stardust reports me for stalking like she wants to, and Eliza gets dragged down with me?

Fuck. She wouldn't. I have to believe that after what we experienced last night, she wouldn't do that.

"Are you fucking with me?" Eliza asks with an edge of impatience, and I don't even have to be there to know she's wearing her signature pissed-off look that makes all our new employees quit within the hour of seeing it.

"No, Eliza. I'm not *fucking* with you," I mutter condescendingly. "I need you to look into any open remote position we have. If there isn't anything, make one up."

Perhaps it would be better to offer her a job in the office. Get her to move out to New York, so I can really keep an eye on her.

No. She'd never go for it.

Baby steps.

"What kind of qualifications does this person have? Do you have a resume?"

"No, I don't, but it doesn't matter. Just find something."

Eliza huffs an irritated breath into the line. "I'll see what I can do."

She doesn't bother closing off the conversation before the line goes dead, and I know I'm going to get my ass chewed out when I go into the office. I don't care, though. It's worth it to pin Stardust into one spot so I don't have to drive all over this shitty ass town to keep track of her.

21

The Lamb

IT'S AN UNUSUALLY busy Thursday morning at Old Soul, and I'm working alone until Rosie gets here to help me close. I typically don't mind handling shifts like this on my own, but something feels different about today. I feel off.

I constantly find myself taking in my surroundings, scanning the cafe for some sort of threat, like the gazelle who senses the lion watching them in the grass. I just know *something* isn't right.

My mystery man, *Bash*, hasn't made any attempts to contact me since the bathtub incident. It feels surreal to have been so intimate with the man who stalks me without the comfortable excuse of him possibly being a dream. Although, even with a new name to call him, I still know next to nothing about the stranger. And yet, I stupidly allowed him to touch me again. To *devour* me, really. Only for him to disappear for over a week. It all seems so… weird. Weird and foreign and alarmingly close to abandonment.

But the weary feeling I'm experiencing now isn't anything like how it feels to have Bash around.

Eventually, I'm knocking orders out as fast as they come in, caught in a rhythm of efficiency that keeps me from looking around the restaurant longer than it takes to count the people lined up out the door. I've overheard enough conversations to gather that there's a training seminar being held at one of the bank buildings down the street. One of the people running it tipped them off that Old Soul was the best coffee in town, and they all congregated here for their lunch break. While I appreciate the tips, I'm swamped. So much so, I had to admit defeat and call Rosie in early just to help manage the line.

We're mid-conversation behind the counter, speculating which of our regulars would have thrown us this business, when a hand wraps around my wrist across the checkout counter.

I had just told the customer standing before me what his total is, hardly glancing up at his unsmiling face before he's shoving his debit card into my hand. It's when I go to grab it that he stops me.

Startled, I lift my gaze up to meet two terrifyingly familiar cerulean eyes staring back at me expectantly, and my heart drops into my stomach.

"Gabe," I greet grimly, frowning at the Cheshire Cat grin splitting his face, and the way his fingers tighten against my skin as his name passes my lips.

"Is there a problem, sir?" Rosie cuts in, dropping the order she was working on to step over to us.

"Not at all. Just catching up with an old friend," he explains coolly, sliding his eyes back over to me in a silent command. He wants me to get rid of her.

Rosie follows his lead, the question burning in her gaze. *Is he going to be a problem?* She wants to know.

I'm torn between the two. I don't want to lie to Rosie, and I don't want to be alone with Gabe. But years of conditioning by my narcissistic sociopath of an ex have taught me that if I don't go along with his antics, there will be punishment.

It doesn't help that his fingers digging into my flesh are serving the perfect reminder of what happens when I don't obey him.

For that reason, I shake my head at Rosie, protecting Gabe like I always do. Gabe gives my wrist another appreciative squeeze, so hard that I'll probably find marks later, and I rip my hand away from him.

He recovers from the rejection flawlessly. "Do you have a free minute?"

Tilting my head toward the dwindling line, I say, "We're busy right now."

A false frown tugs down at his lips, guilting me. But I can tell by the quick, subtle way his eyes darken that he's irritated with me for not playing along as easily as he wants me to. Getting Rosie off his back was as far as my kindness extends to the snake standing before me. I won't be spending any time alone with him. Not when it's so easy for him to manipulate and confuse me.

His lips flatten into a tight, barely there smile as Rosie hands him his drink. The person behind him in line impatiently steps closer.

"Fine. Another time, then." I swipe his card in the POS machine and slide it back over to him, careful not to make any physical contact again.

As the machine processes his card, he releases a dramatically loud sigh, casting his glance over at the crowded cafe. "I suppose I should have kept this place to myself so I could steal a free minute with you. I heard through the grapevine that you moved into your own place and figured you could use the extra customers."

I flinch at that. *Through the grapevine* is a fluffy, casual way to say that he hunted the information down and likely pestered multiple people to find a shred about me. He probably doesn't expect that mine and Halen's friends would rat him out for harassing them, but I'll be questioning them the moment I get a chance to. It's the same method he used to get my new phone number.

To think that every customer who came through here today was somehow tied to him makes my stomach turn. I don't even want to take the cash overflowing from our tip jar home just on principle. Anything that comes from Gabe has invisible strings tied to it, even if I can't see them right away.

Maybe I'll give them all to Rosie.

I pass over his receipt and don't even bother plastering a fake smile on when I say, "Thanks for that, but I'm doing okay. Another time."

I don't give him space to respond and, thankfully, the customer behind him shoulders his way in front of me to pay for his drink. Gabe scowls at the man, but turns and walks out the door, his shoulders a little more tense than before.

There isn't another chance to obsess over what it means for Gabe to have my phone number and knowledge of at least one of my jobs. Or the fact that he's apparently working right down the street from me. The line doesn't go down until it's time to close the cafe, and I end up staying another hour past closing to help Rosie clean up the mess from such a high traffic day.

"That was a whirlwind, huh?" She wipes her brow, setting the last chair up on a table to make room for us to mop. "Sorry I couldn't get in earlier to help. You must be ten times more exhausted than I feel right now."

I shrug dismissively. "I'm fine."

She rounds the counter to stand beside me, waiting for me to move so she can prepare the mop bucket. "Seriously,

Jovie. I don't know where I'd be without you. I mean, you've even got weird exes sending me business."

A hard, boney elbow jabs me in the side jovially. But when I turn toward her with a laugh ghosting my lips, I see the seriousness in her expression.

"Yeah, well, I'm not sure if that's much of a gift. You'll be soaking your feet for the next three days."

Rosie barks out a laugh, then picks up the overflowing tip jar and grabs up the cash so she can count it out and split it up.

"You take it," I tell her.

She pauses, watching me like she's waiting for an explanation. When I nod my head to reassure her, she holds up the wad of cash.

"You want me to take all of this for myself?" she asks in disbelief.

Busying myself straightening a cup full of straws, I nod my head a little too fast. "You didn't have to come in early, but you did." The weak excuse falls out of my mouth before I can think it through. I just don't want Gabe to have any reason to say he helped me, and taking those tips feels like taking his help.

She doesn't bother arguing, though I can tell she wants to. I wouldn't be surprised if she tacked a few extra dollars on my paycheck later on. Either way, she gathers up all the money and shoves it into her purse before we shut off the lights and walk out the door together. This time, I'm looking around for not one, but two men who hunt me.

22

The Lamb

MY MYSTERY MAN returns that night, long after I've fallen asleep. When I got home from the cafe, I went straight to bed and passed out before the sun set. There's something about being around Gabe that does that to me—completely depletes me of all my energy.

I woke up a few hours later to the room blanketed in darkness and a shadow standing over me, peering down at my wrist lying beside me on the bed.

"What's this?" He gently pulls my arm up and turns it so the moonlight shines directly onto me, frowning at the bruises peppering the delicate skin of my inner wrist.

I sit up and try to yank away from his grasp, but he holds me in my spot. Not hard enough to leave a mark or scare me like Gabe, but stern enough to demand an answer.

"It's nothing."

"It's not *nothing*," he spits out the word like it's spoiled food against his tongue. "These look like fingerprints. Who did this to you?"

"You're about to add more if you don't let go," I whine, tugging my arm even harder.

Without warning, he releases his grip, and I go backward, nearly falling onto my pillow. I scowl back at his smug smirk, rubbing the spot dramatically.

But Bash doesn't falter. Once his amusement at my near fall subsides, his brows come together, casting a menacing shadow over his eyes that makes him look murderous.

"Who. Touched. You?" he demands in an angry, gravelly tone.

He looks like he's about to go on a rampage in search of the person responsible for a few bruises on my skin, and I have no idea why it bothers him so much. Just like at the coffee shop with Rosie, I get the urge to protect Gabe from any fallout that might come from his actions. Something tells me that won't work with Bash, though, and lying might end up getting me punished. I have to remember how mentally unstable he is.

With a casual shrug to let him know it's really not a big deal, I simply say, "My asshole ex came to visit me at work."

Apparently, that was the wrong answer.

A low growl reverberates in Bash's chest as he leans toward me again, closing the safe distance my blunder put between us before. All amusement is gone from his expression, and in its place is pure rage.

"And he hurt you like this? Why didn't you tell anyone?"

Another shrug. What's the point of telling anyone when they never believed me before?

Rosie may have stepped in, but then what? I've seen how much collateral damage can happen from one of Gabe's fits. It's best for everyone if I keep them contained to just me.

Besides, this was hardly one of his signature tantrums. He was trying to prove a point that I don't really give a fuck about.

"Has he laid his hands on you before?" Bash asks, breaking my train of thought.

I don't have to answer when my eyes fall to the floor.

"I need your words, Stardust. Tell me that this fucker has hurt you worse than this, and I'll have all the permission I need to handle him."

My eyes snap back up to his face, shocked. "Handle him?"

Bash takes one last step toward me, effectively erasing any personal space I had so he can place his masked lips right against my ear as he speaks in a low, gruff voice.

"I told you, you're *mine* now, and I don't like when people touch my things. Anyone with the balls to do so is going to deal with the consequences. Do you understand?"

I can hear the weight of his fury in the wavering in his words. The struggle for him to keep this dangerous side of him contained. And somehow, I know that he's doing it for my sake. So he doesn't scare me. So I don't run. But I'm too distracted by the fact that, for the first time ever, someone finally believes *me* about Gabe. I'm not the unreliable, irrational, unmanageable girlfriend that Gabe's painted me to be.

I'm tempted to tell him everything. To feed his fire and then direct him to the exact spot where he can find the sniveling asswipe. It would feel so good to know he's finally receiving a taste of his own medicine. I'd love to hear him beg for mercy the same way I've always had to do.

But the part of me that wants to protect the narcissist—the one convinced that everything is my fault, and every mark was earned—stops me.

Shaking my head against Bash's concealed lips, I drop my chin to my chest and sigh in defeat.

"It was just an accident," I lie in a small voice. "I'm fine."

Bash backs away from me, eyes widened. He knows the truth, I'm sure of it. But I have no idea what this man is capable of. What if he hurts Gabe over this? Even if I weren't the one to deliver the blows, I'm just as responsible for knowingly unleashing a rabid dog onto him. I can't have that on my conscience, no matter how badly I've been hurt.

Hurt people hurt people. I'm trying my best to be healed.

"Please drop it," I beg when it's obvious he wants to say more.

After a long, pregnant pause, Bash finally offers one stiff nod of agreement, and I know that's all he'll give.

He blows out a breath and pushes the covers back over me, then climbs into the bed on top of them.

"What are you doing?" I stupidly ask, because this seems like a new step in our odd little relationship he's taking without my knowledge or consent.

"I'm laying down," he states simply, like it's not the weirdest fucking thing that this stranger has once again walked right into my house while I was sleeping and shown himself into my room.

"In my bed…"

"Am I only allowed in your bed when I'm eating you out?"

Scoffing at his boorish remark, I shake my head and send a prayer up above that someone fucking save me from this man who has seemingly been dropped into my life out of nowhere and taken over every aspect of it.

"No, asshole. That's not what I meant."

"Would you like to spread your legs for me now and give me a taste? I thought it might be uncouth of me to lick your pussy so soon after your ex scared you, but I'd be more than happy to chase him out of your thoughts with my tongue. All you have to do is ask, baby."

Turning my back to him, I rest my head on my hands and

tell him, "I'm going back to sleep. Maybe when I wake up, you'll be gone, and I can have peace for once."

His low chuckle vibrates the bed, but he doesn't leave. Instead, he lies there, still as a statue, while I struggle to fall asleep. And when I do, he's there, in my dreams.

23

The Wolf

I KNEW that dickbag ex was going to be an issue.

The moment I saw him creeping around the house, peering into her windows and trying all her locks when she wasn't home, I knew there was something off about the guy. I just didn't suspect that the meathead had actually laid a hand on her. And while it pisses me off that he *ever* had the balls to harm a woman, it enrages me that he did it after she became *mine*.

I knew he was an issue, and I didn't act on my instincts. That's a mistake I don't intend to make again.

She says it's not a big deal. Even lied to me about him having done something like this to her before, but I could see the truth behind her broken expression. He's done far, far worse than a few weak bruises on her wrist. The problem is that everyone else in her life has failed her when it comes to this asshat. Just like we all failed Sienna with Garrett, her useless, spineless ex, who stood back and watched as his friends destroyed her. I'm still deciding how I want to kill him.

Everyone turns a blind eye to the marks, their small minds unable to compute the truth when the snake is standing before them, spinning a completely different story than the one they can see with their naked eyes. I'm guilty of it. I was too detached from my own life to bother acknowledging what was happening right in front of me. I owe it to my sister not to repeat that mistake.

The brute of a man paces in front of the bay window of his modest, suburban home. I can't believe Stardust ever settled for this. That she even believed this is what she deserved.

She deserves the entire night sky and every exploding, magnificent star floating inside of it. No, fuck that. She deserves the *universe*.

My girl is so much bigger than all of this. I hope one day she allows me to give it to her.

I adjust myself against my jeans, my erection growing the longer I think about the little anomaly. Her ex has settled into the couch with a six-pack of beer, making it obvious that he has no plans to move from his spot for quite a while.

With a quick sweep of the area to confirm no one else is around, I recline my seat and unzip my pants, taking my cock in my hand. The illegal tints on my windows make it next to impossible for anyone to see me inside, but it's better to be safe than sorry.

Immediately, my mind strays back to Jovie. To her soft, plump ass, perfectly framed in the tight leggings she's always wearing. The wisps of hair that always seem to be flying into her beautiful, perfectly round face. Her delicious plump lips, always stuck between her teeth as she rolls over some thought inside her head.

Fuck.

I'm finishing into my hand within minutes like some sex-depraved, hormonal, pimple-faced teenage boy.

I need to get laid. But in order to do that, I have to allow her to touch me, and I'm not quite sure she's ready for that.

Once I'm cleaned up, I check on her ex one last time, unsurprised to find that he's in the same spot as before. He'll be an easy hunt. I just need to find time to do it without her knowing it was me. Or perhaps, it would be beneficial to wait and use it as an opportunity to show her the true monster that I am. Maybe I'll even tempt the darkness in her and let her help.

Not yet, though.

I pull away from the curb and head in the direction of the place I actually want to be in.

To the person I want to be in.

24

The Lamb

My PHONE PINGS with an email notification, and I turn away from the counter at Old Soul so the people working at the table across from me don't see me on it. It's an invitation for a phone interview at Lancaster Tech, a cyber security company based in New York. I don't remember applying there, but that isn't saying much. It's hard to keep track of every company I send my resume to when I'm applying to hundreds of positions a week.

I quickly type out a reply, letting them know when I'm available to call, and then shove my phone back into my pocket.

"I saw that," Rosie admonishes, and I jump, sending a frother clattering to the ground. She laughs out loud, shaking her head.

Okay, so I'm still a little jumpy after the other night with the mystery man and the crass way he spoke to me.

"What has you so on edge today?" Rosie wonders. She

grabs a rag from the sink and starts wiping down the workspace that I should be cleaning, and I bend over to pick up the frother, taking the opportunity to get my heartbeat settled back into my chest.

I don't want to tell her about what has happened and risk having her judge me. If I'm being completely honest, I'm still embarrassed that I allowed him to touch me. I wish I had called the police. Or maybe, I could have stabbed him and ran. At least that would make me look like I fought a little. Instead, I played a game with him, then let him wash me and eat me out. And when he came back for more, pretending to care about me like some guard dog, I didn't even chase him away.

Who does that?

"I'm just tired," I mumble the weak excuse into my chest, knowing she'll see right through it.

Instead of bringing him up the way I think she will, Rosie stops wiping and turns to face me, lines of worry etched into her forehead. "You've been working your ass off lately. Maybe it's time to take a personal day."

I'm immediately shaking my head, dismissing the thought. "I can't afford a day off."

"Well, you can't afford to run yourself into the ground, either. If you don't slow down, your body will force you to. Take the afternoon and relax. I'll cover your shift here."

My eyes lift to find hers, questioning whether she's serious or not. Rosie is my friend, but she's a hardass for a boss. She's the last person I would expect to let me off early.

But I *could* use a break.

"Are you sure?" I ask with a mountain of insecurity, waiting for the shoe to drop.

She twists the rag and whips it into the air at me, smacking my ass with the tip. I howl, grabbing the spot she just assaulted. The people sitting across from us scowl our way, but Rosie just laughs at me.

That shit hurt.

"Yes. Get out of here before I change my mind. I had a date with my vibrator later that I'll have to postpone now because of you."

Chuckling, I lift off my apron and scurry out the door before she can reconsider. When I'm settled into the driver's seat, I check my email and find a reply from the hiring manager at Lancaster Tech. She wants to chat with me tonight. Thankfully, my schedule just opened up.

I type out my message, then shift into drive, ignoring the headlights that seem to stay behind me the entire way.

25

The Wolf

My father, in all his infinite wisdom, has taken it upon himself to set up a dinner date with Mallory for me in Styx. He claims he did it in an attempt to rekindle whatever flame might have been between us, but I know that's bullshit. This is his way of letting me know he's well aware of how often I'm spending my time in Styx, and he doesn't approve.

I had to rush from Arthur Lewis, our family lawyer's studio apartment back in Manhattan, where he takes his conquests for the night under the guise of working too late to drive to the suburbs like some Madman from the sixties. He had nothing to offer me about Sienna's case. It's the same regurgitated story as the judge all over again.

A mystery wad of cash was left in his office with a threatening note and pictures of his family. The only extra information he had was that my father refused to let him back out of the case and bring one of his partners on, opting to drop the whole thing instead.

It was a huge waste of fucking time. Once I showed him photos of the seven women who filed police reports against him for sexual assault that somehow disappeared from the police system in the past year, throwing out their entire case against him, I broke his neck and left his dead body there to rot for God knows how long.

Then, I had to gun it into Styx for this dinner to keep up the illusion that my father still holds my puppet strings.

Sure, Mallory and I have hooked up a couple of times, but I have absolutely no interest in pursuing anything with her, especially now that I have my little lamb.

"I'm moving to Chicago after I take the BAR." The words fall slowly from Mallory's supple red lips, as if she's nervously anticipating a negative reaction from me.

"Okay…"

"I think we should take a break from this thing between us." She waves her hand in the air, her long red nails glistening in the low lights above us.

"A break?" I question incredulously. A break from *what*, exactly? We're hardly together.

"Come on, Sebastian. Don't make this harder than it is." I hate the way she uses my full name. It's just another item to add to the growing list of things that irritate me about her. "I know in the end, it's going to be you and me. That's what it's *always* been. But for now, I need to experience life without the weight of a long-distance relationship."

I stare at her, allowing the words to roll around in my head as I piece together why the hell she thinks this means anything to me. What bullshit lie did my dad spew to get her here?

"Why not take a job in the city?" My lips are asking all on their own, because none of this makes sense.

She's right. Mallory has been practically promised to me since birth. Our nuptials would be too beneficial for both of our families to pass up. After all, that's all that matters in our world—money. And making sure that money is preserved and we stay firmly planted in the top one percent. It has nothing to do with my feelings for her or the fact that we're in *love*—whatever the fuck that is. But Mallory was always supposed to come back to New York and settle down with me when she was ready to leave Styx.

So, even though I have no desire to be with this woman in any capacity, I want to know what changed.

"I mean, of course I'll start my own firm there. But it's like your dad said, it'll be such an enriching experience to practice in a completely new city for a little while before I tie myself down–"

"What does my father have to do with this?" I rudely cut her off.

She blinks at me, brows raised at my interruption. I don't bother apologizing, though. Instead, I lean forward and repeat the question, much slower. "What do you mean, 'like my father said?'"

"He's the one who got me the job in Chicago. You knew that," she insists, slowly bringing her wineglass to her lips.

I slam my napkin on the table, and Mallory startles. People seated around us turn to look at the commotion that caused our silverware to clatter against our plates.

"Fuck," I breathe out, running my hand through my hair.

"Sebastian," Mallory hisses, her face contorted in what should be a scowl, if not for the Botox she has loaded beneath her skin. "You're causing a scene."

He knows. He fucking knows exactly what I'm doing in Styx, and he knows how close I am to exposing the truth.

How the hell is he always two steps ahead of me?

Renting out the cabin. Sending Mallory to Chicago. He's trying like hell to steal away all my reasons for being here.

Each move has been carefully calculated to knock me off

my path. I'm not even surprised. I don't give a shit if Mallory leaves the country to practice. I'm pissed at myself for not seeing this coming from a mile away.

"This is exactly why I think we need space. You can't throw a tantrum anytime something gets in your way," Mallory berates me in a low, soft whisper as I work through my dad's process in my mind. I'm obviously not listening, but she's too fucking dense to realize that.

This whole thing has turned into such a tangled web. Each time I feel like I have a grasp on one thread, another one slips through my fingers.

I should just kill my father and be done with it. At the very least, I can assume he had a hand in covering everything up. His own fucking daughter. That's how far he'll go to preserve his social and monetary standing. And now, he's trying to stand in my way of finding the truth.

He's a coward. Death would be a favor. I need to give him something worse.

My thoughts are moving so fast, I hardly notice my prey walk through the dining room before me, taking a seat at a table merely twenty feet away with two other women. Instantly, my attention leaves Mallory and my father and lands firmly on her—my little Stardust, out in the wild.

My gaze locks on her, and my mouth instantly begins to water.

I need a taste.

26

The Lamb

HALEN AND KENNEDY decide to celebrate my potential new employment by treating me to my favorite restaurant. It's one of the most expensive places downtown Styx has to offer and we only come on special occasions.

I tried telling them it really wasn't *that* big of a deal. That my getting a real corporate job for the first time was not in the same bracket as something as significant as anniversaries or holidays. Or that technically, I haven't even accepted the position yet. But they insisted, furthering my insecurities about being their charity case.

Truthfully, though, I'm excited about the prospect of finally rejoining the workforce and breaking out of the constant hustle of taking on odd jobs wherever I can find them. Steady income is a privilege I haven't been afforded in a very long time, and it makes the offer that much more tempting.

No one wants to hire the weird girl with an unexplainable gap in her resume. Unless I want to openly confess that I'd spend that time in a rehabilitation facility, I just had to stumble through that expanse of time on my resume whenever it was brought up. For some reason, the hiring manager at Lancaster Tech didn't even bother asking about my work history. In fact, she didn't ask me much of anything of value. If I hadn't obsessively researched the company myself, I'd think it was a total scam.

I suppose it still could be, but I'm not going to admit that to Halen and Kennedy after I've seen how excited they are for me.

We follow the hostess to a table off to the side and the waiter takes our drink order immediately. On instinct, my eyes scan the room and the faces of the people we'll be sharing our environment with. It's a habit I learned at Sunnybrook, never wanting to be caught off guard by any outbursts or random attacks.

Of course, I doubt that Paul's Chop House would be filled with anyone like the people I encountered at Sunnybrook, but it calms me just the same. Besides, I haven't seen Bash in a while. It's only a matter of time before my crazed stalker makes an appearance.

As I'm about to give up and drop my gaze on the menu, it locks in on *him,* and my breath catches in my throat so abruptly, I nearly choke. It's almost as if my thoughts have conjured him before me.

He's already staring my way, green eyes shadowed by thick eyebrows and the ambient lighting. The mask is gone from his mouth, exposing his sinfully gorgeous features in broad daylight. I'd know that face anywhere. Those haunted eyes. That structured demeanor. I'm absolutely positive it's him.

He meets my confused scowl with a slight tick in his eyebrow—the only break in his unreadable mask.

It can't be.

He can't be here.

He's not even *real*. At least, not in my fragile mind.

Maybe it's not the same *him*.

But that wouldn't explain why he's staring at me that way.

Like by simply existing here, in the same space as him, I've just earned the spot as his newest conquest.

"Are you alright?" Halen asks from my left, but I'm too afraid to tear my gaze away from his face and have him disappear.

He's sitting at an intimate round table in the middle of the room, hardly big enough for two. A blonde woman sits across from him, and though I can only see her profile from here, I can tell she's stunning.

They're obviously on a date.

But *ghosts and stalkers* don't go on dates.

"Jovie…" Halen snaps her fingers in front of my face. When I finally look at her, I'm met with a worried expression. "Are you good?"

Nodding into my lap, my chin tucked firmly against my chest, I answer, "Yeah, just a little claustrophobic."

"It is a little more packed in here tonight than usual," Kennedy agrees easily, sending a warning glare at my sister.

I don't miss the silent argument they have over Kennedy defending me before my eyes swing back over to the middle of the room. To his table.

He's got a whiskey glass tilted back against his lips this time, but his eyes are still focused on me over the rim, instead of on his date. When he notices me looking again, his brows raise in a question.

Am I going to confront him in front of all these people?

The answer is a strong and resounding, *hell no.*

I know better than to start spewing some insanity about a man who breaks into my house at night and buries his face between my legs. That kind of story doesn't bode well for the girl who just got out of the mental hospital.

But, Jovie, if this guy was breaking into your house, why didn't you call the police?

Oh, no reason. I just thought he was a fucking ghost.

What a complete idiot?

So, no. I'm not going to confront him here, in a crowded restaurant, where he appears to be on an intimate date.

But am I going to hide away in the bathroom until he leaves?

Why yes. Yes, I am.

I wait until the waiter comes back to take our orders so Halen and Kennedy aren't stuck waiting to eat, then quickly throw my napkin onto the table and mumble an excuse about not feeling well. I practically fall out of my chair, rushing off to the restroom before they can argue with me. Kennedy's arm flies out in front of Halen before she stands to join me, and I send a silent prayer to whoever is up above for her.

Thankfully, the restroom is mostly empty. There's a woman standing in the mirror reapplying her lipstick, but each stall appears unoccupied. I stumble over to the last one against the wall and close myself in, taking a few deep breaths to stop my heart from beating in my ears. Lipstick lady leaves a few moments later, and I release a long, loud exhale through my lips.

My relief is short-lived. Not even a minute passes before I hear the door open and go completely still so whoever it is doesn't hear me panicking, deciding that I'll wait for them to be done before I step back out. Hopefully, it isn't Halen trying to find me. My ears perk up, listening for whoever it is to enter one of the stalls, but it doesn't seem like anyone is actually there.

Maybe I'm just hearing things.

Still, I linger in the stall for a few more minutes, taking the opportunity to empty my bladder before I gain the courage to leave the safe space.

But as soon as I do, he's in front of me.

"What the hell?" I shriek, wrapping my hand around my throat. My heart stops in my chest, and I don't think it starts back up until he speaks.

"We need to talk."

"Were you there the whole time? Did you hear me?" I hiss, gesturing toward the stall I just walked out of.

And listen, I know having him hear me pee is a weird thing to get hung up on, given the circumstances. But that's what finally sends me over the edge.

He just stares, as if he doesn't even want to dignify the question with a response. Mortified, I turn my back to him and walk over to the sinks, watching him closely in the mirror as I wash my hands.

"We need to talk," he repeats, a little more impatiently this time.

"No shit," I throw over my shoulder, rolling my eyes. "But where do we begin? With you breaking into my home? Or how about you sexually assaulting me in my own bed?"

I look his reflection up and down in the mirror, finally allowing myself to take in his full appearance. For some reason, it's easier for me to face him like this through the mirror than head-on. *Cowardly, I know.* But my feelings about him and this situation are all over the place.

He's dressed in a tailored black suit, his light gray shirt morphing his eyes into an odd, grayish-green color. He's tapping black, polished dress shoes on the floor as his arms cross over his chest. It's a stark contrast from the casual, all black attire I'm used to seeing him in. Although, that's unsurprising, since a custom suit isn't suitable for breaking and entering, and a bandana mask isn't appropriate for a restaurant.

"Sexually assaulting you? If memory serves, you loved every second of it. Never even told me to stop," he counters darkly, leaning his shoulder against the wall. "In fact, you begged me for more."

I flick my eyes back up in the mirror just in time to see the smug smirk that ghosts his lips before he schools his expression again, and I get the urge to smack it right off. I've never resorted to violence, but how far can a person be pushed?

"That was before I realized you were..." I trail off, too embarrassed to finish that sentence.

Before I realized you were real.

He doesn't make me finish my sentence, either because he doesn't care or because he already knows what I was going to say. Instead, he shrugs and tempts his fate by adding, "It's technically more my house than yours."

I narrow my eyes at his reflection. Every time he speaks, he confuses and infuriates me further. "What the hell does that mean?"

"I bought it."

"You *bought* it?" I repeat childishly, and then it all clicks. I did receive a letter about a new owner taking over my lease. But *him*? No way. Why would he go that far to get near me? "No, a property management company took it over... SAL Properties, or something like that."

His lips kick back up in that same simpering smirk, as if there's a joke in there that I'm somehow missing.

"I should call the police on you for what you've done," I weakly threaten, refusing to engage in any sort of banter with this lunatic.

"You won't, though," he says confidently, stepping forward into my back until his breath hits my cheek and sends chills down my spine. My traitorous body instantly reacts to his presence.

He's right, I won't. No one believes the crazy girl who tried to kill herself. But he doesn't need to know that.

"How can you be so sure?"

His nose grazes my jaw as his fingers swipe a few loose strands of hair away, fully exposing my neck to him. Sharp teeth graze against my skin until he nips at my shoulder, and I jump, hating the way it sends tremors pulsing between my legs.

"Because you like it too much."

27

The Wolf

A SOFT GASP passes through her lips when my hand snakes around her hip and tugs her flush against me. She's pissed me off by refusing to face me through this entire exchange. I rest my chin on her shoulder and meet those dark brown eyes in the mirror, making sure to line my mouth up perfectly against her ear.

"You loved having a strange man come for you in the dead of night. To make you scream like no other man has before."

"Bash…" She shivers against me, but shakes her head soberly. "No. You're clearly unhinged."

I smirk at that. "Am I?"

Maybe I am. This whole thing has seemed so fucked up since the beginning, yet when I'm with her—against her—it feels so *right.* Even now, standing in a public women's bathroom where anyone could find us together, I feel a high I've never felt before.

Not even when I kill.

That's got to mean something. Right?

Or am I just completely fucked up, moving from one criminal addiction to the next?

Killing. Stalking. *Sexually assaulting,* as she says. Though I'd never touch a woman without some form of consent. Even now, she hasn't told me to back away. In fact, her hips have begun to slowly rock against mine as my lips trail up and down her neck in featherlight kisses.

"Yes," she hisses, and I'm not sure if it's in response to my question or my hand snaking up her leg and hiking up the sexy, silk minidress she's wearing.

Either way, I continue. My nails graze against her inner thigh and she jerks into my chest as short, quick breaths leave her parted lips. She rests her head back on my shoulder and closes her eyes just as I push her panties over and run my fingers through her slit, spreading the slick arousal all around her swollen pussy lips.

"You're so fucking sexy. So responsive to me," I say into her ear, and she responds with a quiet whimper.

Something slams outside of the bathroom and both of our eyes snap over to the door. My fingers pause right at her entrance as we share a look in the mirror.

I flipped the lock so no one could come in here after me, but that doesn't feel like enough protection from being caught anymore. An employee could unlock the door at any moment. I should pull my hand out of this stranger's panties and rejoin my date for dinner.

But I don't, and she makes no move to get away. Instead, she shifts her hips so my two fingers waiting at her entrance are pushed inside the slightest bit, and all my restraint disappears.

In the next breath, I'm ravaging her. My left hand works against her delectable bundle of nerves as my right hand moves upward, pinching and kneading her nipples through the soft fabric of her dress. Her neck cranes backward as I capture her mouth into a sloppy, sensual kiss.

She isn't wearing a bra. I've been staring at the perky little mounds since the moment she walked past me in the dining room with the hostess. Dreaming about how they'd feel between my fingers.

Of course, I know. I know every inch of this body; in the past few weeks, we've managed to find a fold in time where we could hide away and meld together without the external world influencing us in any way. And every moment I was forced to leave that space and re-enter society, I wished I was back there, with her. I feared things would feel different in the daylight. That the darkness was what fed into our desires, not us.

Yet here we are, somehow finding each other on the other side, and I'm just as obsessed with her as I always have been.

I want to pull every moan and sultry sigh out of her body and absorb it into my own. I want to watch her face in pure ecstasy as she shamelessly watches herself ride my hand in the mirror. To witness as she falls over the edge by my hand.

I thrust my fingers inside her and hook them forward, massaging her clit in small circles with my thumb. She begins to writhe against me, and I have to stop playing with her tits to hold her hips against me so I don't lose my grip on her. Within seconds, she's throwing her head back against my shoulder again with a loud moan that I have no doubt the entire restaurant can hear.

"That's it, baby, come for me," I encourage into her ear.

My voice is hoarse and I'm hardly holding on to my own orgasm as she rubs her ass against my erection. I'm so fucking hard, I can barely move.

Once she's through, she turns in my arms and faces me for the first time. Her dress is completely hiked up in the back, fully exposing her round, supple ass to me in the mirror. But I don't have time to enjoy it before she's tugging at my belt. She raises her brows at me as she sucks her bottom lip into her mouth and chews on it seductively.

And I want to. Holy fuck, do I want to watch her sink down on her knees and choke on my impossibly hard cock.

But I push her hands away and shake my head.

The disappointment from my rejection is immediate. Her face falls and she takes a step away, tugging her dress back down her legs. Now that there's some space between us, I can see that her cheeks are tinged pink—either from her orgasm or her embarrassment—and it brings out the yellow shades in her eyes.

"Not here," I manage to say just as a loud knock raps against the door.

"Is someone in there?" a feminine voice calls out from the other side, and Stardust startles against me.

"What the fuck do we do?" she asks in a low, panicked tone, her eyes darting between me and the door. All the anger and embarrassment has temporarily washed away, and I can't help but feel proud that she's looking to *me* for answers.

My little Stardust knows exactly who her protector is.

"Unlock the door and go back to your table. I'll wait for them to be gone before I leave."

The idea of letting her go, and hiding in the women's bathroom of some shitty chop house doesn't sound appealing to me, but the alternative of being caught is much worse. I have to get back to Mallory anyway.

Stardust nods, then adjusts herself in the mirror. The orgasm she just had is still clear across her face. Her lips are swollen from our kiss and her hair is in a disarray, but she looks as perfect as ever. My cock twitches at the idea that I did that to her.

Before she steps away, I grab her jaw and turn her back toward me.

"I'll be there tonight to finish this," I say, both in a promise and a warning.

She stares up at me, her eyes openly roaming my features for a lingering second. I wish we could stay here, alone in this bubble. But the woman outside the door tries knocking again, interrupting our moment. She rips her gaze away and turns toward the door. It's the only confirmation I get before she's twisting the lock and I'm forced to go into a stall.

28

The Lamb

DINNER PASSES IN A BLUR. I'm sitting in my chair, eating my food, and talking to Kennedy and Halen like nothing is wrong. But my eyes keep finding the dark-haired man seated at the table directly across from us and the beautiful woman he's eating with. They don't appear to have any friendly conversation, though that doesn't make me feel any better about hooking up with him in the bathroom while she waited out here for him alone.

I tried to convince myself she was a family member—a sister or cousin, maybe. But that idea doesn't hold up when their food is cleared away and she reaches across the table to caress his forearm. The moment their skin touches, his eyes flick over to mine, and I have to turn away before my emotions play out across my face.

She's the one he takes out in broad daylight. The one he wines and dines as he keeps me tucked away in the darkness. I'm more furious with myself than anything. I don't support cheating of any kind. Men can be pigs. They'll wring women out for all their worth, and then toss them aside whenever something new and shiny comes along. It should come as no surprise that the creepy stalker dude who crossed numerous boundaries would also be cheating on his girlfriend.

"What's up with you?" Halen finally asks in an irritated tone.

Bash and his date have just walked past us to leave and all thoughts cleared from my mind. Unfortunately, I was in the middle of explaining my new role to Halen and Kennedy when it happened, and had clamped my mouth shut mid-sentence.

"I'm just distracted," I admit, finally able to breathe now that he's gone from the vicinity.

"I'll say," Kennedy mutters.

I force a sheepish smile, pushing Bash out of my mind completely to finish my story. I've allowed him to affect me too much already. "It's just so hard to believe it's true. I've been running myself ragged trying to make ends meet, and then this perfect job just fell into my lap. I'm struggling to wrap my mind around it all."

It's the truth, delivered on a platter of lies.

I am tired, and it's truly unbelievable. But I've hardly been able to focus on anything they've said all night because of Bash. They deserve better than that.

Halen tilts her head, her icy stare thawing a bit. "I know, Jov," she soothes, patting my shoulder. "But if anyone deserves a break like this, it's you."

I hate playing on her emotions, tugging at her heart-strings in the exact tune that will get her to melt into my hands. It's almost too easy to do.

"Maybe we'll have to have a do-over dinner once you're able to rest a bit and actually *accept the job*." Kennedy softly offers the not-so-subtle push, and I nod.

They drop it after that, returning to their usual teasing conversation and I do my best to stay in the moment. It's difficult when my mind wants to obsess over what might happen once I get home, but I somehow manage to make it without any more incidents. We finish our meals and leave shortly after, promising to meet up more often. I end the dinner with the hope that I can lay this whole thing with Bash to rest, so I can return to my normal life.

Of course, all of my resolve melts away when I walk through my front door and his dark silhouette is leaning against the kitchen counter, waiting for me.

.

29

The Wolf

Mallory doesn't make our goodbyes awkward or drawn out. In her delusional mind, we aren't over, we're just on a pause while she *"kickstarts her career and gets the most out of her life before she settles down for good."* Those are her words, not mine.

She has no idea that once she steps out of my car, I don't plan on ever being intimate with her again. In fact, I only agreed to this dinner to keep up appearances and possibly use her in an attempt to get Stardust out of my system. I won't wait on the sidelines for her to decide she's ready to be domesticated and breed more spoiled brats for this gluttonous world.

Fuck our families and their disgusting wealth. None of it is worth preserving.

She was only around because she served a purpose in my plan. I'm not interested in any relationship with her outside of a simple wave when we inevitably see each other at a dinner party. I'm happy to be rid of her. With her gone, I can focus more on Stardust and my kills, like I want to.

I'm closing in on the truth, nearing the finish line for Sienna's justice. This era is coming to an end, and I need to be ready to transition into the next one when the time comes.

And for some unknown reason, I want it to include Stardust.

"How long have you been here?" she asks with a quiver in her voice. She's pinned against the front door, her handbag hugged tightly to her chest.

I watch her eyes scan the room for what I assume is a weapon, and I allow myself to chuckle. That's right, I laugh. It's a foreign sound—one I haven't heard since before Sienna died, I think.

Stardust isn't amused. Her dark eyes snap back to me, a scowl deepening between her brows. "You think any of this is *funny*?" she spits, eyes narrowed.

"You're afraid of me," I point out, refusing to answer her obvious question.

Of course, I think it's funny. I had my fingers buried inside of her less than two hours ago, and now she's looking for an item to smash against my head.

"I'm not afraid of you." She stomps her foot, still refusing to move from her spot in the foyer.

"Then come closer," I challenge.

Stabbing a finger toward the ground, she says, "This is *my* house."

"I thought we already cleared up that this was *my* house," I point out uselessly, because it doesn't matter either way. I just want to irritate her as much as she irritates me.

And I do. My words meet their mark, burying themselves underneath her skin enough to force her to rush toward me into the kitchen. Stopping right before me, she grinds out, "*I* pay the bills. It's *my* home."

From this close, I can see the way her anger darkens her eyes into an even deeper brown. They're nearly as black as my soul feels. Her furrowed brows cast a shadow over them that makes her much more menacing than the little innocent lamb I've come to know.

I like this side of her. I want to pull it out and bottle it up to carry around with me. To shrink the image of her right now down into my locket and wear it around my neck.

I'm smirking at that thought as I deliver another blow that will fuel her fury. "Yes, soon you'll be paying those bills with your shiny new job at Lancaster Tech, correct?"

Her furious expression falls. "How did you know about that?"

"How else do you think you got the position?"

Realization dawns on her all at once. From fury to confusion to terror in a matter of minutes. The rapid transitions have me grinning like a cat.

I do love to play with my meal.

"You didn't… But how… *Why?*" she stutters out, taking a big step away from me.

When she does, my arm snakes around her back and pulls her toward me. Her heartbeat flutters against my chest, kick-starting mine for the first time in what feels like years.

"Have I forgotten to tell you my full name, Stardust?"

She stares up into my face, head shaking in disbelief. And because I know she's done her homework on her new company like a good little employee, I lean forward until my lips graze against her ear and whisper, "Sebastian Lancaster."

30

The Lamb

Sebastian. *Fucking.* Lancaster.

As in, the CEO of Lancaster Tech.

As in *my new boss.*

If he wasn't holding me against his chest, I would have fallen to the ground in pure shock. None of this makes any sense. It's like, while I've been denying his entire existence, he's been burrowing his way into my life until he consumes it completely.

My home. My job. My *privacy.*

He owns it all, and I've given it away willingly.

"Why?" I repeat the same stupid question.

Does it matter why? This guy is obviously out of his goddamn mind and fixated on me for some ungodly reason.

"I like you," he says simply, as if that's enough of an explanation.

"You *like* me?" I repeat incredulously.

This is not the conversation I planned on having with

him tonight. I wanted to ask about the woman he was eating dinner with right in front of me. The one he ditched to follow me into the bathroom. I wanted to know how he came about buying my house after that first night. I was going to demand that he explain how he got into my home and knew my schedule so intimately.

I never expected that his obsession would go so deep.

"Yes, and don't say it like you can't believe anyone could ever like you, Stardust–"

"Stop calling me that," I insist, cutting him off.

Sighing, he looks over my head as if he has no idea what to do with me, and then relents with a stiff, "Fine."

"I need space," I demand, pushing against him in a panic.

He's smothering me. This is all too much to take in. He's bled into my life like a cancer, aggressive and impossible to cure. I'm suffocating on the man I had myself convinced was just a dark part of my imagination mere hours ago.

Bash backs away, albeit hesitantly.

"Don't run. I'll catch you," he warns in a deep, menacing voice.

What the hell does that mean? I don't even have the mental capacity to dissect those words right now. Or the thrill that spikes in the back of my mind and the urge to try it and see for myself.

"Ask me what you want to know," he says more softly.

"I've already asked, and you refuse to answer."

"Ask again."

"No more games?"

He raises his brows as if to say yes, not bothering to actually say it.

I can't help but feel like it's a methodical move. Like he knows what I'll try to use against him later. Everything he does is so calculated, and he's gotten so good at anticipating my moves.

I'm way in over my head.

Still, I have to try. I take a second to think about what to say. At this point, there's so many questions, I can't narrow it down to just one. But I figure a good starting point is, "What the hell do you want from me?"

Shaking his head, he leans against the wall. "It's not that simple."

"You told me to ask, and now you're refusing to answer again."

"That's a complicated question. I don't fucking know what I want from you—that's your appeal. The answer changes constantly."

"Why me?" I try again.

"Because you happened to be here."

"I responded to an ad about this house. Are you telling me that was all coincidental?"

He crosses his arms. "On my end, yes."

"What does that mean? Who else's end is there?"

"My father's."

He's got to be kidding me. "What does your father want from me?"

Bash shrugs, as if this is such a casual conversation to have. Not one where I'm trying to find answers as to why a billionaire even has me on his radar at all, let alone stalking me.

"I don't know," he admits.

I swallow down my emotion, temporarily allowing myself to take a break from that topic to ask the question I really want the answer to, despite how stupid it may be.

"Who was the woman you were with?"

"Were you jealous?"

There's no teasing in his tone, which throws me off a bit, because the question seems like one he would use to humiliate me. Instead, he seems genuinely concerned.

"No," I lie, but he sees right through it.

"She's no one now. A casual hookup. A means to an end. She broke it off at dinner tonight."

"And before? Were you cheating on her when you…?" I let the question trail off, too embarrassed to admit what happened between us on those nights I had no idea who or what he was.

"No. It was never cheating."

Relief washes through me and my traitorous heart leaps in my chest. Such a ridiculous thought. This man has all but admitted to obsessively stalking me, and I'm relieved that he's at least single while he does it.

"Are you done asking questions?" he asks, amusement dancing in his light eyes.

My head tilts to the side as I allow myself to take in all his features without the mask again. I was too afraid at the restaurant, and too angry when I first arrived home. Now, it's like I'm seeing him for the first time.

I was right before. His full lips and dark stubble match the symmetry of his eyes better than I expected. Just standing there, he exudes power. It's impossible not to get swept away in his appearance or masculine energy.

But I have to stop myself from thinking that way. This man is a predator. Just as a wolf or a lion can be beautiful to look at, they'll still rip you to shreds the second they get the chance. The moment you get too close. And I can tell that's exactly what he wants to do when my gaze lifts back to his eyes and sees how much they've darkened as he watches me take him in.

Pulling my lip from between my teeth, I finally answer.

"No." I'm not done asking questions, but his expression tells me he doesn't give a damn.

31

The Wolf

I THOUGHT I could handle taking the time to ease her in. I'm a patient man, and I've already come this far. I don't have many answers for her because I've never done this before, but I was willing to try if it meant wiping that horrified look off her face.

However, when she sucks her lips between her teeth and eyes me like I'm about to be her last meal, I cave.

How is it that she can look so innocent and sinful at the same time? The epitome of forbidden fruit.

My beautiful fig.

Wrapping my hand around the back of her neck, I tug her face right against mine, until our noses are brushing and our teeth clatter against each other. Tilting my head for better access, I clamp down on the lip she was just assaulting and pull on it, earning a surprised whimper.

"Too bad," I mumble in response to her rejection as her blood floods my mouth. "They'll have to wait."

I don't give her a chance to protest before leaning forward to grab behind her knees and hoist her over my shoulder so I can carry her to her room. She lets out a loud squeal, fists pounding ruthlessly against my back as we make our way through the family room I've watched her in countless times now.

She's screaming obscenities and empty threats, but I don't give a flying fuck what she says she's going to do to me. The second I get my mouth on her, she'll settle down. Or she'll begin screaming for a whole new reason.

I slam her back onto the bed and she scurries up toward the pillows, out of my reach.

"You want to play, my pretty little lamb?"

"I'm not *yours*. And I told you not to call me those stupid nicknames," she reminds me in a shaky voice, wrapping her arms around her knees.

When I lean forward with a wolfish grin, she flinches, and the reaction sends shock waves straight to my groin. I had no idea her fear would fuel me this much. I should have been scaring her all along.

"Isn't that what you are? The innocent lamb who happened to cross my path at the perfect time?" I goad, because I can't resist. It's too fucking fun to razzle her.

"No. I didn't cross your path. *You* found *me*, remember?" Her panicked tone is rushed, insistent as her shoulders rattle in a shiver.

"You're so fucking wrong."

I may have been the first to actively seek her out, but she was the one who interrupted me in my kill room. She was the one who placed my hand against her as she pleasured herself. I was ready to kill her, when she enraptured me instead. When she gave me a whole new purpose: to consume her.

"Stay away from me," she says weakly, but I can already

see the fight leaving her eyes as I begin to strip off my clothes.

She tracks my every movement, anxiously waiting for me to grab her up and force myself on her. I won't, though. I'll never take from her without her permission. But I *will* have her crawling to me by the end of this. I'll take everything she has to offer me, and then some, because she fuels a side of me that I never knew existed.

My fingers slowly unbuckle my belt and slip my pants down my legs as she watches with rapt attention, the grip on her knees loosening a small fraction. My erection is fighting against my briefs, stretching the fabric in a perfect outline that leaves nothing to her imagination.

I stroke myself three times before her pupils dilate and her lips part. She wants this—whatever *this* is. It's fucked up and backwards and unprecedented, but that only makes it that much more alluring for her.

"Come to me," I command in an authoritative tone.

She shakes her head once.

"You can deny this all you want, but it will only delay the inevitable and further piss me off."

A daring, bratty scowl twists across her features. "Maybe I want to piss you off."

"Are you sure about that?"

I can see the stubborn indecision in her eyes. Sure, she wants this just as bad as I do, but she's also afraid of it. Afraid of the mysterious man who seems to have taken an unhealthy interest in her. She has no idea how deep my obsession goes, or even that she's the one who sparked it. I would have been fine with killing her. Maybe I'd have taken mercy on her and simply kicked her out of the house. But instead, she revealed a side of myself that I had no idea existed that night she fingered herself in front of me. I won't stop until the need is fully satiated.

All she knows is that she shouldn't want the man who watches her when she sleeps and roams her house without her permission. She *shouldn't,* but she does.

"I'm going to give you one more chance to come to me before I drag you over here myself," I grind out through my teeth in a dark, raspy tone. To prove my point, I dig my finger into the mattress, right where I want her to be. The equivalent of commanding a dog to *come.*

Emotions are warring behind her eyes until fear and desire finally win out. She uncurls her arms from around her knees and starts scooting toward me.

"Crawl," I demand at the last second.

She scowls again, biting back her smart retort when I raise my brow at her in a silent challenge. Then, like the obedient little lamb that she is, she climbs onto her knees.

I smirk at the small victory, staring down at her when she stops right against the edge of the mattress, her face lined up perfectly with my erection.

Jovie doesn't see my triumphant expression, though. Instead, she's gazing at my cock with a hungry look in her eyes. I resist moving, soaking in the erotic scene before me when she sucks that damn lip back into her mouth.

Fuuuck.

My resolve dissipates into a million tiny pieces and falls to the floor around me like black confetti. Primal instincts kick in, impatient and cruel. As if she's floating on the same wavelength as me, Jovie's hands shoot out to grab my erection at the exact moment I shove my hips forward, right into her grasp. A moan rumbles deep in my chest as her fingers wrap around my length, slowly stroking the sensitive skin, enveloping it in her warmth.

"That's right, baby," I find myself praising, thrusting into her grasp over and over again.

She doesn't bother with a response. Instead, she opens

her mouth and takes as much of me as she can, until I can feel my tip hitting the back of her throat as she fights against the urge to gag. I run my fingers through her hair appreciatively when she pulls back, releasing my cock with a loud *pop*.

"Tell me you don't want this," I challenge mockingly as I fuck her mouth, and she eagerly takes every stroke like it's her last meal. "Try to lie to me again, Stardust. I dare you."

Pausing, she fights against my fist holding her head in place to look up at me, lips wrapped fully around my shaft. When I pull out again, she releases my erection and backs away.

"It's not a lie. You're a sick, toxic son of a bitch with an ego the size of this planet. Just another bored little rich boy slumming it with us lower class peasants. Wanting you is the equivalent of handing my soul over to the devil. Dangerous and fruitless."

I'll admit, that surprises me. I stare down at her, stunned silent as her words soak in. She doesn't move, either. Just looks up at me with those round eyes, a mix of hate and longing circling around in them. My hands grab her upper arms to throw her back onto the bed, and follow right behind before she can move away, hiking her dress up her hips in one swoop.

"I'm slumming it with you?" I ask, grinding my cock against her slick center. She's so fucking wet for me, I can't even stand it. "You think that's why I keep coming back here?"

Nodding, she fists the sheets on either side of her body, shaking from the pure ecstasy of our bodies moving together. I haven't even been inside of her yet, and I'm addicted to this feeling. To having her beneath me. If only she'd allow herself to enjoy it with me.

"No, baby. I keep coming back here because you're *mine*, and I'm determined to claim you in every way possible."

With that, I run my tip down her center, taking great care in pressing it against her clit, before I thrust inside, completely filling her in one swift movement.

Our moans meld together in the air, canceling each other out over and over until we're nothing but gasps and breaths and sweat. I lift her leg and rest it on my shoulder, allowing myself to hit her at a completely different angle while opening her up so I can caress her clit and send her nose diving right over the cliff with me.

But my sweet Stardust is closer to finishing than I thought, and the instant my fingers meet her wet slit, she's writhing beneath me as her orgasm takes hold. I've got a front-row seat to watch her fall apart at the seams. She pulsates around my cock, nearly taking me with her, but I draw it out, determined to have her so satisfied when I'm finished with her, she practically falls into a coma.

Brown eyes roll to the back of her head as garbled noises fall from her plump lips, still swollen from being wrapped around my cock.

"I love to watch you come undone," I whisper darkly from above her. If she wants to call me the devil, I'll gladly act the part.

I can tell she's coming down from her high and decide that this is the perfect moment. Thrusting into her as deep as her body will allow, her gasp transforms into a moan as I pull her forward to sit her on my lap, then take her breast into my mouth, swirling my tongue around her nipple as my finger snakes back between our bodies and massages her clit again. I want her to be overwhelmed with sensation—unable to escape it.

It only takes a few moments to send her spiraling back into euphoria, and this time I allow myself to join her. My cock twitches, and then fills her with cum as she cries out, arching her back so her tits are shoved into my face as I bite and lick her nipples.

When we finally come back down, she wraps her arms around my neck and gazes at me, eyes half-mast. I'm still inside of her, my cum oozing out slowly onto the bed beneath me. Without thinking too hard about it—about any of this—I capture her mouth into a sensual kiss, thanking her for offering such an otherworldly experience.

"Rest, Stardust," I tell her as I lie her down onto her pillow, then take the spot beside her, tugging her close to my chest. "We've got all night together."

32

The Lamb

A HEAD OF LONG, auburn hair walks through the doors of Old Soul Cafe, and a heavy feeling settles through my body like someone just dumped a pack of lead weights down my throat. I know it's her before she lifts her face to scan the counter, searching for me.

My mother.

The same dreadful feeling that always follows seeing her snakes down to my back, skittering across my legs like a million tiny spiders. Her dark eyes lock on mine, and I'm frozen to my spot. I should have run the moment I realized it was her. But there's no use. She'll always find me because there's too many people she's collected pity from over how I've treated her in the past year to keep my life a secret from her.

Too many people who don't know the truth about what she did that night.

Keeping me locked in her predatory gaze, she walks

toward the counter with slow, careful steps. As always, she's playing the part of the wounded mother to a T. Pretending to be cautious about approaching me like I'm some sort of rabid animal, though the hardness in her stare paints a different story.

"Jovie," she greets, stopping a few feet in front of the counter.

It's a slow Monday morning at the cafe. Not many people have filtered in for their morning brew, and only one person is working away on their laptop at a faraway table. Unlike with Gabe, I can't shrug her off with the excuse of being too busy.

"How can I help you?" I refuse to greet her in a casual way. To call her Mom or pretend she holds any value in my life.

It's the kindest way I can force her to get to the point, and then get her out of here.

"I tried calling," she begins softly.

I can tell by the fullness in her cheeks and the color all over her body that she's in a sober stint. Probably going through rehab for the umpteenth time and is looking to complete one of her steps.

I've been burned enough times in the past with false hope to believe this time will be any different than the last. That this one will stick.

Still, the little girl inside of me wants to believe there's a chance. But I shove her down and force myself to remember what the woman standing before me did for a handful of drugs. The way she betrayed me—almost killed me. And ruined my life.

"Halen gave me your number. I had to beg her for it," she goes on, cracking a small smile the way she always does when Halen comes up—her golden child who can do no wrong.

I know she's been calling. I've been ignoring every single one, deleting the messages before even listening to them. There's nothing she can say that will justify what she's done to me. The biggest favor I can offer her is to stay silent about it, and even that is killing me. Especially when people like Halen and Kennedy try to pressure me into forgiving her.

"There's nothing for us to speak about." I tell her, my voice cold.

With another tentative step forward, she places her hand across her chest. "That's not true. I have a lot to explain, and so much to apologize for."

"I'm not interested in any of it."

Tilting her head, she closes the distance between herself and the counter, resting her palms on the weathered wood between us. "Come on, Jovie. I'm your mother and–"

"Exactly," I hiss, cutting off whatever guilt trip she was about to send me on. "You're my mother, and you did the unspeakable. There's no turning back from that."

Crossing my arms over my chest, I raise my brows at her, waiting for whatever rebuttal she can draw up.

"Then, I guess I just have to come right out and ask…"

There it is. She didn't come to make amends or apologize. She never does. The only reason she's standing before me is because she wants something.

My inner child shrinks away, disappointed by her yet again.

When I don't respond, she shifts her weight uncomfortably, pretending this is difficult to do. It's not difficult. She has no problem taking from me, she just knows that she's supposed to act a certain way to get what she wants. To feign humility.

"I've run into a little road block and I could use some help…" she begins, and I don't even have to listen any more to know she wants money from me.

"How much do you need?" I cut in, straight to the point.

Glancing down at her hands, she mumbles into her chest, "Two grand."

My eyes widen.

Two grand? That's my entire savings account. Every single dime I've scraped together in the past few months and managed to set aside to get myself out of the pits of poverty.

And she has the fucking nerve to ask me to hand it all over.

"That's a crazy amount," I admonish.

"Well, I really need five, but Halen is helping me with some, and I've managed to save some money from working at The Shamrock. I can't work anymore, though. With my condition, it's just not feasible."

The Shamrock is the same gentleman's club I bartended at when we lived with Gabe. I was always adamantly against getting on the stage and dancing, opting instead to swallow my pride enough to wear the skimpy outfits and stay behind the bar, where no one could touch me—though they always did. My mother never had any issues with using her looks to rake in tips—among other things. Her job as a dancer is what kept her locked into her addictions for so long. Gabe never understood why I wouldn't just join her to make ends meet. It was a toxic environment filled with broken souls and shattered dreams.

If she was working there, it's only a matter of time before her vices suck her back in. Not to mention, she was probably making double what I make in one day. Where is that money going? And what condition could force her to stop?

I don't voice my doubts to her, though. She doesn't owe me any explanation for how she lives her life, and I don't really give a shit either way. I just want her gone, and if draining my savings account is how I get rid of her, then maybe I'll have to do it.

I've been dragging my feet about putting in my two-week notice at any of my jobs. When I first received my offer at Lancaster Tech, I wanted to call each and every one of my bosses right then and there to quit. Thankfully, I waited, because the realization that I only received the offer because of my mystery man's obsession with me has cast my good news into a much darker light. Although, taking the job at Lancaster Tech is feeling more necessary than ever. It seems like I'm going to be forced to work for my stalker, whether I like it or not.

"Five grand? What the hell did you do?" I breathe out, exasperated. My entire future is slipping through my fingers again, all because of my mother's mistakes.

"I know it's a lot to ask, especially after everything that's happened between us. But I've exhausted all my other options. I wouldn't bother you if it wasn't life and death."

Life and death. For God's sake, who the hell is she mixed up with?

We stare at one another in a stony, tense silence where she allows her mask to slip the slightest amount, and accidentally reveals the greedy monster she really is. The way she speaks, it's like she had no control over the situation. It's easier for her to act as if this all just happens *to* her instead of taking ownership of her shitty life decisions. Decisions she'll continue to make so long as she knows we'll be here to bail her out every time.

I don't *want* to help her, but she always manages to say the perfect things to manipulate me into doing what she wants. I may not want anything to do with my mother, but that doesn't mean I'll leave her for dead, especially if I can help it.

It's only two grand. I've managed to save it up once; I'm sure I can do it again.

In half the time, if I accept the position that Bash is offering.

"I'll need a couple days to get things together," I relent, breaking our stare-off when the door opens and a customer walks through.

My mother's face breaks into a wide, triumphant smile. She won. Again. And I can't help but feel like I've just been scammed in some way. Maybe next time, I'll be more successful in shutting her out.

"Thank you so much, Jo Jo. I truly don't deserve you," she gushes, locking her fingers together beneath her chin.

For once, I agree. Her eyes begin to water in a dramatic show of gratitude, and I look away before she gets the satisfaction of having me as an audience to her performance. When the man stops at the opposite end of the counter busies himself with one of our menus, I lean in closer to my mom so I won't be overheard.

"I'll help you this time, but only under one condition: You have to stay away from me after this. No phone calls, no random pop-ins, nothing."

Her shoulders fall forward, brows immediately tugging together in a frown. "Come on, Jo. We can get past this," she tries to say, but I'm immediately shaking my head and holding my hand up to stop her.

"No, we can't. After I get this money to you, you have to leave me alone."

Jutting her lip out, she slowly nods, accepting my terms without a fight. She should be in jail for what she's done. Peace and privacy are the bare minimum she could offer me, regardless of how sad it might make her right now. I shouldn't be guilted for trying to move on from what she did to me in the healthiest way possible.

Without asking if she wants to order a drink, I turn away and walk to the other side of the counter to help my customer, watching as my mother drags her feet across the cafe and out the door.

It may not feel like it right now, but I'm doing the right thing. Even if it goes against everything I've been conditioned to do for her. All the training I've had to protect and serve her.

One day, I'll be grateful for cutting her off.

I hope.

33

The Wolf

THE ORDER IS HOSTING a charity gala. Like all their public events, families are expected to attend. It's the last place I want to be, surrounded by a crowd of narcissistic rapists, murderers, and criminals. If I have to endure one more conversation with a crusty old man flaunting his wealth to me, I'll throw myself off the thirtieth story balcony.

This world is so incestuous and brutal. How is it that we've allowed a small group of people to hold the most amount of wealth, only to hoard it and watch as the rest of the world burns to the ground? How is it that I'm sitting at a table completely covered with rare foods that everyone here is too image-obsessed to eat, while the Star-dusts of the world struggle to make it to their next meal? Mallory and her mother are prattling on about their next European vacation while her father tries to talk my ear off about the failing investments my father roped him into, as if I give a fuck. Sienna has been flitting in and out of the room, inserting her own comments and snide remarks about the people who aided in her murder that only fuel my anger.

I'm not a good man. But I knew that making people like this even *richer* by trampling on those who work hard to earn every dime was going to slowly kill me. It's why I refused to ship off to some expensive Ivy League college and join the family business the second I graduated. Instead, I took what knowledge I already had, and I created something that actually added value to the world. The *whole* world, not just the top three percent.

But I have to show my face at these things if I want to keep them off my scent. I've got a plan for how I'll reveal myself as the one who's been plucking them off. Missing one of their many opportunities to throw money around like it's confetti and giving their pea-sized brains a chance to connect the dots feels too anticlimactic.

For now, I like to be here to hear them speculate. To listen from the outskirts of the room as they quietly take their guesses on who could be hunting them down, then obsess over who might be next. The fact that they haven't already narrowed it down to someone connected to Sienna only further proves what sick sons of bitches they truly are. Every single one of them is guilty of the same crimes committed against my sister, some even worse. They know if their killer is out for retaliation, it'll take a lot more kills to truly pin it on one incident.

"I heard he doesn't take any souvenirs from his victims."

"My friend on the force claims there might be multiple killers, since there's so much variation with how the bodies are left."

"He doesn't even wait between victims like most serial killers. Just dumps the body and moves onto the next."

Their whispered conversations fill my ears as I move through the room. They don't know what to do with the information they have about their killer, and that's what terrifies them the most.

I haven't been sworn in as a member and gone through the insidious hoops to be initiated yet. My father and all my uncles are on the board, so it's fully expected I'll follow behind. They would prefer that time to come sooner rather than later. The *incident* with Sienna, as they so delicately put it, bought me some time to recover before accepting those men as my "brothers." The group of snakes who committed the crimes were given a slap on the wrist, and then initiated within the following week.

They should have known from the start that I would never rest until each and every one of them was no longer breathing.

My mother tried to raise hell, but no one listened to her. How my father can still sit beside those men and protect them from paying for their crimes is beyond me, though I'm not entirely convinced he was as innocent as he tries to claim. I think there was an expected role for him to play as the wounded parent, and he performed it out of necessity. But something about it lacked the heart and contempt that should have been there against the men who butchered and raped his own daughter.

His death will certainly be the most painful.

I'm doing my rounds, slowly walking the perimeter of the room to avoid being pulled into any real conversation, when someone taps me on the shoulder from behind. When I turn, I'm not surprised to find Logan's father, Charles, standing before me with a grim expression. He's been tailing me all night.

"Sebastian," he greets in an unusually melancholy tone.

I still remember the smug smiles that Charles and Logan wore in the courtroom when it was announced that the charges for Sienna's murder were dropped. There was a moment when I seriously considered killing the man standing before me right alongside his son. But in the end, taking Logan from him and forcing him to live the rest of his life without his precious heir to inherit *anything* he worked his long, useless life for is far worse than any torture I could dish out in the workshop.

Charles was always the most boisterous, obnoxious person in the room—especially with his little mini-me by his side. When Logan was initiated, they threw a bash at their vacation home in Cabo, completely ignorant to the fact that multiple families were mourning their losses as a result of his sick ceremony. The shell of a human standing before me is as broken inside as every shattered bone was in my sister's dead body.

It's a rewarding sight, to say the least.

"Charles," I accost with a wide smile, a little too loudly. "How have you been?"

He scowls the slightest bit, taken back by the fact that I haven't fallen all over myself to offer any condolences for losing his son the way everyone else here has done the instant they see him.

I killed Logan weeks ago. There's no reason for him to still be milking his death now. They sure as hell didn't offer us that privilege when we were in the same position. And besides, there're five other families here who have lost their sons in the same manner who are getting by just fine.

They just have no idea the killer is standing among them. Although, Charles looks oddly suspicious.

"I'm sure you've heard about Logan," he says bitterly, wincing at the mention of his late son's name.

Nodding once, I tip my drink toward him. "I did. Sorry to hear that yet another bright future has been stolen away."

The apology comes out as insincere as it feels, but I've gotten my point across. I don't give a fuck about Logan. He's just another name on a long list of people who have been forced to give their lives to this incestuous, ego-driven secret society.

"You two were always close," he pushes, before narrowing his eyes.

I only shrug, tightening my lips into a thin line. "We lost touch when he went away to college, but Logan always made sure everyone was having a good time."

Everyone but the unfortunate soul he deemed his victim that night.

Logan was an asshole well before he graduated college and initiated into The Order. We all knew it, and I'm sure there are far more people relieved to hear he's gone than there are mourning his loss.

Charles leans in, positioning himself so we're standing shoulder-to-shoulder, and it looks like we're assessing the room together.

"They're saying the killer is targeting The Order specifically," he mutters in a low enough tone to avoid anyone overhearing. "The Serpent Slayer is what he calls himself."

No, that's what the media is calling me.

It's got a nice ring to it, though I would have chosen something more original. Maybe less conspicuous. I'm sure one of the board members coined the name themselves. They love to flaunt the secrecy of their society in everyone's faces just to seem interesting.

There's nothing interesting about a group of men who abuse power and destroy lives for the hell of it.

I raise my brows at Charles, playing the part he expects me to play—a shocked, concerned member with no clue if I'll be next.

He knows something. I'm sure of it now. I just need to figure out *how much*.

"Why would they be doing that?" I wonder aloud, my tone satirical.

I'm walking a dangerously thin line, mocking him like this. But I'm hoping that I'll get some sort of accusation out of him, so I can assess what kind of threat he is to my process.

"You and I both know that initiation into our order is quite unique. Seems to me that someone is targeting our younger recruits." He finally turns back to me, scanning his eyes over my body in an open show of sizing me up.

I scoff at the mere thought that he could have a chance against me. Charles just raises his brow and goes on with his rant, playing directly into my hand.

"Perhaps the killer is tied to one of The Order's victims."

Ah, yes. There it is: the nail in his coffin.

He's just guaranteed his own death with one long, sideways glance.

"I wouldn't be surprised to find that's true," I reply coolly, already envisioning all the ways he'll scream as I tear his flesh from his body.

It's not like he's an innocent man. Bring his name up with any of the wives and daughters of The Order after they've had a few drinks, and they'll sing like canaries about how he's raped and molested them or someone they knew.

"When is your initiation planned, Sebastian?" he asks, throwing me out of my thoughts.

"It's not. I'm not prepared to join yet after what happened to Sienna." I'm not going to lie to him. Not when I've already decided he's dead. But I do need to be more careful in case he tries to bring his suspicions to anyone else.

"You know, the punishment for harming another brother is quite harsh. Most don't survive it…"

I watch closely as he brings the whiskey glass to his thin lips and downs the rest of it. Sweat has gathered along the edge of his graying mustache, and his hand shakes when he lowers it back down to slam the glass onto a nearby table.

"I'm aware."

I'm not sure what he's getting at with that comment. Is he threatening me with the punishment, or reminding me that, while I'm not technically a member, I could be harmed without repercussions?

He's indirectly threatened me twice now in the span of five minutes. That has earned him a couple of fingers being cut off, at the very least.

Maybe I'll slice those disgusting, wrinkled lips right off his face too.

"Just keep that in mind." With that, he walks away as if he's just won this weird standoff he instigated.

But his steps are hurried, his body tense.

He's nervous. As he should be.

I'll be the boogeyman stealing him away in the dead of night. But for now, I direct my full attention to following him to ensure he doesn't have anyone else on my trail.

34

The Wolf

STARDUST GREETS me on the front porch as soon as I pull up to the cottage early Friday evening, and my chest tightens in disappointment while my heart kicks up in excitement, twisting me into a mess of emotions I really don't have the time to deal with right now.

My plan was to prepare the workshop for my next kill before walking into the house, but she surprised me by being home earlier than I expected. Usually, she's working at that grungy sports bar on Friday nights.

"Looks like your girlfriend is going to be a problem. Hmm, I wonder who predicted that?" Sienna instigates from beside me.

She knows I can't say anything back to her with Stardust's eyes on me, though it might be worth the risk just to tell her to fuck off. But her disinterest in my little Stardust is stronger than her desire to bother me, and as I stride closer to the cottage, I feel her presence disappear from beside me with a distant, taunting chuckle.

I've been on the fence about bringing Charles to the workshop to kill him. If I'm careful enough, I could time it perfectly to where Stardust would never hear a thing and I'd have full access to my usual tools. It would be so poetic for me to kill the bastard in the same spot I bled his son dry.

But just as she's proven today, she's too unpredictable. A variant I can't control, no matter how hard I try. Surely, there're ways for me to get her away for a day or two. Convincing her to leave would be the hardest part.

"I'm going to follow through with the job," she admits in a soft voice as I walk up to the porch steps.

I can't help the smile that dances across my lips at that news. The job was never meant to be the malicious thing she made it out to be, although her reservations were valid. It *will* grant me easier access to her. And it *will* make her more reliant on me than she already is. But I never planned to abuse that power. Not at first.

She deserves a break. It's clear to me that no one has ever done something for her just to do it. Just because they realized she was suffering and needed the extra hand.

"Get that smug smile off your face," she admonishes, and that cute line between her brows deepens with the scowl she's throwing my way.

I won't apologize for being right, though it would be entertaining to watch her try to argue with me. To see the color drain from her face as I reveal just how much I know about her.

Instead of terrorizing her with the truth, I settle on saying, "Turning it down would have been a mistake."

"That remains to be seen. I just don't have any other options at this point." As if I need any more explanation.

I'm well aware of how dire her financial situation is. I've

checked all her accounts and fought myself on filling them anonymously. In the end, I know she'd rather earn the money herself.

"You aren't wearing a mask," she points out, allowing her eyes to roam across my entire body to take in my full work attire—a stark contrast to my usual black jeans and hoodie I wear around her. I didn't bother changing before I left my office to drive here. My cock immediately hardens at her undivided attention, chasing away any rational thought I had. I don't hide it from her, either.

"I can trust you," I explain quietly. Hopefully.

I fucked up with her in that restaurant last week. Then, I fucked up even worse when I met her here. The loss of control I feel around this woman has my head spinning. I can't seem to find my footing on this rocky, uneven ground we're standing on together. Letting her see my face again in the daylight is a huge risk. But so was buying the cottage. So was offering her a job at my company.

This whole situation is a huge mess of risks wrapped up in a tangle of unfamiliar feelings and a shit-ton of broken laws. I have no idea how to claw my way out.

Stardust seems to be satisfied with my answer, completely ignorant to how uneasy it's made me. Her eyes soften as her mouth relaxes from the usual stubborn pucker it always seems to be stuck in whenever she knows I'm near.

"I guess we're both taking a leap of faith."

If only she knew what a huge leap she was taking with me. She would never go for it.

"Something like that," I agree.

There's a pregnant pause when she openly gazes up at me from the porch step, and I know without asking that she's memorizing every detail of my face to remember later, the same way I've done with her countless of times before. She still doesn't entirely believe that this is real. Or perhaps she just wishes that it wasn't. I do my damndest to show her exactly how *real* it is. How tangible this whole fucking mess is.

But regardless of the dreadful feeling deep in my gut each time I leave, I keep coming back, and she keeps letting me in. It's like each of us is daring the other to put an end to this. *Begging* for mercy from the chokehold this connection has on us, but it never comes. Every time I see her, I fall deeper into her clutches.

"Are you going to come inside?" she asks, breaking me from the spell I was under.

It's the simplest question. An invitation inside her home —the house I own. But it's like she's reached into my brain and turned everything upside down.

Since when do I walk in here with an invitation? Since when does the woman I've stalked greet me with good news and a lustful stare?

None of this makes sense. I don't deserve any of it.

"Is that a no?" Stardust pushes, self-consciously wrapping her arms around her middle at the thought of my rejection.

"No. Let's go inside."

My plan to prepare the workshop is tossed to the wayside as she leads me into the house, her ass bouncing with every step, and I decide I won't be bringing any of those Order assholes around her ever again, shrouding her home in darkness and despair. So long as I can preserve her misplaced, innocent convictions about me, I'll keep her out of this.

35

The Lamb

It's been a week since I've accepted my formal offer from Lancaster Tech. I've finished my last scheduled shifts at the bar, resigned with Mrs. Botless, and have only three more shifts with Rosie at Old Soul.

Everyone has been supportive of my new endeavor, even when they found out I'd have a stint alone in New York to go through training at the corporate office before they let me work on my own. If I'm being honest, I was hoping for more resistance. More people to tell me that this is a mistake, and working for the man who actively stalks me is a bad idea.

I suppose they'd have to be made aware about that part, though. I know that Halen would chain me up in her basement if she found out about Bash and all the things he's done since I've moved in. But I'm not quite ready to sully my one shot at a normal life.

Thus begins the vicious cycle I've been stuck in since accepting the job.

Bash has made no attempt at hiding his smugness on the matter. He pities me on a level that borders on pure shame. In the late nights I've found myself wide awake and thinking about it, I can't help but wonder if he's doing all of this because he genuinely cares, or if he's taken me on as some kind of charity case he refuses to bring around his social circle until I make myself more respectable.

Although, there's nothing *less* acceptable than hunting and stalking the woman you want to date.

And if his friends are so judgmental of those who live *below* them, do I really want to be around them in the first place?

Who said we're dating, anyway?

Calm your tits, Jovie. It's all hypothetical.

Unfortunately, Bash is here to witness my downward spiral this time around. He's staring at me in the same way Halen used to do when I first got out of Sunnybrook—like he's debating if he needs to hide all the sharp objects.

He's come back to Styx for the weekend, even using the front door to enter the cottage when he got here. It's a strange change of pace, and one I'm not quite sure how I feel about just yet. There's something significant about the way we got here. I'm struggling to adjust to losing it, no matter how deranged and unconventional it was.

He turns to face me in my bed, careful not to allow any part of our bodies to intersect. His hands rest beneath his cheek, against the pillow, while those odd green eyes gaze at me. *Into* me.

"Tell me to leave," he urges in a calm, desperate whisper, taking me completely off guard.

"Why?" I whisper back voicelessly.

There're a million reasons why he should walk out that door. Every societal rule goes against what's happening between us right now. Every survival instinct screams within me to run.

To call the police. To get away from this man who has clearly formed an unhealthy obsession with me.

I know all my own reasons for telling him to leave. But I want to hear his.

He doesn't give them to me, though. Nothing with him is ever as straightforward as I hope for it to be.

"Your eyes change colors in the daylight," he begins instead. "Right now, they're the sweetest honey brown. But at night, they turn dark and decadent, like the richest chocolate I've ever tasted."

A small smile pulls at my lips, and despite my attempt to hide the shyness I'm feeling at him noticing such a small detail about me, I know my blushing cheeks are giving me away. No one bothers to take in the little things anymore, always in too much of a rush to get to the next best part to enjoy exactly where they are. I doubt Gabe could even guess my eye color, and we dated for years.

"When it comes to you, I can't resist. I want to know everything." He snakes his arm across the sheet, invading the space between us before his long fingers intersect with mine, turning my hand this way and that in the light.

"I'm hungry for the most menial details, and I'm willing to get them no matter the cost."

I'm realizing this is a new side to him that he's sharing. Another one to add to the growing catalog I'm trying to keep track of in my head. None of them seem to connect—each one is more vastly different than the rest.

Who is this man—truly and wholly—at his core? I don't think any version I've seen fully answers that burning question. The one that keeps insisting I allow him to come back. There's so much more to him than what he projects to the outside world.

Maybe I'm guilty of the same crimes he's admitting to.

"There's nothing wrong with wanting to get to know someone," I rationalize, ignoring the small part where he's stalked and hunted me to do so.

There's definitely room for improvement in his methods.

"That's the problem. For you, I'll never tire. I'll never stop feeding on each and every scrap you give me. I want to devour you. *Own* you. And I'm afraid that by the time I've had my fill, there won't be anything left of you."

Own you.

Those two words dance around my head, sending my heart into a fluttering mess of butterfly wings. They should be repulsing me, but instead I melt into a puddle at his feet.

"I'm stronger than you think," I assure him.

"I know. I'm addicted to your strength. But everyone has a breaking point, and finding yours has become a game to me."

He releases my hand and moves to cup my jaw, his thumb lightly grazing against my bottom lip in lazy circles.

"So tell me to leave. Tell me to stop. Chase me away. I swear to fucking God, Stardust, do *something* other than stare at me with that look in your eyes like you aren't even afraid. You have no idea what I'm capable of—what I've already done."

Shaking my head, I tug my lip between my teeth, away from his touch. And I hate myself, because I can't do it. I can't tell my stalker to go away, no matter how much he begs me.

No matter how much every fiber of my being screams against it.

No matter how many times my mind slams its fists against the walls my heart has built around it, silencing it.

I want this man in ways I know aren't any good for me. But where has doing what's *good* gotten me?

"I can handle it," I insist again stubbornly.

Whoever he is, whatever he's done, I don't care. It doesn't change how I feel.

"You have no idea what you're doing," he warns, though his voice sounds more depraved than angry.

"Maybe I'm not as good of a person as you think. Maybe we're two people cut from the same cloth."

Scoffing, he rolls his eyes away from me. "I doubt that."

"I don't."

He falls silent for a beat—long enough for me to think that maybe I've won this argument. Although, I'm not sure that's a worthy brag. It may have been smarter to listen to his pleas and heed his warnings. To accept his vague admissions as enough of a sign to turn the other way.

"What were you thinking that first night you saw me staring at you through the window?" He asks, a curious lilt to his tone.

The desperation from before has seeped out, allowing his usual smugness to take its place. He's accepted my answer—he knows I won't run from him, regardless of how much he begs. Though, judging by the new twinkle in his eyes, I think the time for begging is over. That door has closed. But I don't know what he's getting at with his new line of questioning.

I think back to that night. The terror I felt at being watched floods my stomach again, coating it like thick tar.

"I was afraid," I admit in a low, heavy voice.

"You didn't seem afraid. In fact, you stared right back at me," he points out, lips upturned in prideful wonder as he recalls that night from his own perspective. "It took me completely off guard."

"I wasn't sure if you were real."

Tilting his head, he clicks his tongue doubtfully. "That's not true though, is it?" Leaning forward to erase what's left of the space between us, his forehead brushes against mine as he rests his head on my pillow beside me. "You knew I was real. You felt something that night. Something that electrified your bones and set fire to your soul."

"What are you getting at?"

"I think you refuse to run because you've become addicted to that rush, same as me. You got a taste that night, and nothing—not even your own personal safety—can get in the way of your indulgence."

Strong fingers skirt up my arm, dancing across the tender, sensitive skin as goosebumps follow in their wake until they reach my shoulder, and then they wrap around my jaw to tilt my head so our lips are perfectly aligned. So close, his breath tickles my lips as he goes on.

"I feel it too, Stardust. Every fiber of my being is clawing to give in—to take the dive. And I want to… *so fucking badly*. But I haven't yet because I can't freefall into this feeling, only to turn back and find that you didn't take the leap with me."

His grip tightens against my jawbone, almost painfully as he rolls his forehead against mine, eyes closed. "This is your only chance to run. The only time I can guarantee I won't chase you, or burn the world down behind you. I can't tell you everything, but I can admit that I've done terrible things. Things that will damn me to an eternity in Hell. So, if you have any doubts about me, you need to run. *Now.*"

His eyes pop open, revealing an odd, steely-green color I've never seen before.

"Otherwise, I'm grabbing your hand in mine, and we're making the jump together. We're burning *together.*"

My gaze slowly rakes over his features as his words roll around inside my head, digging their way directly into my subconscious.

He thinks this is a choice, but that isn't true at all.

I *was* terrified when I found him in my yard, though I've realized it's not only because he was watching me. There was something else present with us that night—something that called to each of us, forcing our attention onto one another. Insisting that our gazes collided at that exact moment. The darkness he claims is inside of him resides in me also, and now that it has found its match, there's no way it's letting go.

Bash stares back at me patiently, allowing me all the time I need to process this. But I don't need any more time. The decision has been made—it continues to be made for me.

"If you burn, I burn," I softly say.

His lips are on mine in an instant, accepting my answer and leaving no room for me to reconsider. Shifting his weight on top of me, he nudges my legs open and settles between them, hands brushing against my skin in various places faster than I can even comprehend. Our clothes disappear in a flurry of movements as our mouths move across each other's skin, like it's our last meal and we're both famished.

This feels different than any other time we've been like this. *He's* different. Before, he was viciously staking his claim on me, whether I agreed or not.

Now, it's deeper than that. He's melding with me, sinking into my body until we become one and the darkness inside of us fuses together into one black cloud. Our souls are connecting above our bodies and dancing together as our skin slips and slides against one another. And when we meet our climaxes, it's like the entire world shakes and tilts on its axis. He falls into me and permanently fills the void that's been present in my life for as long as I can remember.

Nothing will ever be the same again, and I couldn't be more delighted.

36

The Lamb

TODAY IS my first day working at Lancaster Tech. I drove in last night, checked into my hotel, and then laid in bed for hours, obsessing over every single minute of the day. I hate that I was forced to take this position because of my mother's mistakes. Because I have to bail her out yet again.

I can't even wade through the resentful emotions I feel toward her to decide if this is something I really, *truly* want. To join the corporate workforce. To work for the man who has stalked me. All my reservations have been drowned out and pushed aside for the sake of *her*. Just like they always have.

Despite the mile-long list of cons, this position comes with a lot of pros that are just enough to fuel me though getting dressed, throwing on a layer of makeup, and hailing a cab.

The receptionist jabs her fingers into a few numbers on her phone's insanely large keypad after I tell her the name of the woman I'm supposed to be meeting. She quickly mumbles, "Miss Benvenuti is here to see you," into the headset, before pressing the button on her earpiece to end the call.

"She'll be right down. You can take a seat to wait for her."

She offers a tight smile, as if she's irritated that I'm still standing here, then gestures her hand behind me to a waiting area tucked into a corner. I don't have a chance to respond before her phone rings and she's pressing the button on her headset to answer, her attention shifted back to her computer like I don't even exist.

Blowing out a breath, I start toward where she told me to sit and plop down onto a chair, reciting my introduction in my head. I've never worked in an office before. Hell, I've never worked anywhere with a receptionist or a dress code, unless you count the black pants and non-skid shoes rule at the sports bars.

I pick at the uncomfortable, stiff fabric of my simple, thrifted black dress as the elevator dings and a group of women rush out, walking right past me without a second glance. The receptionist doesn't even lift her head to greet them.

"Jovie?" a higher-pitched, feminine voice calls from the elevator.

My head jerks up and finds one of the most beautiful, well-dressed women I've ever seen. Her sheer white blouse and pencil skirt look like they cost more than my car, and they flaunt all her curves in the best way. The colors play perfectly against her smooth, luscious dark skin. She's got to be ten times more put together than I am. When my eyes make it up to her smiling face, I realize I've just been caught ogling her.

"Right this way," she says with a playful grin, like this happens all the time.

I'm not sure what's come over me. I didn't expect to find a bunch of slugs working for Bash, but I'm surprised he's got so many women on his staff. Stunning, well-educated women. I wonder if that's intentional on his part, shoving down the flicker of jealousy that wants to ignite into flames.

He's free to do whatever he pleases. We aren't exclusive. In fact, I'd do well to remember he *stalked* me. If any of these women knew that, I doubt they'd care to be much of a threat.

Following her into the elevator, I stand against the back wall and take a deep breath as she hits the button for the twenty-third floor.

"I'm Grace," she greets as the doors close, holding her hand out.

I take it, shaking awkwardly. "Nice to meet you."

Grace. What a perfect name for her.

"First days are always a little intimidating, but it'll feel like home by lunch. Everyone here is very nice." She winks and nudges me in the side with her elbow. "Especially when the CEO recommends you personally."

The elevator dings and opens, and I'm left wondering if I should take that as some sort of compliment or an underhanded remark. This is exactly why I can't have female friends.

"Yeah, I really don't know him that well," I try to explain, though it's no use. I've already been labeled as his pet, and I've hardly seen the building.

Grace steps out before me and slows her stride so we're walking together through aisles of cubicles. A few people lift their heads as we pass by, though most stay concentrated on whatever they're working on, uninterested. Such good little worker bees he's got here.

"Trust me, I meant it as a good thing. You must have some sort of superpower, though. Most people can hardly get five uninterrupted minutes with Mr. Lancaster."

Superpower? Not quite. I've just somehow found myself in the wrong place at the wrong time. Although, I doubt Grace would see it that way.

She walks us to the end of the aisle, then turns left so we can trail along the wall of offices. Each one is built with floor-to-ceiling glass walls that allow the rest of the floor to catch a view of the city, as well as the people working at their desks inside them. While they're breathtaking, they offer no privacy whatsoever.

I scan the rest of the floor silently and notice there's only one office in the opposite corner, built with large, black walls. I can easily guess that it's his or someone else's of equal rank. The lack of cubicles in that area also gives it away.

"Eliza says you'll be working from home a majority of the time, but we'll be training you here in the office until you get the hang of it. Just to be sure you've got resources close by if you have any questions," Grace explains easily without missing a beat as we power-walk through the building. I have no idea how she's doing it so effortlessly in her three-inch heels while I'm struggling to keep up and breathe wearing flats.

"It usually only takes a week or two for trainees to get a handle on things, but we're here for you as long as you need. Did you have any trouble finding a hotel?"

Her eyes flick over to me, expecting an answer. And for some reason, I blush. I can't help it. I *did* find a hotel room. It was the cheapest within walking distance of the building, and this one week is going to max out my emergency credit card.

"Oh, yeah. No problems there."

Grace just smiles again and continues like nothing is awry. She stops in front of an open doorway at the end and swings her arm for me to enter first.

"This is me."

She sashays around me and behind the large, tidy desk, then falls into her chair and holds up a stack of papers. "I received all your paperwork through email. Thanks for getting those back to me so promptly. I just need to grab copies of your IDs and bother you for a couple more signatures, and then I can bring you over to Eliza."

I nod and take the seat across from her, already digging through my purse for my license and social security card that she requested. We spend the next hour going over new employee paperwork and she hands me my new computer.

"Welcome aboard Lancaster Tech. It truly is a great place to work. And I'm not just saying that because I'm in charge of HR," she adds with a wink.

I laugh nervously, pushing away my doubts about how great of a company it really could be with a man like Bash at the head of it. Looking around, everyone seems pretty content. And I've worked at plenty of horribly run places.

"Eliza will be showing you the ropes today, then tomorrow, we'll get you into the training center to go over your daily tasks and procedures. Your position is a little unique in that you'll be working directly with Mr. Lancaster, so Eliza will coach you on how that will go," Grace explains as we practically jog through cubicles again to get to another office along the perimeter of the floor.

An older woman sits at a large desk in an office nearly identical to Grace's. She's typing away at her keyboard, glasses perched at the end of her nose and a pen stuck into her messy hair.

"Eliza, this is Jovie Benvenuti," Grace pipes up when the woman continues to ignore us standing in her doorway. She's much more reserved speaking to Eliza, which makes me assume this woman is higher up in the ranks.

Weathered blue eyes snap up to address her intruders. She unashamedly does a full scan of my body and I'm forced to stand there quietly as her gaze rakes over me. I decide that having her full attention is much more intimidating than being ignored by her completely.

Once she's finished, she turns to Grace.

"Thanks, Grace. I'll let you know when we're done," she says with a tight-lipped smile. The deep timbre of her voice takes me off guard, though I make an effort not to show it.

Eliza waits until Grace shuts the door before she speaks again.

"So, you're Jovie," she muses in her New York accent, leaning back against her huge computer chair. "Your mom got a thing for eighties rock music?"

My eyebrows fly into my hairline, shocked at her blunt joke. It's not like I haven't heard it before, but it's the last thing I expected to come out of her mouth. She's obviously happy with herself, given the smile she's wearing that widens when she sees my reaction.

"You could say that. My sister's name is Halen."

Eliza barks out a laugh, slapping her desk hard enough to startle me. "That's unfortunate."

Twisting my lips, I nod, unsure if this means she's warmed up to me already or if I'm just the butt of everyone's joke.

"I'm Eliza, Sebastian's Executive Assistant," she explains when she sobers back up. "And you're our newest Community Outreach Manager…"

Her tone is dripping with mockery, as if she knows just as well as I do that I have zero experience in a position like this. But I'm not going to fall into whatever trap she's trying to set. Squaring my shoulders, I plaster on my biggest, fakest smile and nod my head. "That's right."

"I gotta be honest, I didn't expect to see *you* standing before me when he called and told me to find you a job. I figured he was just doing a favor for one of his family friends. You know how these rich, hoity-toity women are..." She scowls and throws her hand up, gesturing at nothing in particular. "I should have known he'd throw me a curve ball, especially after he bought that house for you."

She looks back down at my clothes and smiles, as if the thrifted dress somehow pleases her.

"Thank you… I think," is all I can muster. This is not at all how I thought my first day would go.

"It's a compliment. No one understands how you got on his radar, let alone a personal referral. I can't wait to hear what they all say now that they've seen you. Don't even bother with them, though. They're a bunch of gossips."

"Why is it so surprising that Bash—I mean, Sebastian— referred me?" I voice the burning question out loud, because if she's speaking off the cusp, so will I.

"I don't know what he has you call him in private, but here, he's Mr. Lancaster," she corrects carefully, and I imme- diately want to defy her, just to prove I can.

I'm growing tired of all the insulting assumptions. If these women knew what kind of man Bash really was, they wouldn't be so surprised that he bothers himself with someone as low as me.

What sort of act is he putting on here?

"He doesn't talk to anyone. As far as they know, he doesn't have a social life outside of what his father forces him to do. He's like a recluse. Don't get me wrong, I love the boy like one of my own. He's built this place from the ground up with an honest intention that I've never seen in any of these other New York assholes. But he's been a shell of a person since his sister died."

I consider her words for a moment, realizing how little I know about the man who haunts me. The woman before me seems to provide these details to me as if I've already been made privy to them, but she obviously has no idea what the relationship is like between Bash and I. Essentially nonexistent.

I had no idea his sister died. Or that he had a sister at all. And while I know he owns my house, I can't seem to process the fact that he bought it *for me*. But it doesn't surprise me in the slightest that he's been intentional about Lancaster Tech. That much was obvious when I researched the company before I knew it was his.

"I'm only telling you this because he's obviously got a soft spot for you. Don't go messing it up unless you want to deal with me and about a hundred other women knocking on your door." She levels me with a threatening look, then breaks into a smile. "I'm just messing with you. You'd only have to deal with me," she makes sure to add.

Before I can get out a retort to her insulting lecture, the door swings open. Bash stands in the doorway, looking as flawless as ever in a white dress shirt, the sleeves rolled up to his elbows, and black dress slacks. I assume this is his usual attire when he isn't out stalking women, though I actually prefer the dark jeans and hoodies.

He smiles endearingly at Eliza and walks into the small room, his presence sucking all the air out like a vortex.

"Are you threatening my new employee? Should I find someone else to train her?" he jokes, his tone a tad too heavy.

"I'm just playing," she dismisses.

"Yeah, the same way a tiger plays with its food before eating it," Bash quips. He stops behind my chair, tightly wrapping his fingers around the back of it.

Eliza doesn't deny his accusation, and I'm forced to shove the balloon of irritation that's quickly inflating in my chest again at the easy, familiar banter they share at my expense.

First of all, I can be a tiger too, *thank you very much*.

And second, why the hell am I jealous that my literal *stalker* is friendly with another, much older woman?

Let me say that, again, for the people in the back of my hard, distorted head: he's. My. *Stalker.*

Pull it together, Jovie.

Their continued conversation fades into background noise as I go through my own mental breakdown, and I don't bother tuning back in until I hear Bash say, "Can I borrow her for a moment?"

Eliza looks slightly taken off guard for exactly one second before she recovers herself and nods. "You're the boss."

Bash moves his hand from the chair to my shoulder and gives a gentle squeeze. It's the simplest gesture. So subtle, many people wouldn't even notice. But Eliza does. Her gaze burns into his fingers, so hot that I swear he feels it on his skin. And he doesn't pull away like I thought he would. Instead, he slides that same hand over my shoulder and down my arm, until he reaches my hand and entwines his fingers with mine.

I don't know what game he's playing here, but it feels like the gesture is more of a message for Eliza than it is for me.

She pries her gaze away from our interlocked hands and turns toward her computer, lips pursed stubbornly. "Let me know when I can get back to training," she dismissively calls over her shoulder as we walk out the door.

As soon as we're back in the main area, I pull away from his grasp.

"What was that?" I hiss, crossing my arms.

Bash continues walking a step ahead of me, completely unaffected.

"We'll talk in my office."

37

The Wolf

I'M on her before my office door even clicks shut, pinning her against the wall with my hips as my mouth moves along her neck, her jaw, her ears, and then back to her lips.

I know I caught her by surprise when I grabbed her hand in Eliza's office, but I had to prove a point. I had no doubt Eliza was going to give her a hard time—that's why I came for her in the first place. As much as I love my assistant, she blurs the line between employee and family far too often. But when I actually heard her threaten my little Stardust, I snapped.

No one will ever hurt her. Not even in theory.

Of course, my independent little Stardust didn't like the primal show of affection, but that's a small price to pay for her protection. Eliza got the point to back away, and that's all that matters.

I'm sure I'll be hearing about it from her later.

Jovie's palms press against my chest in a weak attempt to shove me off, though her tongue is still working against mine in her typical dance of want and hate. I take a few more moments to savor her taste before I get chewed out, and then relent. I'm hardly one step away when she begins berating me.

"I can handle myself," she insists.

"I have no doubt that's true," I say slowly, watching the line between her brows dig even deeper with her glowering at my patronizing tone. The same hands that were just against my chest are now balled into fists, ready to strike.

"How is your first day going?" I try again, a little more gently.

I'm not used to tiptoeing around anyone like this. I'm not used to fucking *caring*.

Straightening out her dress, she side-steps me, and walks farther into my office, pacing a burning trail into the floor.

"You told everyone that we know each other," she accuses.

I round my desk to sit in my chair, shaking my head with my arms crossed over my chest. Mostly to stop myself from reaching out for her again.

"I didn't tell a soul besides Eliza. Though, I'm sure she had a field day with it."

"I can't do this. I don't know what I was thinking coming here," she rushes out. Her pacing ceases, landing her directly in front of my desk.

"What does that mean?"

Biting her lip, she raises her pinched brows. "It means that I shouldn't have ever taken this job in the first place."

I scoff, rolling my eyes. "Well, you can't just leave."

"Why not? Everyone expects me to be this bimbo, who only got the job because I'm sleeping with the CEO. The worst part is that they aren't even wrong."

"Yes, they are." My lips flatten into a tight line in an

attempt to stamp out my irritation. Whoever has made her feel like that is going to lose their fucking job today.

"I'll just have to find another way."

Another way? I have no idea what she's talking about, and that pisses me off worse than the idea of her leaving. No matter how much I violate her privacy, I still can't seem to figure her out.

"I'm not going to demand for you to stay, but leaving would be a huge mistake."

I want to demand it. I want to tie her up and keep her here, in my city. I finally got her here, and she's already slipping through my fingers. But if I tell her that, she'll only want to run even faster. And I can't risk having her alone in Styx when my father is so desperate to keep his secrets covered.

What will he do when he discovers how deep things run between me and her? The thought alone is enough to have my blood boiling.

Her eyes drop to her wringing hands and a defeated sigh passes through her lips as she falls into the chair. "I'm so in over my head," she mumbles to herself.

"What does that mean? You have to give me something, Stardust. I don't like guessing games."

"Why did you hire me? I mean, I know it's because you're crazy…" Her eyes flick up to my face, watching for my reaction to her insult. When I refuse to give her one—mostly because she's right—she goes on. "But I'm not qualified for this position. I don't think I'm even qualified to work the front desk of this place, let alone being a manager of something. And everyone here seems to know it but you."

How does she not see that she's better than every single person here? That she may not have the experience or education they do, but she's got more drive and hunger than all of them combined. She's invaluable.

I consider how to get that through to her for a moment,

allowing myself to gaze at her beautiful face while my mouth begins to overshare.

"This company is my life. I built it from the ground up. I threw *everything* I had into it, and continue to do so every single day. You clearly don't understand that I wouldn't have allowed you to come here if I didn't think you could do it. If I thought you were some *bimbo*. So, for once in your life, allow yourself to have something good. To fucking *deserve* something other than the bullshit you've accepted."

Huffing out a disbelieving sigh, she rolls her lips together. "How do you do that? You hardly know me, yet you know exactly how to get right under my skin."

"I know you better than anyone else," I correct. "Stay. Give it a chance. Fuck what everyone else thinks. Fuck what *I* think. Do this because *you* want to."

Her gaze falls to the floor, head shaking. "I don't know..."

"Do you think I'm afraid to get on my knees before you and beg in my own office, little Stardust?" I round the desk, slowly stalking toward her, savoring every bated breath she takes.

Her body goes rigid against the chair, and I wish she'd just let go the way she does when we're alone. It would make things so much more enjoyable for her.

I know she wants this. It's obvious in the way her legs go slack as I stop right in front of her. In the way her chin quivers as I wrap my hands around the armrests and lean forward until our noses brush.

"Do you think I'm above ripping those pretty thighs apart right here and running my tongue along your pussy?"

To prove my point, I get down on my knees before her and place my hands on her upper thighs.

She inhales a shaky breath, those beautiful red lips parted just enough for me to imagine them wrapped around my cock again.

"I'm sure it would break, like, a dozen laws if someone walked in and caught you," she snarks back, surprising me with her quick tongue.

The doubt and shame from before rolls off her shoulders as we fall back into our usual banter, burning me with whiplash. Her reactions always seem to take me off guard.

"No one will have to walk in here to know I'm fucking you. You'll be screaming my name so loud as I worship every inch of this beautiful body, they'll think I'm murdering you," I promise, flashing my teeth.

I can tell she's conflicted. Fucking the boss in her first few hours of working isn't the most traditional introduction to a corporate career. As much as she wants to pretend to hate me, I know she wants this job. But I'm also swaying her in the right direction. Leaning forward, I place a few light kisses across her upper thighs.

"You're sick," she quips half-heartedly, running her nails against my scalp. Her hips push forward, as if her pussy senses its owner nearby and feels gravitated toward me.

Slender fingers wrap around the base of the chair to steady herself as I shove her dress up, grab her ass, and pull her to me in one swift movement. At this angle, my mouth is lined up perfectly to lean in and devour her. All I'd have to do is move her red panties out of the way. Toying with the edges of the fabric, I look up to watch her face, shrouded in pure ecstasy, as I skim the sides of her luscious lips.

A soft, breathy moan slips out of her as I move my fingers over the slightest bit, and her hips buck forward again.

"Please," she pleads in a wanton whisper.

"Tell me what you want, baby," I say into her center, deliberately pushing hot breaths against the sensitive, exposed skin.

She shifts against the seat, unable to find relief from her arousal with me sitting right here. I chuckle, then turn my head to sink my teeth into her inner thigh. Her yelp slashes through the stagnant, stale air, electrifying my office with her addictive energy and jolting her directly against my mouth.

With that single taste, I'm unhinged. My restraint completely dissolves as she moans again, grinding herself into my face. I rip her lace underwear in half, throwing the shredded fabric to the side haphazardly as I stick my tongue inside of her. Relief sweeps through me when she cries out again and I'm sucking and nibbling and licking with abandon.

Anyone could walk by and hear her. She's completely let loose, just like I wanted her to. Consequences be damned.

She makes me reckless.

"Ah, Bash," she cries in a long moan that goes straight to my cock.

"That's right, baby. Remember who owns this beautiful pussy," I praise, adding my fingers inside of her. "Such a good little employee."

"Arrghh," she garbles. "Yes, *Mr. Lancaster.*"

I stop, pulling away enough to see her scowl at my abandonment.

"Did I say you could call me that?"

She looks down at me, confusion tugging down her flushed face. "Am I not supposed to? All your other employees do it. What else should I call you? Sir? *Boss?*"

She's instigating me. Lashing out because I've embarrassed her and chased away her orgasm. I just hate that it's working.

"No." My finger works against her clit again, easing her tension, and her eyes flutter shut.

Mr. Lancaster is my piece of shit father. I've never liked when anyone here calls me that, either. It's also far too formal of a name for her to call me when my tongue is lodged inside of her.

"Tell me you won't call me that again." I warn in a low voice, pulling away to prove my point.

"God… okay, whatever," she relents with a frustrated growl. "Just put your fucking mouth back on me."

Now, I'm a patient man. I let a lot slide with my insolent little lamb. But this entitlement? That's not going to work for me.

Not after she just fucking insulted me with that formal name.

We're well past that, and she knows it.

Rolling back onto my heels, I push myself off the floor and stand before her, ignoring the questioning glare she's burning through me. My fingers make quick work of my belt, pulling it through the loops before I throw it into my desk with a loud *clang* that makes her jump. Next, I m unbuttoning my pants and allowing my erection to spring free from the restricting material.

The image of her staring up at me, mouth ajar, with her legs still spread wide, will live in my memory forever. But I have a point to prove.

Stroking myself, I close the distance between us with a smirk. "I love that smart mouth of yours, but I think it's time that you learned how you're going to speak to me."

I watch as the mask of defiance slips onto her face. As if the mere mention of *teaching* her something makes her want to revolt immediately.

"What's the matter? You don't want my cock down your throat?" I provoke.

She slams her legs shut, turning her shoulders away from me in her seat. I've crowded her enough so she can't stand, but she's still doing everything she can to show me she's not interested.

"That's funny," I continue, running my fingers along her neck and shoulder. "I seem to remember you begging to suck my cock just a few nights ago."

Rolling her eyes, she pushes against me to stand, but I don't budge. "I have to get back to work. For *your* company. Remember that, Mr. CEO? I'm your employee."

"You're not going anywhere."

"Maybe I'll stop at HR on my way. They'd love to hear about this." She drags her hands through the air, motioning toward my exposed body.

But I won't be deterred. When she tries to get up again, I grab up a handful of hair by the nape of her neck and pull back, effectively pushing her against her seat and tilting her head upward to face me fully. Leaning forward until our mouths are perfectly lined up, I capture her lips in another kiss.

She resists at first, tightening her lips against mine, denying me access. But when I give her hair another pull, she's forced to open up for me. It's only when I slip my tongue inside that she finally melts against my touch, returning the kiss with the same reckless abandon she had before.

"Taste that, Stardust? That's *you* on my tongue. Your arousal… your ecstasy. It's what turns me into this primal animal," I say against her lips, between kisses. "I can't even fathom how fucking feral it's going to make me, seeing my cum dripping down your chin in the middle of my office. Watching you take my cock like it was made for you, the same way your pussy did this weekend."

My other hand moves to wrap my fingers around her throat, earning a sensual sigh that goes straight into my mouth and down to my groin.

"This thing between us… it's poetic. *Sacred*. We're more

than just two deprived souls feeding off one another's despair. And you can threaten me all you want with the police, or HR, or whoever the fuck you can think of to give yourself a false sense of security, but we both know you're just as afraid of losing this as I am."

Moving my mouth away from hers, I trail my lips along her jaw, digging little nips into her flesh with my teeth until she's moaning into my ear again.

"You can't escape me. Not in this life or any one that comes after it. My soul has latched onto yours, melding us into one. I'll always find you, Stardust."

She whimpers against me as I suck her earlobe between my teeth and bite down.

"So, you're going to open that beautiful, smart mouth of yours, and you're going to wrap those cherry-red lips around my cock. Because that's what you've been dreaming about since the first time you caught me in your bedroom, and because it's your punishment for referring to me as anything but *yours*."

By the time I stand up straight again, she's grabbing my erection into her hands and eagerly guiding it toward her mouth out of spite, a hateful gleam shining in those darkened eyes.

"Mm, that's my girl," I hum, loosening my grip on her hair so she has room to lean forward and take me into her mouth. I don't care if she fucking abhors me. It doesn't change anything.

But she stops at the last second. She tests the bounds of my patience by looking up at me with an incredulous scowl, fingers wrapped around my base, my tip grazing her lips.

"You can say whatever twisted words you want to pretend this situation isn't as fucked up as it is. That you didn't stalk me, corner me, and trick me. And I'll go along while I'm still getting something out of it. But don't mistake this for anything other than some sick obsession you have. Don't mistake yourself as anything other than a monster."

She smirks, as if she's somehow maneuvered around me and gotten her checkmate. When I don't respond, she flicks her tongue out and runs it along the base of my cock, and I let her believe she's got some semblance of control. At least for a moment.

Ah, yes, she's so fucking cute. But that's enough playing.

"That's a nice little speech, but I think it's time for you to shut the fuck up and take your punishment like a good girl."

Tightening my fist against the base of her scalp again, I yank her head back to open her mouth for me. "And just so you know, I've done far worse than any of that," I tell her, then shove my hips forward and send my cock straight down her throat.

Stardust gags on the sudden intrusion, struggling to adjust herself so she can take me even deeper in an act of defiance. I may have her in my grip, but she's the one in control. She wraps her hands around my thighs, adjusting the pace as I reach down and grab her tit in my hand, kneading it until I feel the familiar tightening sensation sizzling up my spine and weakening my legs.

Within minutes of our argument, I'm coming into her mouth and she's swallowing it all up, ensuring not a single drop escapes. Once I'm finished, she pulls away and leans back into her chair, revealing the hand she's rubbing against her clit. She tips her head back, unashamedly pleasuring herself right before my eyes.

Well, that simply won't do.

Scooping my hands under her knees to cradle her ass, I lift her up and swing her body over to my desk, carefully balancing her on the edge while I clear a spot for her before pushing her backward.

"Such a disobedient, impatient little lamb," I muse, kneeling before her. "Now, let me enjoy my lunch."

She shudders out a breath, as I swipe my flattened tongue along her sensitive slit with the perfect amount of pressure to tease her clit as I pass by it. Her long nails scrape against my scalp again as I nibble on the sensitive, swollen nub, then soothe it with my swirling tongue before I'm assaulting it all over again. My finger slips inside of her, spreading her sweet arousal all around for my mouth to clean up.

Stardust wisely keeps her snarky remarks to herself this time, the only noises coming from her mouth being the whimpering moans she can't seem to contain as I feast on her delectable pussy. In no time, I can feel her body tense up before she stills against me, and then her pleasure fills my mouth.

I'm so fucking turned on by the erotic display, I'm hoisting her up from my desk and carrying her over to the floor-to-ceiling window before my mind can even comprehend what I'm doing. Leaning her back against the glass to bear her weight, I capture her mouth in a wet kiss, sharing the delicious taste of her orgasm with her. My erection rubs between her legs, right against the sensitive spot I just worked on.

She cranes her neck, peering out the window with a worried expression. "Someone could see us," she says, pulling her lip into her mouth. It's a nervous tick she has that sends me spiraling every time.

I swipe my tongue along her jaw, hardly glancing out at the view she's referring to. "No one is looking up here," I promise through kisses, unable to keep my mouth off of her.

Her gaze lingers for another second as she wars with herself before her desire wins out and she's back to giving me her full attention. Her hips grind circles against mine, letting me know she's ready for another round.

And I don't have to be told twice. I'm instantly lining myself up with her wet center, rubbing my tip around to coat it in her juices before I'm slowly pushing my hips forward, filling her with one deep thrust.

She releases a moan directly into my ear, wrapping her arms around my neck as her thighs tighten against my sides. We find a rhythm, and the office fills with the sultry sounds of our bodies moving against each other and our low, breathy moans.

I don't even have to reach between us to caress her clit and help her reach her climax. Our bodies are creating enough friction that, before I know it, she's grasping onto my shoulders and stiffening in my arms as her pussy pulsates around me, encouraging my own orgasm to follow right behind. Just as her juices coat our skin, my cock twitches inside of her and fills her with my seed.

She moans at the warm sensation, grabbing my head to pull me into another sloppy kiss. We each come down from our highs, and it feels like our souls have just returned to our bodies after dancing in the sky together.

With a sheepish smile, she hops off of me and stands on shaky legs, shimmying her dress back down her legs, sans underwear.

We don't bother exchanging any awkward goodbyes. Instead, she mumbles something about needing to get back to work, and then slips out the door without looking back, leaving me alone to sit back in my chair and marvel at how fucked I truly am.

Shifting my gaze out the window, I notice that the conference room of the office building next to us is full of people who could have easily looked over and watched that entire display. I should be mortified. Or at least protective over my little lamb. But I can't seem to muster any feelings other than pride and arrogance.

In fact, I almost hope they did look.

Just before I turn away, I notice a smudge on the glass. Her ass was planted there so firmly, it left a perfect print behind. I smile to myself, leaning farther into my chair to admire it.

I don't think I'll ever let them wash my windows again.

38

The Lamb

BASH FINDS me in the training center at the end of the day, just as I'm packing up my laptop to leave. When I catch him leaning his shoulder against the door jamb, hands in his pockets, a hot blush creeps along my cheeks, the way it always does around him. The memory of those hands on me earlier is still so fresh in my mind, I could practically feel their phantom brushes against my skin all afternoon. It doesn't help that I've spent the past four hours learning all the amazing things Bash has done in his career.

He somehow manages to turn me into a person I don't recognize when we're together, and then he leaves me alone to try to reconcile my feelings. I know I should be embarrassed about what I allowed to happen between us, how he treated me so crassly. But the truth is, I'm not. Not even a little bit.

"Did you have a good first day?" he asks as I approach, slinging my new backpack over my shoulder.

"I did," I admit with a smile.

Regardless of my conflicting feelings for Bash, his company is doing something really great here. Everyone was friendly and welcoming, despite my odd recruitment. This is probably one of the only jobs I've ever had where I'm excited to come back in the morning.

We walk into the elevator together and Bash hits the button for the ground floor. There's a group of people rushing to join us, but Bash slams his finger on the 'close' button and the doors slide shut just as they reach us. He feigns an apologetic shrug as they disappear behind the metal, shutting us off from the rest of the world.

His hand immediately slithers against my ass as he moves behind me, his hot breath blowing over the crook of my neck. And while I know I'm going to hate myself for it later, I lean back, pressing myself against the hardness of his erection. Bash releases a low moan into my hair, and I take it as encouragement to begin slowly swaying my hips against him.

"You're a devious little minx," he growls, splaying his fingers across my abdomen to hold me closer.

The elevator stops, and I manage to step away from him just in time for the doors to open, exposing us to the busy lobby of our office building that serves as the perfect bucket of ice water to cool me off. I'm mortified at how carried away I got after only a few moments alone with him. After one single touch.

Bash snickers behind me as we walk off together, completely unaware of my internal battle as he discreetly adjusts himself in his pants.

That was way too close.

When we break through the glass doors, I veer off to the side of the building and turn to face him, hot rage burning in my chest. "We can't do that here," I reprimand.

Bash rolls his eyes, stepping toward me to brush his

knuckles against my chin. It takes everything in me not to lean into his touch, which has me overcorrecting and propelling myself away from him with more force than necessary. I stumble backward, and his eyes widen as I barely catch myself from falling on my ass.

"I promise, Stardust, no one here gives a shit about us."

"I-I just can't do this with you right now. I'll see you tomorrow."

"Where do you think you're going?" Bash throws his arm across my chest to stop me from turning left, toward my hotel.

"To my hotel," I state simply, confused by the sharpness of his tone.

Shaking his head once, he scowls down at me. "Yeah, that's not happening."

"What does that mean?"

His hand slides down my arm until his fingers lace with mine, completely enveloping them. With a firm, threatening squeeze that nearly cuts off my blood supply, he says, "You're coming with me."

I rip my hand away from his grasp, ignoring the familiar predatory look that's crossed his face. This is the version of him that I'm used to seeing—not the casual, laid-back performance he's been putting on all day for his employees.

Is it wrong to admit I like this one better, even if I'm still a little afraid of it?

"Like hell I am," I growl, hugging my hands to my chest. "I practically broke the bank to pay for this hotel. I'm sleeping there."

Bash isn't deterred by my tantrum, and he doesn't give a fuck about the money he's asking me to throw away just to stay with him.

He leans forward, hunching his back so we're face-to-face, and then lowers his voice so no one else can overhear. "I don't think you understand me, Stardust. There's no way I'm going to have you sleeping anywhere but my bed while you're in *my* city," he grinds out between his teeth.

It's such a terrifying sight, I want to cower down before him and beg for forgiveness.

My pride won't allow that, though. Instead, I muster up every scrap of courage I have left and stand my ground, because the old Jovie would have allowed this man to walk all over me the same way Gabe did, and she quite literally died trying to appease him. Unfortunately for Bash, I'm no longer a living doormat.

"And I don't think *you* understand *me*. I'm not shacking up with my new boss in my first week working for him. There're already enough rumors floating around about us."

He rears back, dark brows coming together in a deep scowl. "And you give a fuck what any of them say? Come on, you're better than that…"

I'm already backing away from him, nearly tripping over a group of people who just walked out of the same building we were just in. They mumble a string of curse words at me, immediately cutting off their threats when they notice Bash standing a few feet away.

"My answer is no. I'll see you tomorrow. I've got to get to bed early. My new boss is a bit of a prick," I weakly joke, but it falls on deaf ears. For a moment, I think he's going to drop this act and let me go so I can begin walking or hail a cab.

In the blink of an eye, he's erased the distance I put between us. With one hand wrapped around the back of my neck and the other securely holding my waist, he tugs me against him. From a distance, it would look like we were just hugging goodbye. No one is aware of his fingers digging into my hip, or the iron-grip he's keeping on my neck to hold me in place as he brushes his teeth against my ear, lightly nipping at the sensitive skin.

It was a stupid, delusional moment.

"You don't get to tell me no," he growls, sending spiders skittering down my spine.

"I can't afford to say yes," I find myself admitting.

I don't just mean financially. There is no scenario where this ends well for me.

"I need my things," I try again, scouring my brain for any logical reason I can come up with for him to just let me go. "I can't wear the same outfit tomorrow."

"We can buy you something new," he offers, his voice ice-cold.

"Please, Bash."

A war wages within him, though he's only giving me a small glimpse of it through his facial features. I haven't uncovered much about him, but one thing I'm positive about is that Bash doesn't like to have his word questioned. Too bad for him, I'm not allowing another man to dictate my every move.

"I'll come with you to get them, then take you to my place."

I want to scream. I'd love to punch him right in the face for being such a prick over this. No matter how much I give him, he always wants to take more.

Dropping his voice, he tilts his head and rolls his shoulders back. "This is my final offer, Stardust. I'm not leaving you alone in this city."

And there's something about the way he says those words that tells me this is about more than him being a possessive asshole with no concern for my privacy. That there may be more to his story that he isn't telling me.

"Fine," I relent. "But you can wait in the lobby for me."

Bash doesn't bother answering, not that it would matter either way. He's made up his mind, and I'm expected to just go along with it. Perhaps I'm just like everyone else and I've fallen for his charms, forgetting how insane he truly is. Or maybe I'm just as crazy as he is, because when he releases me from his firm hold, I don't run. I don't call for help. I don't even take a step away from him.

Instead, I follow my predator like a good little lamb.

39

The Wolf

BEING with Stardust out in the open feels like a sin. She's self-conscious about being seen with me in public, and while one part of me wants to bend her over right in the middle of the sidewalk and show every other asshole around us who she belongs to, most of me is afraid that someone from The Order is going to find us together and use her as leverage against me.

I'm so close to the end. When this whole thing started, I didn't give a damn if I lived or died, so long as Sienna's murderers paid. Now, I stand to lose way more, and it's leaving me on edge.

She thinks I'm insisting that she stay with me just because I want her all to myself. While that's entirely true, I also can't stand the idea of her being so close and not having the ability to protect her from the monsters I know prowl these streets. Styx is like a safe haven. Off the radar for most of the useless, deadly people I've been hunting. I know that when she's there, she's nearly non-existent—exactly how I need her to be right now. I wouldn't have even had her come to New York for this job, but Eliza stomped her feet and pitched a fit until I agreed, claiming it would be impossible for her to be trained remotely.

It takes her twenty-three minutes to grab her bags from her room while I wait in the hotel lobby like she insisted. I have no idea what the fuck she was doing up there in all that time, but I hope she at least had the sense to gather everything, because she won't be returning.

"I was almost thinking you were trying to bail on me, little lamb," I greet as she rolls her suitcase across the glossy lobby floor, a pillow tucked beneath her other arm.

"I wouldn't dream of such a thing," she snarks back as I reach out to take her backpack and the handle of her luggage.

"A pillow?" I tease, raising my brow at the dingy blue fabric case.

A soft pink blush spreads across her cheeks and I want to grab her up right here and make that blush spread all the way down her neck, the way I know it does after she's orgasmed.

"Hotel pillows suck."

"Well, it's a good thing you aren't staying at a hotel then, isn't it?"

"I'm sure your pillows suck too."

She's grumpy. Even when I take her last bag and sling it over my shoulder, relieving her of all the weight, she scowls at me. We walk out the doors and back out into the musky city air.

"How far is your place? Is it a long walk?"

Lifting my arm to grab Sterling's attention, I place my hand on her shoulder to guide her toward his town car.

"We're not walking," is all I say, handing her bags over to Sterling so he can toss them in his trunk.

"You have a driver." It's a statement. One she makes with zero emotion or fanfare. Apparently, she's unimpressed.

"Of course, I have a driver. Have you ever been stuck in New York City traffic?"

I open the back door and gesture for her to climb in first. Naturally, she hesitates, because who would she be if she didn't question every fucking move I make to a frustrating degree?

"What's the worst I can do, Stardust?"

There's a lot worse that I could do to her, actually. In fact, I'm already planning some of it tonight as punishment for her insolence.

She pauses, sweeping her gaze across the sidewalk and all the buildings around us. I understand her hesitance, but there's truly no room for it anymore. We've long surpassed this tentative stage—probably when I found her with her fingers rubbing her clit as she shoved her tit into my hand, although I doubt she remembers that.

Sterling rounds the vehicle, offering me a stiff nod before he falls into the driver's seat and stares ahead, patiently waiting to get on with his task.

"Just get in," I command more harshly, my patience thin.

Stardust huffs out a loud, frustrated growl, but she obeys. When I climb in behind her, I don't miss the fact that she's crammed her body against the opposite door, as far away from me as possible.

Good. I need space from her for a moment, too.

And once I'm finished with that, I'll show her exactly what happens to irritating little girls like her.

40

The Lamb

HE HAS A DRIVER.

It shouldn't come as much of a surprise to me, all things considered. But for some reason, it's the final straw that sends my weakly stacked mind into a rockslide of intrusive thoughts.

Said driver has dropped us off at a ridiculously tall, newer building and handed my luggage back to Bash before driving off again. My next mental breakdown comes when we take the elevator up to the top floor that opens right up to his apartment.

I'm sorry, did I call it an apartment? I meant penthouse. No, worse than that, it's practically a mansion in the sky.

Our elevator ride is nothing like the one we had earlier. He remains stiff at my side, his shoulders tense as he works his jaw back and forth. We're in a silent standoff, each of us too stubborn to be the first to cut through the intense energy radiating between us. There was no warning about what to expect when the doors opened, and while all of this is pretty typical for the CEO of an insanely successful company in a city like New York, it's still unbelievable that someone like *me* could be standing in a place like this, with a person like him.

This entire experience is surreal. I have no idea how I got here.

Bash strolls a few feet into the space before he turns back to face me, hands in his pockets. He almost seems… nervous? Is it possible that my stalker is just as anxious about having me here as I am about being here?

"This is home," he announces, leaning his shoulder against one of the wood columns, a cocky gleam in his light eyes.

Nope, I was wrong before. This man is definitely showing off.

"The guest suites are upstairs. Kitchen and dining are that way. And my bedroom and office are down that hall."

My gaze flits past him, slowly taking in the details of the new space. I'm greedily cataloging every speck of knowledge that I can gather about him in the sparsely decorated room. The walls are a light gray with black accents all around—in the tables and lamps, the framed art, the throw pillows. An enormous white sectional couch sits in the center of his living room, facing a built-in wall of shelves surrounding a large TV.

It's the perfect balance of masculine and feminine ener-gies and, once again, the jealous monster inside my chest begins to rumble to life at the possibility that he may have shared this home with a woman at some point. Perhaps he still does.

"I'm starving." He cuts off my wandering thoughts as he pushes off the column and heads toward the direction he said the kitchen was in. I have no choice but to follow behind him, my chest burning with nervous anticipation of what the rest of his home looks like.

The short hallway he leads me down opens up to an enormous, stark-white kitchen and dining room that look like they haven't ever been touched, save for the two covered plates sitting on the lighted stove.

I'm starting to think there isn't a single speck of color in this place.

"I hope you don't mind, I told my cook to make an extra plate for you. I figured you'd be hungry after nearly missing lunch." He grabs up the plates, then turns to wink at me.

Fire burns up my chest and neck as memories of our lunch together flood my mind. Will he expect that from me again tonight?

I know I shouldn't want him to, especially after this chauvinistic show of control over me. At what point did he decide that I was coming home with him instead of to my hotel? Did he plan it all along? I should be appalled. Still, the dark, starved part of me is hoping for more.

It's been so long since I've indulged myself. Maybe I never have.

Bash pulls out a chair for me at the table, then returns to the kitchen to pour two glasses of wine before he takes the seat across from it. I shyly uncover the plate, my senses instantly assaulted by the delicious scents of various herbs and spices. I think it's chicken parmesan, though I've never seen the dish presented so beautifully.

"It might be a little cold now. We took much longer to get home than I usually do." With a pointed glare, he shoves a piece of chicken into his mouth.

I don't bother voicing the smart retort begging to come out so I can defend myself. Instead, I cut into the meat and wrap my lips around the fork, moaning when the flavors burst across my tongue.

Quickly cutting off another bite, I repeat the motion, not bothering with manners or politeness when my stomach is empty and rumbling. Everything else fades away as I experience true bliss for a few short moments. Maybe I'm not a picky eater, just a bad cook.

I make it nearly halfway through the meal before I realize Bash has hardly touched his plate, his eyes fixated on me like some sort of animal at a zoo. Dropping my fork to grab the fabric napkin he set beside me, I delicately dab at my mouth, mortified to find that my lips were covered in red tomato sauce.

What the hell just came over me?

"You're truly an exquisite creature," he comments, an impressed smirk kicking up the side of his mouth. It seems like it would be a jab, but his tone and expression say otherwise.

"Sorry. This is delicious," I say, as if that explains the grotesque display I just put on.

"I can't wait to taste it on your tongue later."

Gulping down my wine, I raise my brows at him over the rim in response. My thighs rub together of their own accord, naturally trying to relieve the pulsating tension that kicks up again from his words. So, I guess that answers my question from before.

Bash just chuckles at my response, then returns to his meal. We finish eating and he brings me back through the main room, then up a set of stairs I must have missed when we walked off the elevator earlier.

"This is your room for the week," he explains, opening the solid wood door at the end of the hallway to reveal a bedroom that is easily the size of half my house.

It's tastefully decorated in deep shades of red and purple, and I can't help but notice the resemblance to the fruit he left in my home each time he was there without my knowledge.

"Where's your room?" I ask as he rolls my luggage into the middle of the space and tosses my pillow onto the bed.

"Downstairs, across the house. I don't usually have guests here, but when I do, I like to keep my privacy."

Dropping my eyes back to the bed, I nod once, a little disappointed to hear that he'll be so far away. The way he spoke at dinner, it seemed like he expected more to happen tonight, and the traitorous, feral woman inside of me is disappointed that doesn't seem to be the case.

"Feel free to wash up," Bash calls to me on his way out. "I've got a few work emails to answer. I'll be back for you in a little bit."

"Back for me?"

Raising a brow at me like I'm the most pathetic thing he's ever laid eyes on, he nods. "Yes, Stardust. I'll be back."

With that, he disappears down the hall, and I don't bother going after him to ask for any more clarification. When it comes to Bash, asking more questions only seems to get me further from the answer. Instead, I grab something to wear for bed and head into the bathroom for a shower, relieved to have a chance to decompress from the insanity of this day.

41

The Lamb

A SOFT SIGH passes my lips and my back arches into his touch. But *he* isn't here. At least, not in my room. I've drifted off to sleep, and he's managed to dig his way into my subconscious again.

Someone snickers above me, and my eyes snap open to find those menacing greens blazing into me.

"Hi, Stardust," he whispers, finger grazing along the hem of my shirt.

"What time is it?" I ask stupidly.

How long have I been out?

Bash shifts his weight and moves away from my side, spreading my legs to make room for himself between them on the bed. Once he's settled in with my calves resting on each of his thighs, he hooks his fingers into my thong and drags it down, fully exposing me to the cold night air.

I could swear I had shorts on when I went to bed...

"It's late," is all he says, lifting my legs so he can pull my thong all the way off before he gently rests them back in their spots against him. Next, he places his hand just below my belly button, applying the smallest amount of pressure as he slides it down, right over my bare pussy.

"Bash," I moan, unable to bother with coyness or feigned shyness anymore. There's no time to play games. I just want him to fuck me.

I waited at least two hours for him to come back like some lovesick puppy. The urge to roam his house on my own was strong, but it didn't outweigh the possibility that I'd get lost or find something I didn't want to see.

"That's right, baby. Tell me who this pussy belongs to," he praises, rubbing my clit.

My hips buck forward, shoving his whole palm into my slick center to chase the high he's teasing me with. One hand holds my hips down while the other plunges inside of me, hooking upward to hit the perfect spot and have me screaming his name even louder. Within minutes, I'm seeing stars, the familiar burn of an orgasm crackling down my spine as it builds.

And like the cruel bastard he is, Bash withdraws from me, shifting his weight onto his ankles as he straightens up and takes his front-row seat for my blue vulva.

"What are you doing?" I groan, my body attempting to recover from the building waves that never met their crest.

"You've been a very bad girl today," he chastises, his lips pursed. "I think it's time I teach you how this thing is going to work between us. You've been spoiled."

Spoiled? For fuck's sake, this guy has some balls on him. My jaw is still sore from earlier. Another "lesson" from him sounds absolutely horrible right now.

Rolling my eyes, I prop myself up onto my elbows. "If you aren't going to do it, I'll handle it myself."

My hand quickly replaces the spot he just left, circling

and rubbing in search of the release he cheated me out of while he tracks my every movement, an indistinguishable look in his eyes.

I'm so turned on by having him watch me pleasure myself, my orgasm quickly catches up to me, nearly hitting me at twice the force I can usually muster on my own. I can feel it *right there*, creeping on the edge. Until a large, strong hand wraps around my wrist and pulls it away.

"Like hell, you will."

"You bastard," I cry out in a high-pitched voice, thoroughly irritated.

Bash grabs up my other wrist, unbothered by my attempts to fight against him as he leans forward and pins them above my head. With our bodies at this angle, his erection grazes against my sensitive, pulsating center, and I lift my hips to grind them against it, desperate to release this agonizing tension.

"You're ravenous," he chortles, but doesn't pull himself away. Instead, he bucks his hips forward and grinds against me with equal fervor, his breaths growing uneven as the pleasure builds.

"Such a naughty girl, yet you can't even handle a little punishment for your smart mouth."

"I think you like me better this way."

That earns another breathy laugh, and then, with zero warning, he grabs my hips and flips me around onto my stomach, lifting my hips so my ass is stuck in the air before him.

"We'll just have to do it the old-fashioned way, then."

A large palm gently smooths over the supple skin, fingers squeezing and shaking as my ass jiggles before him. Then a loud *smack* pierces the air as he slaps me with his whole hand, sending burning flames dancing across my flesh. His soft palm returns, soothing the ache before he repeats the motion three times over. By the last strike, I'm screaming his name into the empty, dark air, my arousal practically dripping down my legs.

"Fuck," I whine. "I'll do whatever you want, just stop teasing me. I can't take it anymore."

I feel him pause behind me, then his fingers lightly graze against my swollen pussy, and I jump forward, unable to handle the overstimulation that results from that small touch.

"You want me to let you finish, baby?"

"Yes. Please, Bash," I beg without an ounce of shame.

His presence behind me shifts, then I feel his large hands wrap around my sides as he pulls me back toward him, until our thighs are flush with each other. His erection rubs along my sensitive flesh as he moves his hips around teasingly, fingers tightening against me from his own desire.

"Promise me you won't give me any more shit about staying with me," I hear his low, husky voice plead from behind.

At least I can rest well knowing this is torturing him just as much as it is me.

It doesn't take a second thought for me to turn my head backward, sighing as he rubs his tip across my dripping slit. "I promise. I'm not going anywhere."

That's all the confirmation he needs to line himself up and slowly ease in, instantly relieving the pressure that's been building since he woke me up. I cry out, incapable of holding my relief in any longer as Bash quickens his pace, using the hand on my hip to steady me as the other reaches around and pleasures my clit.

An orgasm begins rolling through me embarrassingly quick as I fall forward into the mattress, incapable of even holding myself up as he drills into me from behind. Once the wave passes, he flips my body over again and nestles himself between my legs, capturing my mouth into a mind-numbing kiss as he proceeds to make me orgasm three more times before we pass out beside one another.

42

The Wolf

WAKING up beside Stardust feels like I've somehow cheated my way into Heaven and stolen a slice of it to bring back down to Earth with me. She feels right in my arms. More right than anything I deserve in this turbulent waste of a lifetime. A good man would let her go. He would free her from the burdens she has no knowledge of by staying with me.

I suppose it's for the best that I'm not a good man.

I was late meeting her up here last night, caught up in a string of emails I found on my father's account. I'd hacked into it weeks ago, but haven't had the time to comb through everything as thoroughly as I'd like. Finally, I found a deleted thread of emails from the week before Sienna was killed, and time stood still as I read through each and every incriminating message that served to guarantee the deaths of at least three more men—my father included. Hours later, I made my way up to Stardust's room, thoroughly irritated, to find her fast asleep, and I couldn't resist. I needed the release and, as always, she was more than willing to help me find it.

We've each just reached our respective climaxes, exhausted from a long night of discovering each other's bodies like a familiar, distant land that we're only just returning to. I got a solid three hours of sleep before rolling over and finding her there, and then started all over again. I've spent so much time inside of her, we're dangerously close to walking into the office late and conjoined together.

Not that I could give a fuck what anyone thinks. But she does, and if something matters to her, I'm realizing that my brain suddenly makes it a priority for me as well.

"Tell me more about you," she says with a jovial lilt to her voice, and I can't help the way my stomach drops at her request.

I'd do anything to keep the content glow radiating off of her right now. To make the sparkle in her eyes more permanent. But I can't give her what she wants. The more she knows, the higher the chance she'll want to run in the other direction. At one point, I couldn't have cared less what she did. But now? Now, I'm afraid that losing her would be like having the air sucked right out of my lungs. And while I absolutely refuse to let her go, it's entirely possible that this strong force of a woman might manage to knock me down and leave anyway when she finds out the truth.

"Didn't you already have a crash course on me in your training yesterday?" I ask, smirking, though the whole idea of her sitting through a presentation that practically outlines every time I've taken a shit in New York makes me want to vomit. That's another argument I lost against Eliza.

You're building more than a business here. You're building a community. These people want to know who they're working for, and Lord knows you won't be leaving your office to show them," she had said when I argued against it. In the end, she won and, of course, she was right. My employees feel much closer to me, and I've hardly had to lift a finger.

Although, now that Stardust has gone through that embarrassing presentation, I'm considering the idea of revisiting that argument with Eliza.

"Yeah, but all of that was stuff I could have found out about you with a quick google search. I want to know more. You practically know my entire life story, and all I've got is your resume."

With a heavy sigh, I lift my eyes to the ceiling and try to pull some menial fact about myself out of thin air that won't make her want to scream.

What are my hobbies? Torturing and killing people.

What do I do in my spare time? Hunt the people I plan to torture and kill. And occasionally stalk you.

What's my relationship like with my family? Well, I'm currently running through a list of people to torture and kill because they murdered my sister. Oh, you want to know about my parents? Well, my mother is practically catatonic and my father's danced his way onto said list of people I want to torture and kill.

See how this might get a little sticky?

"I've already told you, I'm not a good person. There's nothing else to tell."

A frustrated groan vibrates against her chest, and she sits up against the headboard, pulling the sheet up in a hurry. She doesn't notice when the soft fabric slips through her fingers, exposing her left breast to the brightening morning light. My eyes linger on her chest for a long moment, appreciating the soft milkiness of her skin.

"Why do you do that?" she asks, pulling me from my thoughts.

I'm too amused by her comical show to remember what I said to frustrate her so badly. "Do what?"

"You pretend that you're this horrible person, yet you've done all these amazing things. It's like you *want* me to hate you."

"You've said so yourself: I'm a monster," I remind her, throwing her words back into her face.

When she tilts her head and stares at me impatiently, it's as if her cruel words from less than twenty-four hours ago don't count anymore. But they do. They count more than anything, because that was her opinion of me before she had every bullshit lie shoved down her throat by my assistant. It's easy for me to accept that the rest of the world may perceive me that way. It's harder when it comes from someone I care about. My natural defense is to lean into it—to push her away before she destroys me like she inevitably will.

Working my jaw, I narrow my eyes at her. I don't know when she's going to get it. Why does she insist on seeing this imaginary side of me?

"For every good thing I've done, there's a much worse thing to counter it. Sure, I can throw money at charities and offer my employees livable salaries. I can create a company that helps people, and pretend to be some honorable philan-thropist, just like every other rich asshole in this world. But I'm not a saint. No matter what I do, you can't rationalize my sins with a few weak attempts at redemption. I'm still the monster lurking in your shadows."

"Something tells me that's just the mask you choose to wear to push people away..."

"No, it's not a mask. It's the real me, Stardust. I've done horrible, unthinkable things in the name of revenge."

I can see I've upset her, though she's trying like hell to hide it from me. Despite her best efforts, a single tear leaks from her eye and rolls down her cheek, and my strong little lamb doesn't even bother wiping it away. She tucks her chin into her chest stubbornly, eyes cast down at her wringing hands.

"I don't know what's wrong with me," she says brokenly into her lap. "You tell me all these horrible things, expecting me to run in the opposite direction, and I know that's what I should be doing. Anyone in their right mind would run straight to the police after what you've done to me. But I can't fucking do it. It's still not enough to make me bail on you, because I know you. I know you probably have a good reason to do all of that. And I think that says more about me than anything else."

"Look at me," I command, placing my fingers beneath her chin delicately to guide her head upward. Once those beautiful, mahogany eyes land on mine, I tell her, "There's nothing wrong with you. You're perfect in every single fucking way."

More tears spill over, and her face crumples. "Then why can't I walk away?"

"For the same reason I can't seem to stay away to keep you safe: we were made for each other. Even though you're the brightest fucking star in the galaxy, and I'm just a black hole that sucks the life out of everything. Even though being with me could completely implode your life. You make everything feel less hopeless."

"That makes no sense," she says through a sad chuckle, tears still streaming down her reddened face.

"No, it doesn't, but who said anything has to make sense? If it feels good, why can't we just run with it?"

Who the hell is this mushy bastard speaking for me right now? Sebastian Lancaster doesn't spew shit like this. But Jovie has changed me, and I can't decide if it's for the better. It was easier being a shell of a person, void of emotions or responsibility to anyone else. To walk through life and do the things I need to do without the constant fear that the things that matter the most to me won't be taken away.

Maybe a part of me died with Sienna, and Jovie has stumbled along to bring it back to life.

"What time is it?" she asks in a sudden panic, her back shooting straight up to look around for a clock.

My gaze slips over to the alarm clock sitting on the dresser across from me, and hers follows. As soon as she sees that it's past seven, she jumps out of bed, a string of cuss words falling from her mouth that makes me smile as she hops over me and begins running around the room, gathering her clothes.

"Turns out, I know the boss. He doesn't give a shit if you're on time," I try to reassure her, taking my time to swing my legs over the side of the bed and strolling toward the bathroom for a quick shower.

"I already know you're perfectly content walking into that building an hour late with me at your side, looking like I just rolled out of your bed. But I caught enough shit yesterday about you. There's no way in hell I'm walking in late, especially like this."

That gives me pause. "Who gave you shit?" I'm asking from the doorway, ready to fire whoever disrespected my little lamb on her first day.

Shaking her head, she hugs her clothes to her chest, effectively covering her beautiful tits from my view. Her hair is a tousled mess on top of her head, her cheeks painted a deeper red now that she's been rushing around. I don't think she could look any more fucking perfect.

"No one. I need to shower."

"Save time and shower with me," I offer, leaning my palm against the top of the door jamb to give her a full, uninterrupted view of what I'm offering. My smile falls when she rolls her eyes and blows out an exasperated breath.

"Something tells me that will take far more time than I have." She shoulders past me into the bathroom, ignoring me completely. The water turns on, and I'm long forgotten as she hops into the spray and begins lathering soap into her hair.

I head wordlessly down to my room to take a shower *alone* and get ready for another day of work with Stardust, grateful I managed to bullshit my way through her interrogation.

One day, I'll tell her everything. I'll lay it all out and give her the chance to decide what she wants to do with me—a sadistic murderer driven to madness in my unrelenting quest for revenge. Until then, I'm savoring every single moment she offers me.

43

The Lamb

I'm ready to pass out and fall asleep on my desk by 3 p.m.

Bash kept me awake all night, and while I was a willing participant in his escapades, I'm certainly paying for that decision today.

My training session is being led by Grace, who is going over all the amazing things Lancaster Tech has to offer its employees. It's an enormous part of my job, knowing all these benefits, but it's insanely boring and hard to retain when the man they speak so highly of robbed me of all my rest the night before. I feel like if anyone had suspicions about me and Bash before, they're more than certain there's something going on between us now.

It doesn't help that he insisted on walking in with me this morning instead of letting me hang back for a few minutes the way I wanted to. He truly doesn't care what anyone thinks of him, and he fails to understand why I can't seem to take on the same attitude.

Probably because there's about a billion-dollar difference in our bank accounts, my guy.

He had to work through lunch, so I had a chance to check out the cafeteria and socialize with my new coworkers. Despite being seen as Bash's pet, everyone has been really nice. Most of my fears about taking this position have been pushed away as time goes on, and I feel like it's something I'm completely capable of. For the first time in my life, I feel like I might be okay. My resentment for my mother fades away with every hour I spend here, part of a community I probably wouldn't have otherwise been a part of without her push.

It's still sad to see my bank account so low from bailing her out, but soon that will be rectified as well.

"You look like your brain has been fried," Grace comments with a teasing smile. "Let's wrap it up for today and pick up where we left off tomorrow morning."

I stare at her disbelievingly, debating whether or not this is some sort of joke, or if she's really letting me leave early. At all my previous jobs, it was more likely that you'd be asked to stay later than your designated shift than to be released early simply because you looked tired. Rosie is the only exception to that, and my reasoning was a far cry from being kept awake all night by a man with a never-ending sex drive.

Once I confirm that she's serious, we each pack up our laptops and head out for the day. But as soon as I step into the main office area, I realize I have no idea where I'm supposed to go.

Do I tell Bash I'm leaving early? Am I expected to go to his apartment and wait for him? Does he even care?

I think my hotel room is still reserved. Though, I've always wanted to explore the streets of New York...

"Heading out?" Bash calls from the elevators beside Eliza, who stands with a large bag strapped across her shoulder.

When I nod at him hesitantly, he mumbles something to her, and then walks over to me, turning us away from the rest of the lobby so no one overhears. I take note of Eliza stiffening behind his back, though she keeps her mouth clamped shut.

"We're going to grab a coffee. You look like you could use one," he says with a wink.

"I'm okay," I tell him, ignoring his assistant's eyes burning holes into the side of my head. "I was just going to walk around for a bit. I've never been here before, and I've always wanted to see the square."

Bash's eyes crinkle in amusement, and he chuckles lightly, like there's another inside joke I'm missing out on.

"Time Square is still quite a ways away," he says, tilting his head at me pitifully. Then, his face falls as he looks around us, lowering his voice. "Are you sure you don't just want me to have Sterling take you back to my apartment so you can rest? I don't like the idea of you being alone…"

"Wrap it up, lover boy. We've got a meeting to get to," Eliza calls across the lobby, earning even more unwanted attention.

"I'll just stay close, then," I rush out, my tone a little too close to a question. I shoot him an irritated look, silently pleading with him not to make a big deal over this. I'm not asking for permission.

Hanging his head, he blows out a breath. I can tell he wants to insist that I go to his place, but Eliza yells another warning, jabbing her finger on the elevator button. When it immediately dings and the doors open, he lifts his head, those intense eyes pinning me to my spot with their silent warning.

"Stay close. Don't talk to anyone. I'll be back for you in an hour—two tops."

I nod, frustrated with myself for even allowing him to

think he can make these terms, and his gaze lingers on me for a moment too long before he turns away and jogs toward Eliza.

She hits the button to close the doors before I can join them, and I'm forced to wait for the next ride down.

Bash finds me window shopping at a jeweler a few blocks away from the office two hours later. I don't even want to think about how he managed to hunt me down so efficiently, though I wouldn't put it past him to be tracking my phone or something equally as unsettling.

I regretted my decision not to go back to his penthouse within twenty minutes, but I refused to admit defeat to him so quickly. Instead, I wandered around with absolutely no direction while the crisp autumn air nipped at my skin.

What was I thinking, anyway? I couldn't even afford a hotel room in this city. I sure as hell can't afford to shop in any of the stores, especially the ones surrounding blocks of office buildings filled with a bunch of rich people.

And no one here is very kind, either. It's no wonder he was bred into a psychopath.

"See anything that catches your eye?" he asks from beside me, gazing in at all the beautiful, expensive pieces.

I point to a golden, heart-shaped locket that's studded with diamonds. "My mother had something like that once. She kept a picture of mine and my sister's father in it and wore it every day," I find myself telling him.

Seeing it here in the window sparked the memory, and my mood instantly went downhill after that. "He died when we were young and she didn't keep many pictures of him around. She said she'd give it to me when I turned thirteen. But then one day, about two months before my birthday, she pawned it to pay the rent. I was so mad at her, we didn't speak for a week."

Sebastian isn't looking at the locket as I tell him my pathetic story. Instead, he's staring down at me with a look I've never seen him wear before, and I quickly turn away as soon as I notice it. I'm not sure I have the mental capacity to deal with another overbearing version of him right now.

But when a few seconds pass and his gaze lingers, I turn my head to ask what he's doing when he shifts his feet to fully face me, forcing me to do the same. I track his movements as he reaches into the pocket of his pants and pulls out a golden, heart-shaped locket. It's nearly identical to the one in the window, save for all the diamonds.

"This was my sister's," he explains, holding it up in front of his face with a look of pure misery.

"It's beautiful."

Those gorgeous green eyes, now a shade lighter than I've ever seen them, flick from the locket to me in a silent debate. Until, without warning, he grabs my shoulder and spins me around, swinging the necklace in front of my face so he can put it around my neck.

"I want you to have it."

Stepping away, I shake my head adamantly. "I can't take this from you, Bash."

But he pulls me back, clasping it together before I can protest any more. "I want it to go to someone who appreciates it as much as she did, and I can't do that. There's a picture of me and her inside. You can toss it and put your own in there."

His shoulders stiffen, and he looks off in the distance behind me, as if someone has just called his name. I turn to see what caught his attention, but no one is anywhere near us. When I turn back to face him, he shakes his head and looks back down at me, smiling.

"Thank you," I tell him genuinely. "I'll make sure it stays in good hands."

That same proud smile graces his lips as he grabs my hand into his and leads me down the street.

"Your sister meant a lot to you, but you never talk about her," I point out, hoping I'm not prying too much.

Ever since Eliza told me about her, a million questions have been burning in the back of my mind. Questions I've been too afraid to voice for fear of him shutting me down. This feels like the perfect opportunity to learn more about my mysterious man.

"Were you close?"

There's a brief pause when I think he's going to shut me down. "She meant everything to me," he admits, surprising me. "And we were nearly inseparable since birth. She was my best friend. I wish I could talk about her more; it just still hurts too much."

So, they were twins. That explains a lot.

"I'm sorry I brought it up, then."

"Don't be. You remind me of her. You're both extremely hard-headed."

I swat his arm, and he laughs lightly, chasing away the heaviness of the moment.

"I'd like for you to tell me more about her one day."

He turns his head to me, still smiling as a new twinkle appears in his eyes. "I'd love to."

We arrive at the front of our office building, and he releases my hand, signaling his driver toward us.

"Let's go home," he mumbles to me, then leads the way to the town car.

44

The Wolf

"You've milked this long enough," my father's stern, husky voice warns.

Stardust and I have managed to steer clear of him throughout the week, avoiding all his usual spots and routes whenever we ventured out into the city. She wants to explore New York. The problem is that she's blissfully ignorant to all the demons and monsters who lurk around every corner. The last thing I need is a weakness for him or anyone else in The Order to exploit in efforts to control me, and she's become my Achilles heel.

He found us on Thursday afternoon at a pizza stand one block from his penthouse. I knew it was risky to bring her there, but it was the middle of the day. I assumed he'd be off fucking anything that moved under the guise of work.

Our eyes locked across the street, and I knew I was fucked. Ushering Jovie back into Sterling's car and out of view, I nodded to him once in a silent confirmation that we would speak soon, then climbed in behind her.

He called me within the hour, insisting we set up lunch to 'catch up'. I opted to meet him at his office, where he immediately began spewing his bullshit.

"I've already made my answer clear," I say evenly, turning in my seat across the desk to face him fully so he can feel the difference between our sizes.

He's old and decrepit now. More so than he should be at his age. Life has punished him for all the horrible things he's done—both to himself and to others. I can't wait to watch his soul escape his body, only to be pulled into the deepest bowels of Hell, right where it belongs. I only hope Sienna will be able to get her hits in when he gets there.

"You sure about that?" He stamps out his cigarette into the full ashtray sitting between us, filling the air with a horrible chemical smell as the old butts begin to catch fire. "Last I checked, you've got a hell of a lot more to lose now than when you initially told me you weren't joining."

Jovie. Of course, he's going to threaten my little Stardust. She's the only thing he can hold against me anymore. He's so fucking predictable, it's almost too easy. But he's underestimating how far I'll go to protect her, especially after I failed so miserably at protecting Sienna from this fucked-up life.

Ignoring the possessive ache that's taken hold of my chest, I relax my shoulders and do my best to appear unaffected. "I won't be pressured into joining a secret society just to jack off the rapists and murderers who took my sister from me over some bad business deal. My answer is final."

"You think they targeted Sienna over a *bad business deal?*" A nefarious laugh erupts from his mouth, and I wait in silence while he recovers himself to explain further. "You've got it all wrong, son."

Son.

He truly has no idea the significance and meaning of that word. He's always treated his family like pawns. Little rewards he collected throughout his lifetime, just to say that he did it. Achievements unlocked, and then forgotten about in his quest for the next one.

That's why he allowed them to kill Sienna without a second thought. It's why he continuously betrays and cheats on my mother between whatever open legs he can find. And it's why he's never once attempted to connect with me outside of his weak commands to follow in his footsteps.

Initiating me into The Order is yet another item to check off his list of things that make him appear human. Decent.

He's never wanted me to follow after him. That would just run the risk of me being *better* than him. Because no matter what I do in this life, I will *always* top him. I'll always win for the simple fact that absolutely nothing he does in life is done honorably.

"Enlighten me."

"They didn't target her to get to me. I would have gladly given my life if that were the case." Shaking his head slowly, he levels me with a broken, stoney look that has my heart rate kicking up a notch.

And his next words send it to a skittering stop.

"They went after her to get to *you.*"

I don't bother hiding my confusion, too caught up in trying to make sense of what he's just told me to worry about masking my emotions in front of him.

"Your refusal to join The Order has cost us a lot more than you know," he continues, basking in my agony.

The room falls completely silent, and I swear he can hear the exact moment his words penetrate my psyche and my soul shatters into a million pieces.

I had no idea. I would never have put my family at risk if I knew how desperate they were to get me to join.

But *why?* That's the burning question that fuels my every move.

Why have they set their sights on me so pointedly?

Why is it so important to them that I join their cult that they would go this far to send me a message?

In my moment of weak desperation, I ignore every signal in my brain warning me against it, and I ask the enemy sitting before me.

"What do they want from me?"

I hate the way my voice breaks at the end. I can't stand the vulnerability it reveals to him. But I have to know, and if it means making sense of Sienna's death, I'll do it. I'm willing to go to any lengths to bring my sister justice and peace.

"You're putting me in a difficult position," he admits, changing the subject with a non answer, and the worried creases above his brow deepen as he considers his next words carefully. "They know you're the Serpent Slayer."

I can tell that's hard for him to admit, stuck between his duty to his brothers and his weak need to manipulate me. Though, I'm not surprised to hear that they know. Honestly, it took them long enough to put the pieces together. I practically signed the past three deaths off and led them straight to me, even without my usual tools at my disposal. For a group of Ivy League educated men running the corporate world, they sure aren't that sharp.

"Good," I say with a crazed smile, flashing my teeth. I feel out of my mind right now. "It's about time they start playing the game with me."

My father isn't impressed with my egotistical display. He slams his fists onto my desk, leaning forward so we're nose to nose.

"You have no idea what you're getting yourself wrapped up in, Sebastian. They'll destroy you. They don't even have to kill you to do it. Your business, your home, everyone you love. It'll all be at risk," he warns in a low rumble, and if I didn't know better, I'd think he actually cared.

I've prepared for this. The Order has the resources to take anyone down with very little effort, but they're also disgustingly predictable. I've been working up to this day for over a year, while they're still playing catch up to all my crimes against them. Even with my newfound information about Sienna's death. Everything I care about was protected before I even made my first kill.

Everything except Jovie, of course. She came out of nowhere and continues to fight me on every step. She's the only person I'm genuinely concerned about when they make their first move.

"I'm prepared," I assure him, shoving away all my doubts and refusing to be the first to break eye contact.

With a long, disappointed shake of his head, my father stands and backs away from his desk, adjusting his suit coat.

"You can't say I didn't warn you."

"What about you, *Dad?*" I spit the title sarcastically. I haven't referred to this man as anything but 'asshole' since I graduated high school and he tried to stop me from opening my own company by blocking my inheritance. "You've been fraternizing with your daughter's killers for a year now. When everything goes down, which side will you be standing on?"

He has the nerve to look taken aback, though the question quickly causes his mouth to tighten into a flat line as he considers his answer. I lean back in my chair, relaxing my arms on either side of me as I watch him war with what he should say.

The appropriate thing would be to support his son. To defend the accusation that he's remained close to the men who stole his most precious gift. To protect what's left of his flesh and blood. That's what a *father* would do, especially after already losing one of his children to the power-hungry psychos he associates with. But his need to appear successful and loyal to them fights against that. The two sides can no longer exist cohesively, and it's splitting him in half.

"You don't understand. I've taken an oath," he finally says, and those last four words serve as the final stroke of the ax hacking away at our relationship.

He'll choose them. Just like he did when they killed Sienna. Just like he has as they've bled my mother dry of everything she cares about.

"Then you'll go down with them."

I watch him struggle again, wanting to defend himself without giving too much away to his new enemy. The Order's oath is considered top secret until the night of initiation. As a prospective member, you're expected to jump through their satanic, humiliating hoops without ever truly knowing what you're signing up for until you're already in. It's ridiculous and archaic and while there're stories about men having their doubts at the last minute, no one has ever backed out for fear of the punishment that comes along with doing so.

So, he's correct in that aspect. I truly have no idea what he agreed to when joining their brotherhood. But I don't give a fuck. I'm going to take great pleasure in watching each and every one of them suffer as I burn their secret society to the ground. And my father just ensured that he'll be there screaming right alongside the rest of them.

45

The Lamb

My week in New York comes to an end far sooner than I'm ready. Despite my lack of rest each night, I'm able to pick up all the information I need to start doing my job on my own, and have managed to build a great support network within the company if I have any questions.

It's the oddest thing. I've brought myself to a place of being *completely okay,* all on my own. If you told me a year ago that any of this was possible, I'd probably laugh in your face. Even more, I handed over my entire savings and bailed my mother out along the way. That alone deserves some sort of reward after what she's done to me.

Of course, I would be remiss not to acknowledge Bash's hand in my path to independence. If it weren't for him, I'd still be slinging coffees at Old Soul and walking dogs for Mrs. Botless. My skepticism and hesitancy toward him are beginning to be overshadowed by dangerous admiration. He spews all this nonsense about the horrible things he's done, and while I'm perfectly aware of how he tends to blur the lines between inappropriateness and personal boundaries, I can't imagine a man who does so much good for the world is capable of anything as bad as he tries to say.

It's not like he moonlights as a serial killer, right? At least, not when he's busy stalking me at night…

"Don't go back," he begs on Sunday evening as I'm packing up the last of my things from my guest bedroom. I haven't stayed in here since that first night. Each night this week, Bash has carried me into his room and we've spent all hours of the night christening his bed together.

Where the rest of his living spaces are decorated in sterile whites and grays, his room is a bruised cave of black and blue. The most comfortable black duvet lays across his enormous bed, and the curtains remain pulled shut so no sunlight gets in until he opens them.

He grabs both of my hands up into his, cradling them delicately like I'm the most precious thing he's ever held. His brows are pulled together tighter than I've ever seen them, and his full lips are turned down into a sad pout.

My mind quickly adds this version of him to the ever-growing list.

"I have to."

"Says who?" he asks, his tone edging on desperate.

"It's my home."

It's a weak excuse. I know it is. But it's the only thing tethering me to the ground right now to stop me from floating away in the oblivious cloud with him after the week we've shared. The only thing stopping me from dropping everything and running away with the man who stands before me.

"Fuck that. Styx doesn't have anything good to offer you, Jovie, and you know it," he spits incredulously, his eyes wild. This is a man who isn't used to being denied what he wants.

"My family is there," I whisper brokenly.

Another paper-thin excuse. Halen and Kennedy would understand, and they're the only people who matter. Would it be such a tragedy if my mother couldn't ever find me again? If I dropped completely off of Gabe's radar?

"Stay with me," he repeats, a little more insistent. "I need you to stay with me. You aren't safe there alone."

"I don't know what that means," I admit honestly. The only real threat in my life was him, and I've fallen right into his clutches.

This monster standing before me is the reason my entire life has imploded, but I can't even muster up a shred of resentment toward him for it. I only resent myself for not seeing the warning signs before I fell for him.

He doesn't bother arguing. Instead, his gaze darkens and his voice drops.

"Stay," he commands.

"I can't stay with you Bash. I don't even fucking *know* you."

I'm convincing myself more than him. Taking the job, renting my home from him, staying in his penthouse—all of these were concessions I made against my better judgment. How far can I allow him to bend my will until my life is completely unrecognizable?

"That's bullshit. You know me better than anyone else."

I shake my head, rolling my lips into a firm line before I say something I don't mean. I can't fucking stand that he's ruining the amazing week we had with this silly argument.

"I'm not going to ask you again. If you leave today, the offer leaves with you."

My mouth goes slack, my eyes widening in complete shock that he's putting me in this difficult position.

"That's not fair. You gave me this job so I can work it remotely. *From Styx*. Because that's where my life is."

"Goddamnit, Jovie, this isn't about the fucking job. It's not about your shitty family. It's about protecting your life. It's about reaping the consequences for laying down all your inhibitions and allowing a monster like me around you."

"Protecting my life? Bash, you aren't making any sense. What the hell are you wrapped up in? What changed this week?"

"Everything," is all he says. His entire demeanor shifts back into the man I first met—the dangerous stalker who speaks in code.

And I realize, without a shadow of a doubt, that by tangling myself with him, I've stepped into a world I can't fully understand. One I have no self-governing over. No freedom.

If I stay with him, I'll become a prisoner.

46

The Wolf

"Just fucking go then, Stardust," I roar, pointing my finger toward the door behind her.

She peers at me with tear-stained cheeks and shakes her head, once again refusing to acknowledge the truth staring right back at her.

That death incarnate has claimed her as his own. That the version of me she's made up in her head is nothing but smoke and mirrors, her mind protecting her. That she's being given *one last shot* at running away before I take her down with me.

And there's no guarantee I won't chase her when she does.

When that doesn't seem to sink in for her, I double down, my tone more harsh and cruel than it ever has been with her.

"Want to know the truth?" I shout like a madman, my face reddening as my blood pressure rises, my body's way of warning me against what I'm about to do.

"Don't do this, Bash," Sienna warns from the corner of the room.

Skirting my eyes past her ghostly form, I snarl, then mentally will her away.

"I've hunted and tortured and killed for no other reason than I *wanted* to. I fucking *crave* my victim's blood like an addict craves their next hit. I *stalked* you, for fuck's sake. I've lived in your house beside you, stayed in your spare bedrooms for days at a time, and you had no idea. You can't just ignore that part of me to make this seem more viable."

"I'm not ignoring anything," she mumbles into her chest childishly, flinching at the sheer volume of my voice.

"Yes, you are. But it's time for you to face reality. It's time for you to decide if you're in this or not. because I'm not fucking around anymore."

I've been on edge since seeing my father, watching my back and double checking around every corner like some kind of paranoid freak. Her departure has loomed over our heads for the past two days, though each of us has had entirely different reasons to dread it. Now that the time is here, I'm scrambling, throwing out ultimatums and confessions like I've officially lost it.

I didn't want this. *Any of it.* There was no plan for me beyond killing the men who brutally murdered my sister. No future. I had tunnel vision, and it made me blind to her until she was standing right in front of me, offering an alternative I never envisioned. If she isn't willing to brave the storm with me, I'm not sure what I'll do.

"I don't know what you want from me. What am I supposed to say to all of this?" she cries out, the dam finally bursting as she releases the reaction I've been trying to pull from her all along.

What do I want from her? *Every-fucking-thing.*

I want her anger, her fear, her joy. I want to feel every

single emotion that flows through her because I've been so depraved in the past year, denying myself all of it. I just want to feel *alive* again, and she's the only one who does that for me. But my message is getting muddied.

I'm confusing her. I'm confusing *myself*.

Taking a long, deep breath, I pinch the bridge of my nose and gather my thoughts as she sobs uncontrollably, trying like hell to do the same.

"I *want* you to have a normal life, free of stalkers and murderers. You deserve peace, Stardust. The kind of peace I can't give you. But the selfish side of me wants to hold you in my grasp for as long as possible. To throw you in a cage and feed off your innocent soul because mine is so tattered, I can hardly recognize myself."

Stardust takes a brave, large step forward into the gap I've intentionally placed between us. "Fine. I want *you*, Bash. No matter the cost. But I can't just drop my whole life and never return. We can do this together the right way."

"We don't have time for all that..." I'm trying to convey the urgency of the situation without scaring her, but that feels impossible when my heart feels like it's going to burst out of my chest at any moment.

"What's the rush? Just tell me, Bash."

What's the rush? There's a society of dangerous men with nothing but resources at their disposal to come after her and destroy her with zero consequences.

But telling her that will only make her want to do something stupid, like go to the police. I can't have that. "I had a plan, and it didn't include you in it. The only way I can keep you safe anymore is by having you beside me."

It's not enough. I can tell by the stubborn set of her jaw and her stiffened stance that she won't be cooperating. Not tonight. Not anytime soon.

"I'm going home. We'll figure out a way to make this work."

"I'm afraid it'll be too late." With that, I turn my back to her and walk out of the room, locking myself in my office to cool off before I do something crazy like tie her up.

When I've finally cooled down and am ready to speak rationally, I climb back up the stairs to find her room empty.

She's gone.

Instead of following her to Styx the way every fiber of my being is itching to do, I decide its best to watch my enemy instead. If I can't keep her safely tucked under my wing, then I'll just have to kill every threat that stands against her.

47

The Lamb

A LOUD BANGING on my front door startles me, sending my fresh plate of chicken nuggets flying all around the kitchen floor. On instinct, I look out the sliding glass doors for Bash, unsurprised to find nothing but the open grass and cold lake.

He hasn't been back since I refused to stay in New York with him. Since he made his crazy confessions. It has taken me days to sort out the things he admitted to, and every time the puzzle pieces lock into place, I find myself spiraling a little further.

All the creaks and groans I grew so used to seem to have disappeared, further digging the knife of his admissions and confusing me. Were they all him? Was I ignorantly living in this home while a stranger coexisted down the hall?

For some reason, that feels worse than him being a murderer. It's more personal. *Violating.*

In all the time Bash was around, I never felt unsafe with him. Not in a way that made me think he would take my life.

If I'm being honest, I don't think my brain is fully comprehending that he's capable of such ugly things. I'm still too fragile to obsess over that part yet and connect the dots. It's like there's a block against it, protecting me from a full-blown mental breakdown. Though, I know the time will come where I have to.

We've each remained firmly planted in our stubborn argument, neither one willing to admit we're wrong or reach out. He appears to be giving me space after his ridiculous ultimatum. It's odd how much I grew used to having him around, lurking in the shadows. If I didn't receive emails from him daily for work, I might even miss my stalker.

But he would never knock, especially like that.

Once my heart returns back into my chest, I round the corner of the kitchen just in time for my visitor to begin assaulting the door again.

"I'm coming!" I yell, glancing out the front window to catch a peek at who it might be.

Everything stops when I see Gabe's face peering back at me through the glass. He smiles at my alarmed reaction, pointing to the door and mouthing for me to let him in.

In all the chaos of Bash, I nearly forgot about Gabe.

There's a long moment when I hesitate behind the steel door, considering my options. I could refuse to open it. He would probably make a scene, but it'd be worth it to keep him out of my space. Or, I could invite him inside to hear whatever he has to say that he deems worthy of trampling over every single boundary I've placed against him.

He doesn't deserve that courtesy from me, but I know he expects it, nonetheless.

"Come on, Jo Jo. Open up," the voice of my nightmares shouts from the other side of the door, reminding me that he and my mother shared the same, ridiculous nickname for me. I'm forced to make a decision.

What can he really do to me that he hasn't already tried? That I haven't already survived?

Taking one last moment to gather myself, I suck in the biggest breath I can muster before swinging open the door and allowing Gabe to come in and steal it from me.

"How did you find out where I live?" I ask, not even bothering with any sort of polite greeting.

"It's not hard to look people up these days," he replies condescendingly, his eyes roaming over my body.

When I don't make any moves to open the door farther and let him in, he gestures behind me.

"Aren't you going to invite me inside to see your new place?"

No. I want to say. I don't want any part of him infecting my safe space after the months it took for me to build it out of the rubble he created of my life.

"I'm busy, Gabe." Leaning my hip against the door jamb, I block him off from the entrance.

"It'll only take a minute. I know you don't have to work today…" His tone is confident and testing. He knows he's got me caught in his net. Part of the game is catching me in a lie, so he can turn around and use it against me.

I want to ask him how he could possibly know that. Why did he feel the need to look up my address after I made it clear that I didn't want to speak to him by ignoring his countless threatening calls and text messages? What is it about me that gives him the impression he has any power over my life anymore? And when will his iron grip on me loosen?

"Just let me in," he urges again, his voice so low, it almost comes out as a growl.

With a relenting sigh, I swing the door open in defeat, stepping out of the way so he can push past me triumphantly, just like he always does.

I follow behind as he walks himself through my sacred space, and I feel like having his eyes brush against all my things is somehow sullying them forever. Like a child who walks through an art gallery and can't resist running his grimy, sticky hands over all the preserved paintings, Gabe takes his time violating my home. And as the submissive little girl he's trained me to be, I watch each and every one of his reactions as he absorbs the things that matter most to me, unable to stop the pangs of hurt when his eyes flit over them dismissively, or his lip curls up in disgust. It's like he knows precisely which things to do in order to get a reaction out of me.

"So, this is where you've been hiding out all this time." His eyes pause at the overripe fig sitting in the middle of my dining table, then continue with their ruthless scan, deeming it insignificant.

"It's cute," he offers patronizingly with a sarcastic lilt in his voice.

Gabe leads us straight back to my family room, and I can't decide if the move was intentional because he somehow already knew the layout of my home before coming here, or if the flow of the house brought him here naturally. Either way, he stops in front of the couch, and I walk past him in an attempt to block him from moving any farther, into my bedroom.

That's my first mistake.

48

The Lamb

"I've been trying to get a hold of you again," Gabe says in an eerily even tone. At first glance, he appears relaxed and non-confrontational, but I know better than to believe that.

His eyes are a little darker than usual, his lips turned down the slightest bit. Even if I wasn't trained to notice all the little micro expressions to avoid riling him up, his anger would be glaringly obvious in the forward set of his jaw and flared nostrils, as if he needs to make more space so he can breathe through his fury.

"I've been busy," I reply in a calm, flippant voice, refusing to allow my fear to take hold of me. The fear is his favorite part of this game we play.

How is it that Bash is the murderer, but Gabe makes me feel more on edge?

He chuckles humorlessly, rolling his neck from side to side in a dramatic display of irritation at my attitude. I take the opportunity to map out an escape, though he's managed to make that nearly impossible with his burly figure blocking the only path to any of my exits.

"Ah, yes. With your shiny new job…"

Nodding, I mumble a noncommittal, "Something like that."

There's a weighted moment when he just stares at me, head tilted and a creepy, fake smile planted on his lips that doesn't reach his eyes. I fight the urge to cower under his watchful glare, refusing to break eye contact. Finally, after what feels like forever, he sucks in a breath and drops his gaze to my chest.

"Where is the man you've got living here, Jovie?" he questions, unbridled jealousy lacing his words.

I still. There's no way he knows about Bash. Not unless they've somehow run into each other outside. But Bash would have mentioned that to me. He's too curious not to.

"What man?" I pry, careful not to let my expressions give anything away more than they may already have.

"The one shacked up in your spare bedroom." Gabe tilts his head backward, toward the bedrooms I never touch, and I release a relieved breath. "I can tell a man is sleeping there. It reeks of cologne."

I've lived in your house beside you, stayed in your spare bedrooms for days at a time, and you had no idea.

Bash wasn't lying before. He really was staying in my house. Despite the open admission, there was still a part of me that wanted to deny it. But Gabe somehow knew…

He doesn't know about Bash, specifically. He's just fishing. Trying to frame me for a crime so he can punish me for it later.

But there is no crime. And he's not my judge and jury. I need to remember that.

"I haven't shown you my spare bedroom, Gabe." *So how would you know what it smells like, you creep?*

My question from before about him knowing the layout of my house has been answered. Every feeling I should have had about Bash watching me comes creeping in tenfold at the idea of slimy Gabe doing it.

In true Gabe fashion, he doesn't own up to anything that has my stomach turned upside down.

"Let's just make this easy for both of us. You've thrown your little fit and had all your fun, now it's time to come back home."

Home. What an odd way for him to describe the prison he created for me in the years that we were together? The place I literally died to get out of. There's no way in hell I'm going back there. Not without a fight.

"I *am* home, Gabe," I say in the kindest way I can muster.

It's not as convincing as I hoped and my voice wavered on his name, but I doubt he'll see past his own rage at my words to notice. I just need to be careful not to rile him up when he's got this crazed look in his eyes.

"I think you should leave."

Shaking his head, he levels me with an evil glare. "I'm not leaving without you, baby," he rasps.

"Well then, I'll have to call the police on you for intruding." I hold up my phone to punctuate the threat.

But Gabe doesn't even flinch. His brows come together in an angry scowl as he challenges, "Go ahead. Let's see who they believe."

And there it is. All his work is paying off. I know now for a fact that he won't go away without a fight. He'll do everything in his power to get me back to that house with him—if that's even really where he wants to take me—including destroying my reputation more than he already has to convince the world I'm the bad guy and he's just doing his best to deal with my insanity.

That's what he told the people in Sunnybrook. That's

what he told the hospital staff when he came rushing in like the worried, dutiful boyfriend after they brought me back to life. The most terrifying part was that they all believed every lie he spun for them. No one had any idea that *he* was my cause of death, not me.

"You know, I meet a lot of people in my new job. A lot of rich bankers from the city. People who know the market and can give my clients a leg up. It's a small world, really."

He shifts on his feet, opening the gap even farther. "Imagine my surprise when one of those men comes to me with a proposition… a shit ton of money in exchange for my mousey little ex-girlfriend."

I squint my eyes at him, completely lost. What would some investment banker from New York want with me?

"At first, I wasn't going to do it. It felt like a betrayal to myself if I just handed you over. You belong to me, afterall. But then I realized: what if I took my money, I took my girl, and we both just disappeared? What could they really do?"

He chortles, proud of this little plan he's concocted. Too bad I'm not going anywhere with him.

"So that's what we're gonna do. I know you're mad about Sunnybrook, but it's time to get over that and come back to me. We can start a new life together and forget about all this."

Like a trapped animal, I start to feel like the walls are closing in on me. Every possible scenario runs through my mind as I consider what the best option is. Kindness isn't getting me anywhere. My nerves feel like electrical wires that have been splintered, the current still jumping out of them in every direction. There's no way I'll be able to stave off the panic for much longer.

My only choice is to run. I know it's the most realistic chance at survival, especially with the wild look in Gabe's eyes telling me that if he gets to me, I won't be coming out alive again. This is an attempt to clean up his own mess, and he doesn't plan on failing.

Before trepidation can infect my muscles and slow me down, I crouch into a ball and shoot through the small gap on his left, between him and the couch. I overshoot the space a tiny bit, bouncing off the couch and into him, but it ends up working out in my favor. Gabe is thrown against the wall and a burst of profanities escape his lips as he loses his footing from my abrupt departure. Luckily, I'm able to recover faster than he is.

I ricochet into the dining room, the sliding glass doors in clear view. Once I'm outside without any obstacles, I know I've got the endurance to outrun him. Gabe has always only focused on building muscle mass. It's turned him into a heavy, slow-moving boulder.

I'm so fucking close.

My hand reaches for the handle, when I'm stopped in my tracks by his arm wrapped around my stomach and yanked away. Gabe throws me to the ground on my back like a sack of potatoes, and all my breath leaves my lungs in one big *whoosh* from the impact. His face appears over me as his foot crushes my abdomen, and I struggle to take in oxygen.

"You know better than to run, Jovie," he chastises breathily. "I've always been stronger."

To prove his point, he jams his foot against my ribs. I swear I can hear one crack as he does it, and then he chuckles. He thinks he's crippled me enough with that to loosen his hold and gaze around the room, considering his next move.

But I won't lose to him again. I won't die by his hand a second time.

I gather every ounce of strength I can muster, refusing to succumb to the pain radiating from my back and side, and use it to grab his ankle and shove him off of me. The motion takes him completely off guard again, sending him straight to the floor beside me with a loud roar and a thundering thump. Rolling away, I go to climb to my feet, wincing when my rib screams in agony at the pressure.

I'm so pissed at myself for not taking more self-defense classes when I wanted to. For not fighting harder when it mattered and proving to him that I'm not some ragdoll for him to throw around. What the hell have I been doing this whole time that was so important? Why did I ever allow myself to get so complacent? What's the point of being given a second chance at life when I'm just wasting away?

Stop.

I've got to stop thinking this way. I'll never survive.

I'm only able to take half-breaths, and my lungs feel like sad, deflating balloons, but I push myself to run across the house toward the front door. I hardly make it three steps, when a hand wraps around my ankle and swipes me off my feet.

I go down hard and fast. My elbows bounce off the hardwood floor and my nose takes a direct hit, nearly knocking me unconscious. I can hardly see straight through the stars in my eyes when Gabe gets back up and sends his foot flying into my side.

"Stupid bitch."

He kicks again. And again. Then he leans over and slams his fists into my back. Then my legs. Then, he lands a few blows into the back of my head.

I cry out in agonizing pain, my face still shoved against the floor in the puddle of blood pouring from my mouth and nose. My head feels like it weighs a thousand pounds. I can hardly hold it up enough to breathe, so I turn to rest on my cheek instead as my body takes the beating. Blood is gushing onto the floor and into my mouth, making the few shallow breaths that I can take wet and soggy.

I'm about to give up. There's no way I can break away

from him for a third time in this condition. Especially when he's hardly taken any hits and has likely broken nearly every bone in my midsection.

He's stopped hitting me now. I'm wading in and out of consciousness, losing track of time. I have no idea where he went, but I don't feel his presence above me anymore. He must assume I'm knocked out. Or dead. I can't even fathom what he'll do to me now.

Death calls to me with her familiar, slow lullaby. She sounds so inviting, so peaceful. I want to drift away and escape all this pain and suffering. She agreed to give me a second chance, but it's only made me even more sure that this is what I want. To be with her…

I *need* this.

Just as I'm about to reach out and touch my old friend, a blur of blonde hair flashes in front of my eyes, forcing me to turn and focus my eyes above.

The blur appears again, faster this time. As if it's urging me to see something… to *do* something. Death's song fades farther away, and I can hear Gabe's heavy footsteps trudging up and down the hall. I could swear a woman yells something above my head, snapping my attention back to the counter, where I can now see my butcher block is sitting right on the edge. I blink at it slowly.

That's weird. I don't remember moving it there. It's always lived by the stove.

Gabe must finish whatever he's doing down the hall, because I hear his footsteps coming closer again. The feminine voice has become so shrill, it's turned into a high-pitched ringing in my ears.

She's urging me to grab a knife. I've put that much together in my foggy mind. But how the hell am I supposed to do that? Every breath takes concentrated effort.

I have to make a decision. Death's song has become so

drowned out by the ringing, I can hardly hear it anymore. Gabe must have turned back again. He's rummaging through my linen closet for something—probably a sheet to wrap my dead body up in.

In one last feeble, begrudging attempt at surviving, I use all my strength to throw my arm up toward the counter to grab a knife.

But it's at least six inches too short to reach the block.

"Fuck," I breathe out, positive I'm going to die now.

But what happens when Death doesn't come back to guide me? Where do I go then?

The ringing gets louder again and the flash of blonde hair bustles past me with a quick, frantic energy.

She wants me to try again.

"I can't," I wheeze out brokenly.

Angrily.

She chased Death away, and now I'm all alone.

The ringing somehow becomes even louder. As if she's arguing with me, provoking me.

Fine.

If it will put an end to this incessant ringing and bring Death's siren song back, I'll try again. Just to prove that I can't.

The linen closet door slams shut at the end of the hall, and I know I've only got seconds before he breaks past the wall and sees me alive. Using the blood pooled beneath me to my advantage, I slide my chest across the floor to get closer to the side of the cabinet. With everything I have to give, I jam my arm back into the air. And by some strange, inconceivable miracle, my fingers graze the counter and wrap around a cold, metallic blade.

The ringing turns into a satisfied hum when I pull the knife down to the floor with me. I'm holding the hilt so tight, my fingers are going numb. A burst of adrenaline has flooded into my veins, taking up the empty space left behind by my lack of blood. Gabe rounds the corner and, just as I predicted, he's holding a dark gray sheet. Just the right shade to hide the blood that would blossom through the fabric and incriminate him.

He leaves a wide berth around my body, carelessly throwing the sheet onto the floor beside me. My head is awkwardly turned in the opposite direction, feeding into the illusion that I'm more than half-dead, but I can feel his eyes grazing over me like talons. He *harrumphs* smugly, as if he's proud of his work.

Fucking bastard. Doesn't even feel any remorse for what he's done.

I want to lash out and stab him right now, but I know my body can't exert the effort it would take to reach that far. Instead, I have to lie as still as possible and wait for the perfect time—for him to come to me—hoping the blade is hidden far enough beneath me until then. I'm relying heavily on stupid luck, playing the unattainable game when my head is swimming, blood and adrenaline swirling around like the most toxic mix of fear and delusion. But any time I allow any negative thoughts to infiltrate my headspace, the ringing in my ears becomes more shrill, as if my guardian angel is clearing them before they take root inside my brain.

What is Gabe doing, anyway? He's been standing over me quietly for a suspiciously long time.

Wait a second.

The subtle, deep groan he releases from his chest vibrates against the floor beneath me.

Is that… *is he…?*

Oh, God. The sadistic asshole is jacking off over me. Over what he thinks is my dead corpse.

I'm going to be sick.

Well, if I had any doubt about stabbing him before, it's

washed away with every grotesque grunt he's released through this entire psychopathic display.

I know he's finished when I hear the elastic waistband of his sweats snap back into place. His steps approach me again—probably to clean his jizz off his hands in my kitchen sink, the sick fucker—and I know I'm about to get my one and only shot.

Lucky for me, the universe is on my side for once. Gabe makes the grave mistake of stepping over me, and I watch with excited anticipation as the stars align perfectly, and I get a clear shot of his crotch.

Throwing every ounce of hate, betrayal, hurt, and anger that I have for this sad excuse of a man, I spin onto my back just as he's got his first leg over me, effectively trapping him in his spot. Then, without an ounce of hesitation, I jam the knife straight up.

Right into his dick.

Check. Mate.

Gabe roars, his voice reverberating off every surface in the house and amplifying against my ears. His cum-soaked hands grab at the knife that's still lodged inside of him, but they're too slippery to get a good grip. Blood is gushing out of the wound and falling directly on my stomach. He doesn't even acknowledge that I'm here anymore. He collapses onto his knees, then rolls onto his back, still releasing a series of agonizing screams that mine couldn't even compete with.

What a spineless bastard?

His pain has somehow staved off my own, sending another bolt of adrenaline through my veins. With slow, weighted movements, I climb up to my knees and peer down at him. His eyes are squeezed shut, his face screwed into a broken, tormented expression.

Men are so weak. Women are capable of enduring days of labor pains, then pushing entire human beings out of their bodies, nearly splitting themselves in half in the process. We shed the linings of whole-ass organs and bleed quarts of blood every month, yet we're still expected to do the same jobs as men during that time. *For less money*, I might add.

And here he is, crying because of a little cut to his manhood.

Pathetic.

The blonde blur is twirling laps around me, her high-pitched noises resembling something more akin to giggling than the screaming she was torturing me with earlier. If I catch sight of her long enough, I can almost make out her feminine form, but it's like she's going out of her way to ensure I don't get more than half a second to see her.

As if my hands are moving on their own, they reach out for the knife, magnetized to it. The girl laughs louder as I pull the knife out, inch by torturous inch, pulling even louder screams from Gabe's mouth.

I should be running from him. His hands are fully functioning, and with this injury, he'd never catch up to me. But my body is far more beaten than my mind is allowing me to comprehend. Each breath feels like swallowing nails, and I can feel one of my ribs bent inward, probably scraping against some vital organ and causing severe internal bleeding.

If I ran, I wouldn't make it far enough to find help. Not way out here.

I don't even know where my phone is. My memory of everything before Gabe's attack feels blurry, the thoughts swirling in the same way as the ghostly girl, close but just out of reach.

I'm going to die here.

I've already resigned myself to the fact. So I might as well fight.

Gabe's eyes grow impossibly wide as I hold the knife

above him, his limbs paralyzed in fear. Without a second thought, I drop my hands and jam the knife into his neck. This time, there's no screaming. Instead, blood pours out of the wound, dropping down the side of his mouth as he makes distorted gurgling sounds.

Something about the sight breaks an integral piece inside of me. It severs a part of my conscious, and I turn into an raging beast.

Perhaps this is the sweet addictions my mystery man feels when he kills. Maybe we're more alike than I thought.

My hands lift again, then dig the knife back in. Repeatedly. In his stomach, his face, his arms, his legs. Everywhere. More times than I can even track. Not that I want to track. I don't care if there's nothing left of this shell of a human being. It still wouldn't be enough of a punishment for what he's done to me in all the years I've known him.

Only when there's nothing left lying beneath me but an unrecognizable, bloodied corpse, I drop the knife and fall back onto the floor. Death's song returns and, this time, the blonde girl doesn't bother chasing her away.

49

The Wolf

I'M ABOUT to dig my blade into Charles's thigh for the third time when Sienna appears behind him, eyes wide and mouth open in pure panic. The horrified scream that erupts from Charles's mouth as my knife assaults him drowns out whatever Sienna is trying to say, stealing away any satisfactions I may have gotten from his agony.

I'm instantly infuriated with her for interrupting this cathartic moment. I'm so close to getting him to admit the list of names working against me in The Order, and the last thing I need is to have her here muddling it all up. She knows better than to appear beside me now.

"What do you want?" I grind out once the asshole before me settles down his sobbing enough for me to speak.

He doesn't bother lifting his head to respond to me, though I doubt he can hear anything after the way he's been shrieking for the past hour. My ears are still ringing from the sheer volumes he was able to reach as his broken voice echoed off the metal walls of the shipping container I dragged him into. If I attacked him in his apartment like I originally planned, we'd definitely have been caught.

"She's in trouble," Sienna rushes out, almost seeming out of breath.

That's new. I didn't even know she has breath.

"Who's in trouble?" I push, buying time. I already know who. But I'm confused about why Sienna would be here telling me. She hates Stardust.

Charles finally raises his slumped head enough to shoot me a questioning glare, but I ignore it. I don't have to explain that I'm speaking to my dead sister. He'll be joining her soon enough.

"Jovie." Her appearance flickers for a moment, then evens out. "You have to get to her. The ex is there."

"Ah, I imagine there's trouble in paradise," the decrepit man before me says, a wicked smile spreading across his bloody lips.

"Shut the fuck up," I bark at him.

"You'll be too late. She's already as good as dead."

Pulling my hair in every direction, I spin in place, completely flustered. I don't know what the fuck is going on with Sienna, or why she's speaking in fragmented sentences, but her panic is a living, breathing thing that seems to steal all the oxygen out of the room.

And what the fuck is Charles mumbling about? How could he know what Sienna said?

I knew the ex was going to be a problem. I let him slip through the cracks, too distracted with everything else.

My hands are working faster than my mind, quickly sliding every knife into its corresponding pocket of my roll bag. I'm using disinfecting wipes to clean the ones coated in blood, but I've got to remember to double back and properly wash them when I get home.

Speaking of blood...

Swinging my gaze back over to Charles, I realize I've still got an audience to witness my downfall. Blood dribbles out of the slices I've made into his paling skin—on his legs, arms, and face. I've left his entire torso for last. He looks depleted, but his eyes are still full of stubborn life that I planned to drain out of him slowly and painfully. *Fuck.* I really wanted to savor this one, and now I'm stuck rushing through yet another kill for my little Stardust.

I'm going to make up for this with her piece of shit ex.

"Sorry, Chuck," I begin in a surprisingly even tone, because I know how much he hates being called that. "I have to *cut* our little meeting short."

Smirking at my punny joke, I slide my largest knife from the roll and hold it up while Chuck begins frantically fighting against his restraints again, as if he'll somehow be able to break free. He's sputtering out a string of curses and empty threats, which turn to promises and guarantees that he'll never be able to fulfill in the remainder of his useless life.

"Tell me who you've been working with, and I'll let you go," I offer, dropping the hand with the knife to my side.

Charles nods, straightening himself in his chair, as if that would give him any shred of dignity after the display he just put on. He takes a few deep breaths, and I roll my eyes at him, stepping forward with the knife raised. My girl needs me, and this prick is playing games.

"It's not as simple as you think. There're quite a few people–"

"Names, Chuck," I interrupt with a growl. "You better start listing names in the next three fucking seconds, or this knife is going straight through your heart."

"You father. Your grandfather. They tried to screw Andrew Black and Greyson Brower over with their investments. They knew there was an initiation coming up, so they threw her name in at the last second. Logan didn't want to do it, but he had no choice. They wanted to prove a point to your family not to cross them."

So all that bullshit my father spewed about them targeting me was a lie.

"Who dropped the charges?"

"The board told your dad he had to drop them, or risk being removed and punished."

It's exactly what I expected, but it still stings to hear that my own father and grandfather sacrificed Sienna for their own gain.

My father knew all along.

He fucking knew they had his daughter killed, and he let them get away with it like the coward that he is instead of giving her the justice she deserved.

"They're going after your little girlfriend next. She'll be dead before you get there."

The wet crack of my knife piercing through the skin and bones of Charles's chest fills the air beside his surprised grunt before his last words find their way into my ears and embed themselves into my brain. I almost feel bad for the sorry asshole. He thought he was going to have a shot at walking out of here. Instead, I channeled every ounce of anger I have into that one shot, tearing through him with more force than necessary.

But he was no better than my father. He knew what happened and didn't say a word, just like the rest of them. He let his own son kill my sister over a bad deal. Over fucking *money*—the root of every evil there is.

Ripping the knife out of his slumped body, I quickly wipe his fresh, crimson blood off and put it back into its spot, then roll the sheath of knives up to tuck it into my back pocket. I scan the small space, taking inventory of what's left for me to do. I've covered each surface with plastic and taken every effort I could think of not to leave any trace of DNA behind, but I can never be too sure. I thought I'd have more time.

I planned to scrub it all down and remove his body from the site so no one came across it, effectively erasing any trace of myself here. Instead, I'm pouring the can of gasoline I brought as a precaution onto every surface, taking great care in soaking the still-warm body that sits in the middle of the shipping crate.

Sienna appears again beside me, urgency burning in her eyes.

"You need to hurry, Bash," she screeches.

I strip down to my boxers and throw the blood-soaked, black clothes into the crate, then toss the gas can on top of them.

"I'm fucking trying here. Tell me what's going on."

"He's at the house. He wants to kill her. I can't keep her safe, Bash. She needs you."

He wants to kill her.

They're going after your girlfriend.

She'll be dead before you get there.

Those fucking bastards. They found Stardust.

Tugging a box of matches from my oversized boot, I light one and toss it into the metal container, running backwards as the tiny flicker immediately ignites into a sea of flames before me.

I'm running through a dark maze of containers, careful to stay away from any major aisleways that I already noted cameras in. Sienna has disappeared again, but I didn't expect her to come along for this part. She told me enough to get my blood boiling hotter than the quickly growing fire blazing behind me. Alarms begin to sound off all around the shipyard, and I have to stop a few times as employees rush toward the container I just left on their utility carts. Hopefully, Charles's body is mostly incinerated before they can control the fire, or I might face the serious risk of being caught.

I'm tripping on the toes of the boots I wore, irritated strings of curses leaving my lips every time I stumble. They're two sizes too big in case anyone comes across my tracks and tries to pin me down based on my shoe size, though that won't matter when they catch me falling on my ass. My knees and palms are getting scraped up from constantly catching myself in the gravel, but I can't stop.

I thought I was being so careful with this one. I planned everything out down to the second. Everything except Stardust.

This is why having her around is such a fucking risk.

A burner vehicle I purchased for cash yesterday sits at the entrance of the shipping yard in the same spot I left it in earlier. I paid one of the shipyard attendants to use his cart for an hour, and then shoved Charles in the back of it to avoid leading any trace of him back to the car. I'll ditch this one in a parking garage that doesn't use cameras down the street, where I left my own vehicle and a change of clothes. Then, it's about an hour before I can make it to Styx—forty-five minutes, if I really push it. It'll be a miracle if I don't want to catch any police attention with Charles's blood splattered all over me.

I try to summon Sienna once I'm on the expressway, but she doesn't appear. It only feeds my panic, and the drive turns into a blur of lights and cars as I race to help my little Stardust, mentally planning for every scenario.

50

The Wolf

The house is eerily quiet.

That's the first thing I notice.

The front door is closed, and everything appears to be normal from the outside, but I can feel the staunching stillness as soon as I pull into the driveway. Sienna appears beside me on the front porch, a solemn look on her face as I twist the knob and find that it's unlocked.

Stardust never leaves her doors unlocked.

"I did everything I could think to do, Bash," she says, and her words sound more like an apology than an explanation.

An apology for doing everything she could, but still not doing *enough.*

I'm stuck on that thought when I open the door and the messy front room comes into view. My eyes land on every imperfection and piece that's out of place. I've memorized this house over the last few months—taken note of each menial detail. And all of it is shifted. As if someone picked up the house and gave it a good shake before setting it back down again.

My feet take me through the rooms in search of her. The kitchen is even messier than the front room, and the dining table and chairs that my mother and Sienna picked out have been smashed to pieces.

That's where I find them.

Jovie's lifeless body lies beside the coward who attacked her, their blood pooled beneath them in a way that makes it impossible for me to locate the source of it. He's a bloody, mangled mess, and she has dried blood matted in too many spots for me to count.

Both of them have clearly put up a fight. I only hope she has a little more left in her than he does.

I walk to her side, crouching to press my fingers against her neck and check for a pulse.

It's hardly there—the weak, thrumming beat of life still pumping through her veins. But it's enough to have me blowing out a breath and sending a prayer of gratitude up to the imaginary man up above. Quickly pulling my phone out of my pocket, I dial the number and hold it up to my ear, lightly grazing my knuckles against Stardust's cheek.

"911, what's your emergency," the operator's feminine voice answers after one ring.

"My girlfriend has been attacked in her home. She's hardly breathing. We need an ambulance as soon as possible," I explain in a detached, low tone.

The panic wreaking havoc on my chest doesn't infect my speaking at all, and I'm sure the operator is taken off guard by my peaceful demeanor.

This is just the calm before the storm.

I recite the address to the operator, answer a few of her questions, and then hang up. I want a few moments alone with Stardust before the chaos begins. I want a chance to make sure her attacker is truly dead, because there's no way in hell I'm allowing another asshole with a god complex to hurt someone I love and get away with it.

Someone I love.

The intrusive thought gives me pause. I shove it down before it can grow legs and take off.

"Jovie, baby," I begin, leaning forward so my lips are right against her ear.

My hand carefully wraps around her upper arm, giving it a reassuring squeeze so she knows I'm right beside her, but not enough to cause her any pain. I don't want to move her too much and disrupt her injuries before the medics get here.

"Hold on for a few more minutes. I need you to stay strong until the ambulance comes and fixes you up. Can you do that for me?"

Tears roll down my cheeks as her lungs make a horrible wheezing noise, desperate for oxygen that can't seem to make its way through her windpipes.

"I can't lose you, Stardust," I go on. "I refuse to let you go without me."

Sienna appears behind me, and while I can't feel her touch, I know she's placed her hand along my shoulder in a show of support. Whatever she witnessed here—whatever she did to stop it—it's taken a toll on her.

There's a pounding on the door before it's thrust open and heavy footsteps enter the house. I call out to them, letting them know where to go before I lean forward and place a soft kiss on Stardust's cheek, and then back away from her to allow them access.

The police arrive a few moments later, and then a fire truck pulls in, filling the yard with emergency vehicles and flashing lights. They try asking me questions, but I can't give them any answers. Sienna is beside me the entire time, spouting out replies to their line of questioning. Of course,

I'm the only one who can hear her, and I'm not in a position to offer what she's saying without negating my entire argument that I wasn't here until I called them in.

Once they're gone and both bodies have been cleaned up from the floor—hers to be taken to the hospital and his to be taken to the morgue—I stand in the middle of the kitchen and take the scene in. It's not my first time standing in puddles of blood, surrounded by remnants of chaos and struggle. But this is the only time it's ever taken a toll on me mentally.

Crouching down to the spot I found Stardust lying in less than an hour ago, I swipe my finger through the blood, caking it with the thick chunks that have almost fully dried out.

I could lose her.

It would be my fault, too. I knew she wasn't safe in Styx after being seen with me in New York. I should have done more to get her to stay with me. I should have tied her up and forced her. I should have set my ego aside, ignored the sting that came with her rejection, and come back to Styx to make sure she was still okay.

All of this is my fault, and I don't fucking know how to fix it.

Being in her life has gotten her attacked. Staying away made her an easy target.

What do I do now?

51

The Lamb

A SYMPHONY of voices surrounds me, hands pushing and pulling against multiple spots on my body.

The pain is so intense, it cancels itself out. My lungs hurt worse than my head, which hurts worse than my legs. I've fallen into a constant state of agony—a new baseline for pain that buzzes into numbness.

There's someone standing over me, but I can't ask what's going on through the tube stuck down my throat.

Each thought flutters in, hardly landing before the next one comes and chases it away.

I'm tired. So, so tired.

It's time to rest.

Just as the idea flows into my brain, Death's lullaby begins softly playing in my ears.

I'm so happy she's back…

The music grows louder, the beat thrumming loudly in my ears as something pushes against my chest, crushing me.

Instead of focusing on the affliction, I follow the music as it grows louder and louder.

All my pain slowly disappears, flying away like grains of sand.

And for once, I find peace.

52

The Wolf

Stardust is gone.

I had no idea what to do when they took her, so I followed the ambulance to the hospital and planted myself in the waiting room, hopeful that the blood splattered across my skin would be mistaken as hers and not my recent victim's.

The pained, regretful look the doctor wore as he delivered the news to me in a private waiting room after only a half hour in surgery is still etched into my brain. It replays over and over—a permanent fixture on my subconscious.

They should have done more.

They should have tried harder to save her.

There had to have been something else they could have tried.

They hardly gave her a chance.

There were so many things I wanted to scream into the doctor's face at that moment, but I held it all in.

I've killed over a dozen people now with my bare hands with hardly a second thought, but it's her blood that has stained my soul for all of eternity. It's her life that has stolen away my purpose. If I could have given mine to spare her, I would have done it in a heartbeat.

After all, it's my obsession that brought her to this point.

I didn't wait around at the hospital for them to deliver the news to her family when they arrived. Not when there's so much left to do.

My rage burns hot enough to scorch my path to my father's office. I'm blind to everything around me, hyper focused on finding the root of every evil that's been committed against me and cut it off at the head like the poisonous snake that he is. Then, I'm going to burn The Loyal Order of the Serpent and every single person in it to the ground.

She's gone.

She's gone.

She's gone.

My mind repeats the mantra, a constant reminder for why I'm doing this. The two words that break my subconscious in half and steal away any humanity I had left.

No one stops me on my way to my parents' penthouse. As if they know that stepping in my way will only result in them getting caught in the crosshairs. My mother is nowhere to be found when I walk off the elevator and into their foyer. In fact, no one is around at all. The place is quiet and still.

My feet take me up the stairs, past all the bedrooms, and right up to the door at the end of the hallway. His office. Once a forbidden room that no one could ever enter without his permission, which he didn't dole out generously. I hadn't even seen it until I was fifteen years old and he began grooming me for The Order. Now, I'm confidently twisting the knob, letting myself in with zero regard for his privacy or the rules I no longer abide by.

His weathered, glum face stares back at me from behind his long, elegant desk. It's almost as if he's expecting me—a fact I should find disturbing, but I'm no longer surprised by.

He's always been two steps ahead.

"Sebastian," he greets, leaning his elbows onto his protruding belly and placing his hands together in a steeple.

I don't bother with false pleasantries. Instead, I close the door behind me and approach his desk, my hand resting on the knife at my hip.

She's gone.

"Come on, son. There's no need for any of this. I've already told you, it was *you* they targeted with Sienna's death. That's why this has happened again."

He's trying to deflect. A classic narcissist, unable to accept blame or the consequences of his own actions.

"You really thought I'd take your word on that, *Daddy Dearest?*" Offering a wicked smile, I pull my knife from its holster and hold it up in front of my face, taking care in ensuring the light catches the cold metal at the perfect angle.

"It's interesting what a man will admit to when he thinks his life will be spared for the truth," I go on, stepping closer toward him. "I've uncovered quite a few of your secrets from members of your beloved brotherhood this week. Secrets I'm sure were expected to die with them."

"I've got nothing to hide," he insists proudly, puffing out his chest.

But I see the underlying fear in his eyes. The defensive way he leans into his chair, preparing his body to thwart off an attack. He thinks he has a chance against me, and that's got to be the most pathetic, gratifying thing I've ever witnessed.

"That's bullshit. You've got more to hide than anyone else. Your whole life is a lie, isn't it?"

He shifts in his chair uncomfortably, his eyes locked in on me like he's waiting for me to strike at any moment. I don't even need to torture him at this point. My mere presence before him is enough to have him pissing his pants.

She's gone.

"Don't do this. You clearly need help healing from her death. From *both* of their deaths. Look at what you've become." His hands reach out in front of him in a dramatic gesture.

How could he already know about Stardust? I received the notification less than an hour ago. He's only proving my instincts were correct, and he was at the helm of her attack.

"I'm simply a product of my own upbringing, wouldn't you say?" Rounding the corner of his desk, I lean my hip on the corner, taking my time before getting too close to him.

"You're a cold-blooded killer."

"Ah, yes. *The Serpent Slayer.* It's got a nice ring to it, doesn't it?" I reach in front of him to pick up the paperweight that Sienna gifted him for Father's Day one year. Her smiling face stares up at me through the bubbled glass, forever frozen. "A little derogatory, if you ask me. I would have gone with something that had more… pizzazz, but what can you do?"

"Sebastian, we can work through this. We can get you the help that you need. Join The Order, and no one will tell the police it was you butchering all those men. No one else will have to get hurt."

Throwing my head back, I bark out a sardonic laugh that has him jumping out of his skin. "When I'm done, The Order will be nothing but ashes on the ground," I promise him.

I've lost so much to that worthless society. It's only right that I'm the one who gets to tear it all down, piece by piece. Starting with the pathetic man sitting before me.

She's gone.

"Some parts of your story weren't adding up. After I talked to a few people, I was able to confirm that *you* were the one who dropped her case, thus letting her killers roam free."

"I didn't have a choice. They destroyed the evidence and were threatening everyone who was willing to prosecute," he rushes out, spewing the same story as the judge and Arthur Lewis.

But there's one piece that doesn't add up. Something I've otherwise ignored until now.

"On Sienna's last night, at our final dinner with her, you told her not to go out," I remind him, pointing the tip of my knife at him. "You knew what was to come, didn't you?"

"There was nothing I could do. At that point, they were already–" He starts to raise his voice, but I step toward him, threatening my attack if he doesn't shut the fuck up.

His lips clamp shut and from this close, it's impossible for him to hide his trembling.

"You let her go, knowing there was a group of men there waiting—planning to kill her," I accuse calmly, though there's a storm brewing in my chest as the accusation is made out loud and he does nothing to deny it.

"What was I supposed to do, Sebastian? They wanted to get to *you*."

"Then you should have sent them to me. You should have fought harder to get her to stay home."

"If they didn't do it that night, they would have just chosen another," he rationalized, and I realize this is how he's allowed himself to get off the hook. This is how he's managed to live with himself after what he did.

"You set her up for slaughter."

"As if you would have done anything differently," he rebukes.

"I would have gladly stepped in and taken her spot. I would have cuffed her to her chair and refused to let her leave. I would have killed those assholes *before* they had a chance to touch her. She deserved to fucking live. She deserved a life full of happiness, and it was all stolen away from her."

"Because of you," he reminds me again.

Running my finger against the blade to test its sharpness, I shake my head. "I'm not arguing anymore. You've dug your own grave, now it's time for you to lie in it. Your time is up."

I make the move toward him, my arm suspended in the air and ready to strike. I didn't want to tie him up or drug him and make it easy. I need to see him fight—to give him a big enough shred of hope that he can escape, so when the life force fades from his eyes, every ounce of faith he has leaves, too.

Just like he did with my little Stardust.

But he won't escape. He'll die tonight, at the hands of his own son for the sins he committed against his family.

My knife is mere inches away when his arm shifts, then quickly slips a gun out from beneath his desk and points it at me.

And as my blade penetrates his skin, a concussive blast echoes throughout my body, and I fall on top of him in a heap.

PAST & PRESENT

53

The Wolf

BEEP-BEEP. *Beep-beep. Beep-beep.*

The sound echoes throughout my otherwise empty mind, its pace quickening as I grow more irritated with it. I attempt to open my eyes, but it feels like they've been glued shut.

Beep-beep-beep. Beep-beep-beep. Beep-beep-beep.

The noise grows faster and louder as I quickly fade back into consciousness, my chest tightening in panic. My arms feel like lead weights at my sides when I try to lift them, and I finally pry my eyelids open enough to see that I've been strapped down with various cords and restraints. I begin fighting against them, rattling the entire bed I'm lying on. White blankets slide off my legs, falling onto the white floor in a heap.

White, white, white.

Everything here is stark white.

"Someone call the nurse for room 1122. Our John Doe is awake," a male voice calls from somewhere out of my vision.

In the next breath, he's standing over me, holding my shoulders against the bed to incapacitate me. The beeping noise picks up a dangerous speed.

"Calm down, sir," the man urges into my ear. "Or I'll have to sedate you."

"What's going on?" an older female voice asks from somewhere behind him. She briefly steps into my line of vision long enough for me to see her pulling on a pair of blue gloves. Then, she moves back out of my sight.

"Not sure. I heard the machine going off, so I came in to check on him and he was fighting against the restraints. Might need to pop a sedative in there to calm him a bit."

As he says the words, I feel the woman's gentle touch on my wrist and stop fighting for a brief moment. I turn my head to watch her twist my arm around, examining the maze of IV lines shooting out of me.

"Are you going to chill out on your own, or do we have to drug you?" she asks me, her brows raised above her pointed stare.

My gaze lazily slips back over to the man who still has his hands wrapped around my shoulders, sizing him up. He doesn't make any moves to let go, and his stare remains hard on me, prepared for any outcome.

Resolving myself to the fact that I'm too weak to do anything, I shrug out of his touch.

"Let go of me," I tell him, relaxing my head against the pillow.

"Sir, do you know where you are?" the woman questions from my other side, but I don't have the energy to look at her again. Instead, my eyes shutter closed, my body already exhausted from the fight I put up.

My head gives a weak, negative shake.

"You're at Cottage Hospital in Cherry Grove, New York."

Cherry Grove. That's just outside of Styx. What the hell am I doing in Cherry Grove?

"You've been in a coma for about six weeks now, sir," she tells me, all sentiment gone from her face. She knows better than to get emotionally involved in a case like this. "Can you tell me your name so we can call your family?"

My name? I've been here for six weeks, and no one even knows who I am?

Instead of answering her question, I ask, "Why am I restrained?"

Instinctually, my arm raises and fights against the straps. The skin they're wrapped around stings and burns from the fabric rubbing into it before.

"You were brought into the emergency room with gunshot wounds and zero identification. It's hospital protocol until the police can rule out that you're a threat to our other patients or staff," the nurse calmly explains, and the man shifts uncomfortably from my other side at the mention of me being a potential threat.

"Sir, if you remember your name, I could expedite the process for getting those removed from your wrists and call your family. I'm sure they're worried about you."

My mind races with possible scenarios for what would happen if they call my father in here and he realizes I'm still alive after he shot me. I'm trying to muster up any memories from that night that would explain why I was found an hour from the last place I remember being, stripped of all my identifiable belongings.

Did my father try to dump my body after he thought he killed me? Is he such a colossal fuck up that he didn't even check to make sure I was *dead* before leaving me behind to be found?

Maybe I should play dumb for now until I can gather more answers…

But then, my mother's face pops into my mind. How worried she must be. Unless he's convinced her that I'm gone. Then, she's likely gone into cardiac arrest from the sorrow of losing both of her children. Sienna's death almost killed her.

She doesn't deserve any of this.

"Sebastian Lancaster," I finally answer the nurse in a strained voice.

She and the guard lock eyes, a silent conversation crossing into the space between them before he nods his head once and walks away. Probably to look me up.

When his wide form disappears out of the door, she rubs her fingers over the medical tape that's holding my IVs in, and then pats my arm.

"Well, Mr. Lancaster, you're very lucky to be alive. If that civilian hadn't pulled over on the side of the road when they did, it may have been too late. We're going to contact your family right away and let them know that you're safe."

I DRIFT in and out of sleep in the next few hours, my rest constantly interrupted by the slew of doctors, nurses, and police officers who want to update me on my condition and ask me questions about how I got here.

They've been attempting to get a hold of my parents to notify them about me. It's been a seemingly impossible feat, since all the numbers I had listed in my emergency contacts file were out of date. Finally, I was able to pull Eliza's phone number from somewhere in the deep recesses of my mind, and the nurse left a message with her. I haven't heard back, but I assume my assistant will be happy to hear I'm not dead.

While I'm eager to see my mother and find answers about whatever lies my father spun, there's only one person I'm truly missing. The only one I'll never speak to again.

My Stardust.

"Your name popped up in our database as a missing person," the middle-aged detective explains that evening. He's already been in and out of here three times, always with a new line of questioning that leads us right back to the same spot. I'm staring at the TV across the room, mindlessly flipping through channels while he speaks.

"The report was filed about five weeks ago by a… Sienna Lancaster. So, the timeline checks out. Are you sure there's nothing you can tell us about the gunshot wounds? You have no idea who could have shot you?" he asks for the millionth time today.

But when I hear her name, I'm whipping my head at him so fast, it nearly spins right off my neck.

"*Who* filed the report?" I ask in disbelief, my brows pulled together in a scowl.

He squints down at the clipboard he's holding in his hands, an unsure look crossing his face. "Sienna Lancaster," he reads off slowly. He lifts his gaze back to me, eyes widening in alarm at my sudden reaction. "She's listed here as your sister. Is that correct?"

How the fuck did my dead sister file a missing persons report?

"Yes, Sienna is my sister," I find myself vaguely agreeing.

Before the detective can say anything else, there's a knock on the door and my nurse—I've learned her name is Julie—strolls back in with a warm smile on her face.

"Good news! I finally got a hold of your family." She walks over and busies herself with checking my IV stand again.

Since they've discovered who I am and my family's wealthy background, they've been more than accommodating. I'm sure it helps that the potential for me being a psycho serial killer has been proven wrong by the police. Now, they think I'm just some poor victim who lost weeks of his life to a senseless attack.

"They're in the waiting room right now, so as soon as you two are wrapped up, I'll bring them back."

The detective nods at her appreciatively, his eyes lingering on her ass for a moment too long as she walks away.

"I want to help you find your attacker, Sebastian. But I need more answers. If any memories or flashbacks from that night pop up, feel free to give me a call. Day or night." He nods toward the business card sitting on my bedside table from when he offered it to me earlier with the same speech.

"Will do, Detective," I say, lifting my hand in a wave as he turns to head out the door.

Unfortunately for him, I know exactly who did this, and I'm not going to rely on the law to take care of it for me.

TEN MINUTES LATER, nurse Julie comes strolling in with my mother in tow, her face red and swollen as if she's been crying, but a smile lights up as soon as she sees me lying on the bed.

"Oh, thank God, you're alive!" she cries out, throwing herself against my chest in a warm, comforting hug.

She looks nothing like the shell of a human she was the last time I saw her. Of course, her face is marred with signs of worry and sadness. But her blonde hair is still bright and freshly done, her nails painted a shiny red. She's wearing one of her usual, flashy outfits instead of the loungewear she was stuck in when I visited her last. No longer the sullen woman who has been mourning the death of her daughter for the past year.

As soon as she moves away from me, Sienna's face comes into full view behind her. Not the ghostly form I've grown used to seeing in the past year, but a flushed, full version of her I thought I'd never see again. Her lively eyes glower at me, cheeks stained red, and eyes puffed out like my mother's.

She's fucking *here*.

Alive.

"What the hell, Bash? We've been going crazy looking for you. You couldn't wake up from your coma a little earlier?" She leans forward and grabs me up in a rough hug, then pulls away to assess me. "You could have spared me a few wrinkles, you asshole."

Our mother swats her on the shoulder, quietly chastising her for her lewd language.

"How are you here? What the hell happened?" I find myself blurting out, my confusion bypassing the filter in my brain that would usually stop me from asking questions like that. Questions that might have them questioning my sanity.

"We hauled ass over here as soon as they called," she tries to explain, ignorant to what I'm really asking her. "Dad got stuck at a work thing, but he'll be close behind."

"Tell him not to come."

My mom blanches. "Come on, Bash. Don't be like that. He was just as worried as we were..." Her head tilts to the side as she considers me. Pities me.

Who knows what bullshit story he spun about my disappearance? I doubt he admitted that he shot me because I came to kill him for having his daughter murdered.

His daughter... who is somehow standing before me.

Fuck. None of this makes any sense.

54

The Wolf

ONCE WE GET past the novelty of being together again, my mom and Sienna begin rattling off what happened from their limited perspective. And none of it seems plausible.

According to them, less than two months have passed since the original date Sienna died. I've probably asked them for the date ten times by now, still shocked when they say a day nearly ten months earlier than I remember—dating my attack to the exact time Sienna would have been killed. My father, who is still a workaholic bastard, got into a fight with me on the night I was brought into the hospital because I told him I'd never join The Order. When they didn't hear from me for a week, my mother checked my apartment and found out that Eliza had also been trying to get a hold of me. She and Sienna filed the police report that afternoon..

That's it. That's all they can give me.

I feel like I've been dropped into an upside-down reality. One I would have fucking killed to have a year ago, after

Sienna supposedly died. But I'm struggling to find relief or happiness when the only person I've ever been able to find any of that in appears to be missing from this version of my life.

I don't mention any of this to them. In fact, I'm careful not to speak of anything I've gone through in—what I feel like—the past year of my life. The last thing I need is them trying to get my head checked and thrown into a mental facility because I'm spewing bullshit about a parallel reality where my sister is dead, my dad tried to kill me, and I went on a murdering rampage.

When my father arrives, there's none of the resentment and malice in his eyes that was there the last time we saw each other in his office. Nothing that would allude to the fact that *he* was the one who shot me. That *he* left me for dead. He even apologized for putting The Order before us, claiming these last few weeks have given him time to reflect and promising that he'll drop my initiation for a while.

I can't tell if he's just a really good actor, or if this is somehow another mind fuck.

It takes me two days to ask about Jovie. In that time, the doctors have slowly unhooked me from my IVs and monitors, dwindling them down to just one for pain management. They're talking about sending me home in the next couple of days, and the thought of going back to that penthouse with all the memories she and I made in our short-lived time together, only to find out that she didn't come along with me into this odd reality, nearly kills me.

But I hate not knowing. So, I wait until it's late, well after my parents have gone home for the night and Sienna is preparing to leave. If I told anyone about my secret affair with my little lamb, it would be Sienna. She knows everything about me.

"Did I mention a woman named Jovie in the weeks

leading up to my attack?" I ask her, deciding to jump right in instead of beating around the bush.

Sienna stops packing her purse to think for a moment, her head tilted toward the ceiling as she tries to recall. "Jovie? No, I think I would remember that name."

My shoulders sag forward, all hope lost. She's still gone. My Stardust didn't come with me.

The crushing disappointment that flows in with that realization nearly makes my heart break in half. My soul longs for its missing counterpart—so close, yet ions away.

"Why do you ask? Do you think she's connected to what happened?" Her voice raises as her suspicions grow. Suddenly, she's been hit with a jolt of energy as the possibility that I've somehow remembered any detail from that night grows more plausible.

Shaking my head, I look up at her with a strained smile, ignoring the pain radiating in my chest. "No, I was just wondering."

"Who is she?" Sienna falls onto the bed beside me, her eyes softening.

"No one, I suppose." Not anymore.

"The look on your face tells me she's *some*one." Patting my arm, she levels me with her bright green eyes—eyes I never thought I'd see again outside of my own reflection. "I know you, Bash. You never talk about anything with that look on your face unless it has to do with work or… well, that's it. Whoever it is must be important. You can tell me. I'm here for you—no judgment."

"It's a confusing situation," I explain vaguely, looking away so she knows I won't be elaborating any further.

Sienna sighs in defeat, and then her hand raises to play with her locket—a nervous tick she's always had. Except, the jewelry hanging off her neck is *not* a locket. It's the first time

I've noticed the simple, round pearl that sits perfectly against her chest.

"Where is grandma's locket?" I ask her.

I can tell she's taken back by the question and the seemingly abrupt change of subject, but she still rolls her eyes in frustration, dropping her hand into her lap dejectedly.

"Oh, you must not have heard I lost it a couple months ago… probably right when all this happened. Went to bed with it on and woke up to find it missing. I've torn through our whole apartment looking for it. Mom has been pissed at me."

It's… *gone?* Disappeared into thin air, right around the time I seemed to have jumped into some sort of alternate reality and gave it to Stardust.

That can't be a coincidence.

"I'm really glad you're still here, Bash." Sienna's voice softens, her blonde hair falling over her like a curtain between us, protecting her from allowing me to see her in such a rare, vulnerable state.

"All those weeks you were missing… it was really hard for me to imagine what I would do without you. I dreamt of you every single night—some of the wildest dreams I've ever had. I would have been destroyed if things ended badly."

I wrap my arms around her shoulders, squeezing her into my chest and she burrows her face against me, hiding it from view as small, quiet sobs wrack through her body. Placing my lips at the crown of her head, I assure her, "None of that matters now. I'm not going anywhere."

And my broken, despondent heart breaks all over again as that reality settles in. I'm *here*, not *there*.

Tears burn behind my eyes as I remember living the nightmare she was so afraid to face. As the faint sorrow and despair take hold of my being again, just for a moment. Just to show me how horrible it was and remind me how many times I wished for this exact thing. To hold my sister—my other half—in my arms again.

And as much as my soul aches for its mate, I have to be grateful that I at least get this. At least Sienna gets a chance to live, and I get the opportunity to hold her again.

55

The Wolf

I'M LEAVING the hospital today. They've moved me into a private room while completing the last of my care. The nurses say I did most of my healing while in my coma, so it's really just been about reacclimating my body to moving on its own and watching for any potential damage from the bullets that they may have missed before. My new room is larger than my last, a shit ton more expensive, and not as close to the constantly buzzing emergency department.

Sienna and my mother were relieved to have peace and quiet, although I know both of them have been missing the drama. They lived for overhearing the far-fetched stories from patients who have landed themselves in the ER like some cheap reality show. Half the time, I wasn't allowed to have my TV on because it interfered with their eavesdropping.

So to commemorate old times, they've taken me for a short walk around the halls while the nurse writes up my discharge paperwork, and we've landed right back into the epicenter of chaos.

We're resting on a bench just outside of the nurses' station because my body is infuriatingly weak and sore. Sienna has just started to broach the subject of her staying with me in my apartment for the summer while I recover, when one of the nurses quickly hangs up the phone and stands to speak to the other three women loitering around her. All of us turn to watch as she makes her announcement.

"We've got a team about three minutes out with a potential overdose. Patient is a twenty-five-year-old female. That's all they were able to get out over the phone. Prepare a bed for her and grab all the free hands you can find. I have a feeling this is going to be a messy one."

A rush of hospital staff runs past me, toward a door at the end of the hall filled with far more medical equipment than the rest of the curtained rooms have. Just as that door slams shut, a burst of cold air hits my neck, and I turn to see the emergency entrance doors have been propped open as they roll in a gurney.

My mom and Sienna share a look, glancing between me and the gurney like they've just realized that my entrance to this hospital probably looked very similar to this woman's. I push away the guilt blossoming in my chest at the fear neither of them can seem to shake that one minute, they're going to blink and I'll be gone. I can't dwell on it right now, or on the fact that I feel the same way about them.

But all of those worries slowly drop away like petals of a dead flower when the medics roll the stretcher past us and I see the pale, lifeless face that's lying on it, and my deadened heart begins to bloom back to life in my chest. In the blink of an eye, I'm standing from the bench, chasing them down the hall so I can get a better look. Not that I need one. I'd know that face anywhere.

It's her.

My Stardust.

My confirmation comes when the medic tries to push me away, but I continue toward her.

"I just need to see her," I'm telling them, over and over again. *I just need to know what the fuck happened.*

And almost as if the sound of my voice temporarily pulls her back to consciousness, those beautiful browns snap open and immediately find me.

"Bash," she whispers brokenly, then sputters out a cough.

"It's me, baby. I'm here," I find myself telling her through all the chaos that's ensuing, but a nurse is pushing me away as they roll her through the door to her private room.

I don't get another chance to talk to her. A male doctor has stepped into my path and stands rooted to the ground, refusing to allow me access to the one thing that matters in this twisted, upside-down world. But at the very last second, just before the door slams closed and shuts her away for good, a glint of gold on her neck catches onto the fluorescent lights, drawing my eyes to the small locket lying against her chest.

I know then with every fiber of my being that all of it was real.

And just like any other predator who is presented with a new prey, I'm back on the hunt.

EPILOGUE

The Lamb
Three months later

"You should just stay with us for a while," my sister suggests for what feels like the millionth time as she and Kennedy walk through my new home. "At least until you can afford something in town."

By some strange twist of fate, I managed to find a furnished, three-bedroom house, situated perfectly on a private lake with all utilities included. It's a deal I couldn't possibly pass up. Halen and Kennedy have been letting me stay with them since I got out of Sunnybrook a couple of weeks ago, but I knew that wasn't a sustainable living arrangement.

Regardless of how many times I tell her, or how many doctors sign off on my psych evaluations, or that fact that I was released from the facility early after I explained what Gabe did and they determined that I'm not a threat to my own well-being, Halen refuses to truly believe that I didn't try to kill myself.

I can't really blame her. Gabe planned that night out well in advance, slipping me low doses of various drugs every day to build them up in my system so that when I inevitably landed in the hospital, my blood panel would look like I truly had a problem. Halen struggles to separate me from my mother now, her brain convinced we share the same addictive personality.

I don't remember anything that happened that night after I stepped into the shower. Not the ambulance ride, or the emergency room, or the first two days they kept me hooked up to machines to ensure my organs wouldn't fail on me.

It's just lost time I'll never get back.

But I can't move on from this nightmare if I'm in an environment like Halen's, where I feel like I have to prove myself at every turn. So I started looking at places to live right away. I never expected to find such a perfect deal this quickly, especially when I've hardly begun working my new job at Old Soul Cafe. But I couldn't pass it up.

Recently bought by a property management company based in New York City, the home was once a vacation spot for some rich family who can't make it out here anymore. It works out perfectly for me, since my asshole ex-boyfriend is still holding all my worldly possessions hostage because I refuse to speak to him after what he and my mother did in a psychotic effort to try to control my every move. Hopefully, we'll be assigned a court date soon, and I can prove to a judge what an insufferable, abusive asshole he is. Besides, everything in here is worth at least ten times what I have, so it's a win-win.

"I've already signed the lease, Hales," I remind her patiently, resisting the urge to throw her out when she runs her finger along the surface of my kitchen table and her face contorts into a look of disgust.

Swiping the dirt onto her jeans, she peers through the sliding glass doors and into the shady backyard.

"It's just so far from home," she whines, looking back at Kennedy for backup. "We would hate for something to happen again and we wouldn't be close. Besides, it's really creepy out here."

"It's not creepy," I interrupt her before she can start spewing a bunch of nonsense about serial killers or something.

Halen sends an exasperated look to Kennedy, silently begging for her to step in, but her wife just shrugs it off.

"It is a little creepy," she agrees, and Halen can't nod her head fast enough, latching onto that point for dear life.

With wide eyes, she points her finger toward the woods. "You have no idea what could be lurking out there. There could be a serial killer—"

"Okay, I think you guys have seen enough," I cut in, this time with my voice a little higher. I grab each of them around their shoulders and usher them toward the front door. "I've got a bit of cleaning to do before we bring my stuff over this weekend, so unless you two want to grab a rag and get to work, you should head on out."

Neither of them volunteers, just like I knew they wouldn't. With a rushed goodbye and a death-grip hug from my sister, I promise them I'll be back home in a couple of hours, then close the door and get to work.

It's really not as bad as Halen thinks. Everything is just coated in a small layer of dust, but once I get all of it cleared away, the home looks ten times as beautiful. I've been having odd bouts of deja vu all evening and can't seem to shake the feeling that I've been here before. Like this place truly is my real home. There have already been quite a few times I was looking for something and instinctively knew exactly where to find it. The familiarity only further convinces me that this was all meant to be.

I wish I could spend my first night here tonight, but I know the impulse decision would only send Halen further into a tizzy. Plus, I don't have any of my things, and I've got a shift to work tomorrow. Instead, I resign myself to waiting just a few more nights.

In a silent resignation, I put away all my cleaners into the linen closet, throw my new comforter onto my bed, and then turn to head out. I'm just about to flip the kitchen lights off, when a speck of purple catches my eye on the dining room table that I just cleared off. I huff out a breath, irritated with myself for not properly cleaning up my garbage, and stomp over to it.

But my steps slow as I realize it's not garbage, but a piece of fruit.

Not just any fruit, though.

It's a fig.

PINKY PROMISE

Hey, friend.

I'm so happy you've chosen to read my book out of the sea of amazing novels available to you. Thank you for giving me this sliver of your life to soak in my words and immerse yourself into my imaginary little world. As the former lonely kid who no one ever listened to, it means so much more to me than you could ever imagine.

Can I ask you for a favor?

An agreement, of sorts...

Prey Drive has taken you on a thrilling, suspenseful, spicy ride. There were slow parts, fast-paced parts, and parts you never saw coming! I'd love to preserve that experience for every reader who opens this book. To allow them the chance to follow this special journey and acquaint themselves with the characters all on their own.

So, here's my request: Now that you're read the last page—the last word—I'm hoping you'll keep this story and all the twists and turns it offers to yourself.

It'll be our little secret.

Of course, I want you to talk about it. Share your favorite quotes and gush over your favorite characters (hopefully, if I did a good job, that's Sebastian Lancaster). You can even talk about the parts you hated.

Just please be mindful of spoiling anything.

And that's it! I hope you enjoyed it!

This one turned me to dust and then built me back up again.

Maybe it'll be a little easier on you.

ABOUT JEN

Jen Stevens was born and raised in Michigan, where she enjoys the weather of all four seasons in a single day. After obtaining her Bachelor's degree, she quickly realized the corporate world wasn't for her and instead took on the daunting role as her children's snack maid. Reading has been an obsession for a long as she could remember, while writing has always been an escape. Jen could quote The Office word-for-word and proudly refers to herself as a romance junkie. She could live off anything made of sugar and has recently obtained the title of Lady. Most of all, she loves connecting with readers!

Check out Jen's website and socials for the most up to date publishing information: www.jenstevenswrites.com
or scan below

Socials: @authorjenstevens

A B O U T   J E N

Jen Stevens was born and raised in Michigan, where she enjoys the weather of all four seasons in a single day. After obtaining her Bachelor's degree, she quickly realized the corporate world wasn't for her and instead took on the daunting role as her children's snack maid. Reading has been an obsession for a long as she could remember, while writing has always been an escape. Jen could quote The Office word-for-word and proudly refers to herself as a romance junkie. She could live off anything made of sugar and has recently obtained the title of Lady. Most of all, she loves connecting with readers!

Check out Jen's website and socials for the most up to date publishing information: www.jenstevenswrites.com
or scan below

Socials: @authorjenstevens

ALSO BY JEN

<u>Dark Romance:</u>
Ugly Truths (Grimville Reapers Book One)
Untold Truths (Grimville Reapers Book Two)
Prey Drive (Parallel Prey Duet Book 1)
Fallen Prey (Parallel Prey Duet Book 2)

<u>Contemporary Romance:</u>
Advice from a Sunflower

<u>Urban Fantasy Romance:</u>
Calling Quarters (Beacon Grove Book One)
Counting Quarters (Beacon Grove Book Two)
<u>Catching Quarters</u> (Beacon Grove Book Three)

Switching Graves (Ravenshurst University Book One)
Splitting Secrets (Ravenshurst University Book Two)